The Blue Bike Murders
by
Ron Parker

The Blue Bike Murder
© Ron Parker 2010

Rolyart Publications

Revised Edition
2019

ISBN: 978-1-84799-842-2

This story is a work of fiction. Any resemblance to any real character, living or dead, is purely coincidental.

<u>Warning</u>
While nothing is explicit, this story does contain some scenes involving child abuse. Anyone offended by stories of this nature should refrain from reading this book.

The Blue Bike Murder
by
Ron Parker

Chapter 1

Jake Swift walked, in good spirits, along the canal towpath with his buddy, Brian Churcher, who trudged along, causing Jake to have to keep waiting for him to catch up. Brian ignored Jake, dragging his feet like someone with a problem.

They were enjoying the long summer school holidays. At least, Jake was.

It wasn't difficult for the twelve-year-old to see something was bothering his pal. Brian was never this quiet.

"What's up wi' you, Brian?" he eventually asked, boredom at his friend's silence changing to concern.

His companion, face pale despite a warm sun shining, turned to him. "I can't tell you."

"Why?"

"You wouldn't understand. You're not old enough."

"I'm almost as old as you!" Jake responded.

"No, you're not. You're two years younger, and your puny size makes you look even younger." The start of a smile spread across his face for the first time that day as he teased his pal.

"Well?"

Brian didn't answer, and the younger boy stayed quiet. Brian was known to have quite a temper, and Jake didn't want a thumping. He'd mind his own business–for now.

All red-haired kids are prone to losing their tempers, Jake's dad told him once. He didn't understand since he knew other teens with red hair who were easy going. Only Brian lost his rag sometimes, and even he was calm most of the time. But when something ruffled him, he'd lash out at anyone within reach. Jake was often within reach. They walked on for a while. It had been hot and dry for some time, and the sun had baked the usually muddy track hard. The boys kicked stones as they passed by old mills which had once used the canal to dispatch their products. Now, the buildings were silent, towering up into the skyline, broken windows dotting their length. The mills stood on the opposite side of the waterway to the boys. Their side opened out onto an area of rough grassland, one of the few open regions left in their small town. Even that would be developed soon. Already a housing estate could be seen encroaching onto the fields the boys had often used for recreation. The smell of the stagnant water from the canal didn't bother the developers any more than it bothered the lads. Jake kicked a pebble into the water and tried to talk to Brian again on a different subject.

"Why didn't you bring your fishing gear?"

Despite the impurity of the water, the local fishing club managed to keep the canal reasonably well-stocked.

"Couldn't get it. I'm not supposed to be out. He'd have seen me," Brian answered.

"Your dad? Is that what's bothering you?"

"He's not my dad. He died when I was eleven. Frank's my step-dad."

"Oh, yeah, sorry, I forgot. You don't like him much do you? Anyway, what can he do? Ground you. Big deal."

"I'm not worried about getting grounded. I couldn't care less."

"You should be, you know." It was a man's voice, and it caused both boys to turn and see that a bearded man of about thirty had ridden up behind them on a blue bicycle. He dismounted and joined the boys.

"I heard what you were saying," he continued. "You should obey your parents, y'know."

"What's it got to do with you?" Brian retorted. "Anyway, he's not my parent."

Jake edged away in concern. "Come on. Don't talk to strangers."

"That's for kids. He won't hurt us."

"No, I won't," The adult said. "But your friend's right. Tell you what, my name's David Ewan. Now tell me your names, and we won't be strangers."

"Get lost," Brian shouted.

"Charming."

Jake shuffled his feet. "Come on, Brian. Let's go."

"You still think I'm here to harm you, don't you? Well, all right, I won't disappoint you." The cyclist leant his bike against the fence then put his hands around Brian's neck, pretending to strangle him.

"Get off me, pervert," Brian protested, pulling the stranger's hands from his throat. The man turned to the younger boy who backed away looking anxious.

"Don't touch me, I'll tell my dad," Jake said.

"I'm just playing," the stranger responded, but seeing the boys were not interested, he retrieved his cycle.

A small red ball whizzed past Brian, followed by a little black and white mongrel that came dashing from the bushes at the side of the towpath. The dog plunged into the waterway to retrieve the ball, scrambled out and shook itself over Brian and Jake.

For the moment, Jake forgot his fear of the stranger and laughed. But Brian wasn't happy at having dirty water shaken all over his clean jeans.

"My mum'll kill me," he complained.

"I'm sure she won't," the man said. "Kids are supposed to get dirty."

"You don't know my mum."

Jake was still laughing.

"It's nothing to laugh about," said Brian. "I'll knock those freckles off your face if you carry on."

"Bruce!" An elderly man appeared, diverting the boys from their potential fight and seizing control of the dog. "Sorry kids," he said as he assessed the situation before taking the animal in the opposite direction to the one in which the boys were going.

"I'll see you again, boys." David Ewan remounted the bike and went on his way.

"Pervert!" Brian shouted after him as they resumed their walk.

"Shush," said Jake, embarrassed.

"Well, he is. It's obvious. What do you think he was trying to do 'till that other bloke came along?"

"You were the one talking to him."

"Only to get rid of him. I wouldn't have let him do anything."

"And you think I would?"

"You're too little to stop him. Besides, you don't know what it's like."

Jake stopped mid-stride and stared at his friend. "'Course I don't. Neither do you, do you?"

"Oh, I know. Jake, if I tell you something, you've got to promise never to tell anyone else, not as long as you live. Swear."

Jake looked into his pal's face. This was going to be something serious. He thought he saw tears forming in Brian's eyes. But Brian never cried; he was too old for that.

"All right, I swear," he said.

"My stepfather has it off with me."

"What!"

"He has it off with me. He's queer, he bums me."

Jake couldn't take this in. He'd known Brian almost all his life. Brian wasn't the kind of kid this happened to. He stopped walking and stared at his friend. Brian didn't stop, and Jake ran to catch him up.

"You're having me on."

"I wish I was."

"You've got to tell someone. A grown-up, I mean. Your mother?"

"She wouldn't believe me. She'd belt me one for telling lies about her dear husband."

"The police then. You have to tell someone."

"No, I can't. And you mustn't. Remember, you promised."

"You'd batter me if I told anyone, I know that. But I still think you should."

"No. Forget about it. Okay?"

"Is that why he wanted you to stay in?"

"I said forget it."

"I was only asking."

"Don't."

They strolled along, silent for a while until Jake couldn't contain himself any longer.

"What does he do to you? Exactly, I mean."

"Shut up about it. I wish I hadn't told you now."

"Sorry, it's just that I don't understand what bumming means properly. I know it's bad, and som'ut to do wi' sex, but what is it?"

"You don't need to know."

"Tell me, please."

"If you don't shut up about it, I'll shove you in the canal."

"All right," Jake said, remembering that hot temper of his friend and not being too sure whether Brian would carry out the threat.

They continued their walk in silence again for a while. A pair of swans approached them and swam away when they realised they would not get food from the youngsters.

Jake watched the birds go and looked into the murky water. Brian wouldn't be mean enough to push him into it. Or would he?

A few minutes later, he took the chance.

"Does he–"

"Right, I warned you." Brian didn't push his friend into the canal, but he did crash his fist into the younger boy's cheek.

Jake put his hand to his face, was silent for a moment, then burst into tears as he ran towards home, leaving Brian alone on the towpath.

"I'm sorry. Come back!" Brian shouted after his companion, but Jake continued to run, still crying.

* * *

Much later that evening, Leonard Mason took Bruce for his second walk of the day along the canal towpath. The young dog was in a playful mood, and Leonard periodically picked up a stick to throw for him. Not wanting the dog to finish up in the dirty water again, he threw the sticks into the fields leading away from the towpath. Bruce was happy to chase after them, sometimes retrieving them for Leonard to throw again, sometimes coming back without them, leaving his master to find a new toy.

Apart from looking after Bruce, Leonard had little to do since he retired, especially after his wife died soon afterwards. Bruce was the only other living thing in his life. "You daft dog," he said when the mongrel again came back empty mouthed. Leonard removed the flat cap always worn when outdoors and pretended to throw it. The dog chased after the invisible missile, turning and barking at his master when he realised He'd duped him.

"Oh, all right," Leonard said, this time picking up a stick and throwing it into a clump of trees.

Bruce followed it into the trees, where he stayed, barking frantically.

"Come on, Bruce," Leonard commanded, but for once, Bruce did not obey his call.

"Must have found a rat or something," Leonard muttered to himself. He took the dog lead from his pocket and groped his way into the bushes.

"You must stay on the lead if you don't come when I call you," he shouted over the noise of the incessant barking. "I don't care if it's a rabbit, or whatever, you've found."

When he saw what Bruce had found, he stopped in his tracks. There lying deep in the dense bushes was the body of a young boy. That was enough of a shock, but what disturbed Leonard, even more, was that he recognised the kid. It was one of the boys he'd met on the towpath that afternoon.

Chapter 2

Detective Inspector Tom Jackson parked his Ford Mondeo close to the hump-backed bridge and made his way down onto the canal towpath. One thing to be thankful for was the recent dry weather meant the path was not in its usual muddy condition — no need to put on boots.

He didn't have to walk far before seeing his sergeant, Harry Abercrombie. The expression on the sergeant's face told Jackson the reports from uniform were not exaggerated.

"What do we have, Harry?"

"Young lad, fourteen or fifteen. Strangled."

"Do we know who he is?" Jackson kicked his toe against the ground, observing how hard the hot sun had baked the mud.

"Not yet. There's no ID on him, not a bus pass, or a library ticket. There was loose change in his pocket and the usual junk kids collect, but nothing to tell us who he is, not even a mobile phone. 'Course the murderer might have taken that."

"Or he might not have had one. Not everyone does, you know, even these days," Jackson said, stroking his short grey moustache. "No kids reported missing?"

"Not yet. Of course, parents don't worry too much about kids this age for a while."

"No. Any obvious motive?"

"The doctor needs to confirm it, but he's almost sure the kid's been sexually assaulted although he was fully dressed when they found him."

"Why would anyone bother to clothe him after abusing him if they were going to kill him? You've talked to the guy who discovered him?"

"Just briefly. Leonard Mason. Over there - the chap with the dog." Abercrombie pointed to where a shocked-looking man leaned against a fencepost stroking the panting dog. Jackson and Abercrombie made their way over to him.

"Down, Bruce!" Mason ordered as the dog lunged forward to greet the men. He pulled the animal back and Jackson bent to pat it as he spoke to the man.

"I'm Inspector Jackson. I believe you've already met my colleague. Finding the body must have been quite a shock to you."

Mason nodded.

"You don't recognise the boy?"

"No, but I've seen him before. Earlier today with another kid. They were with a fellow on a bike."

"They were riding bikes?"

"No. Just the bloke had a bike. The kids were on foot. I don't think they knew the chap. He rode off in the other direction."

"So, they weren't with this man, then. Can you describe him?"

"I didn't take that much notice. He was white and had a beard, a bushy black one. He looked a keep-fit type, middle-aged. The bike was blue."

"That's pretty good. Don't suppose you noticed the make of the bike?"

"I didn't take much interest." Mason had stopped stroking Bruce as he spoke, and the dog now nuzzled his hand to remind him.

"Can you say what sort of bike it was?" Abercrombie interjected. "I mean was it a mountain bike, racer, BMX or what?"

Mason responded to the dog's demands for attention as he replied, "I wouldn't know the difference. In my day, a bike was a bike."

"What about the other kid? What did he look like?" Jackson asked.

"He was younger — about ten or eleven. Blond hair, nice-looking kid. They were fighting–well arguing, anyway." As Mason stroked the dog, Jackson noticed he had well-manicured hands, but ones he had once used for hard toil. A wedding ring embellished the hand used to do the stroking.

"And the other boy was definitely smaller?"

"Oh, yeah. I don't think it's likely he murdered him if that's what you mean."

Abercrombie beckoned Jackson towards him and moved out of earshot of Mason.

"The lad was strangled," Abercrombie said. "I don't consider a ten-year-old would be strong enough to do that."

"No, you're probably right," Jackson said.

He returned to Mason, "We'll need you to come to the police station and make a full statement, but that will do for now. Your information's very helpful, thanks."

Jackson left Abercrombie with Mason to arrange the statement and went to look at the body, where the pathologist was still carrying out his preliminary on-site examination. Police officers were busy searching the area which was now cordoned off with tape, and a tent had been placed over the victim.

"Hi Neil, Harry tells me you think the lad was sexually interfered with?"

"I can't be certain yet, but because of the boy's age I had a brief look while the body was in situ to establish if that was the motivation. I'll need to do proper tests back at the morgue. That might not be your motive, though. I mean–I do believe he's been assaulted, yes, but before today."

"Poor kid. That will make things more difficult."

"One fact I can tell you already is that whoever murdered the boy had small hands. You can see from the marks on his throat."

"Small hands? Could it be another child?"

"It's not impossible, but unlikely. Strangling takes rather a bit of strength - though, like us all, a kid in a violent temper could find extra energy."

"And the killer used his hands, not his arms?"

"It looks like it, yes. That surprised me too. Didn't even use gloves, hence the scratches. Your forensic people might get prints from the lad's neck."

"That's something, anyway. We should be able to get it wrapped up fast."

Jackson looked down at the dead child. The boy was lying on his back, and Jackson saw what Neil meant about scratches. There were fresh ones on the victim's face.

"Anything significant about the scratches?" he asked Neil.

"Funny you should ask that. Most of them were undoubtedly made when the culprit dragged him into these bushes, but there are some that seem as if they've been made by human fingernails, before death."

"Fingernails! You mean he was deliberately scratched?"

"Well, you're the detective, but my theory is that his assailant at some stage clamped his hand over the kid's mouth to stop him screaming. The lad put up a struggle during which the scratches were inflicted. Does that help?"

"It might. It tells us the murderer is someone with long fingernails."

"He's most likely cut them by now. Or will before you catch him."

"It shouldn't be long before we get him. All we have to do is find someone who owns a blue bicycle."

"There must be hundreds of blue bikes in Staffington," Abercrombie said, hearing Jackson's last remark as he entered the tent and approached from behind.

"And hundreds, if not thousands, of men with black beards, but there won't be that many combinations of the two," Jackson answered.

"We've got to find the other kid."

"Yes, but he won't be in there," Jackson replied, following Abercrombie's look back towards the canal.

"You don't think so?"

"No. The murderer hid this boy's body in the bushes because it wouldn't be found as quickly as if they had dumped it in the canal. They wouldn't go to that trouble then leave the other one in the water."

"Well, uniform have found nothing else around here."

"Good. Let's hope it means the other boy's still alive. You're right, though. We have to find him - and quick. The murderer could still be holding him, or he might be a witness. Either way, he's in danger."

"You can get the body moved now. I've done all I can here," Neil interrupted as he closed his briefcase then walked off towards his car.

"Right. Harry, go back to the station and set up an incident room. Organise a briefing in forty-five minutes. I'm just going to visit home first. It's my daughter's birthday."

"And something like this comes up. I'm sorry."

"She'll understand, she must. Get an appeal out for the bloke on the bike and the other kid. I'll see you shortly."

* * *

In a small town like Staffington, it didn't take long for word to get around, especially after the local radio announced an appeal for anyone who knew someone fitting the description of the cyclist to come forward.

David Ewan listened to the broadcast and for once was glad he was on his own. He'd been a loner now for a long time. No relatives who wanted to know him, few acquaintances and definitely no friends.

His first act after hearing the appeal was to shave off his beard, significantly altering his appearance. He was glad whoever gave his description to the police, doubtless the other kid, had omitted his most distinguishing feature - his diminutive height.

After he had shaved, he rode his cycle to the canal where under cover of darkness; he let it slip gently into the water to sink into the mud and weeds below.

* * *

Jackson arrived home. His wife, Sheila, greeted him at the door and they kissed briefly.

"Sorry, love, I need to get straight back. There's been a homicide. I'm going to have to miss Karen's birthday."

"Yes, I heard it on the local news. You must tell Karen yourself, though."

"fair enough. It's why I came home."

They went inside the semi-detached house, and both Jackson's children came running to meet him.

"Hi, kids," he greeted them, picking up and playfully swinging eight-year-old Daniel for a moment before turning to his daughter.

"Well, sweetheart, happy birthday. Almost grown up now, eh. What does being twelve feel like? I've forgotten, it's been so long since I was twelve."

"Okay. You're not staying in, are you?"

"You already know?"

"It's all right. You have to find a murderer, and that's more important than my birthday tea."

"How did you know?"

"Mum told me someone's been killed, and you'd probably have to work late."

"I'm sorry, Karen."

"It's all right, really. You will come to my party on Sunday, though?"

"Nothing will keep me away, I promise. We will put the murderer in prison by then."

"Don't make promises you can't be sure you can keep, Tom, particularly to a child." Jackson turned to see his wife standing in the doorway.

"I'm not a child, Mum. I'm a young adult!" Karen said in indignation.

"No, you're not. You're a kid, so there," Daniel teased. Karen chased him out of the room.

"It's all right, Sheila," Jackson said. "We really will get this chap soon, and it'll be over. I have to go back, though, and get things started. We need to find another kid who was with the victim. They'll need me."

"Another child? You don't think -"

"I don't know what to think yet, but I have to go."

"Yes, I know. We'll see you, eventually."

"Don't wait up."

* * *

Jake Swift was a frightened boy. He'd heard on the radio about the murder on the canal. The body was found just yards from where he had been with his friend that afternoon. It could have been them. The thought kept running through his mind. He wondered whether Brian was thinking the same thing. Who was the kid they'd found, he wondered? If they were playing around the canal, it could be someone who lived nearby, someone he might know, perhaps even a school friend.

The appeal on the radio had asked for anyone who'd been near the canal to contact the police. Should he tell his parents he'd been there? No. What if the police thought he and Brian had killed the kid? But what if Brian had heard the news, and he went forward? That would make it look as if he had something to hide. He had to call Brian to find out if he knew and, if so, what he was going to do. His parents would never allow him to go out this late though. They wouldn't let him use the phone either. What should he do?

* * *

When Jackson arrived at the police station, there was a commotion going on in reception.

The largest woman Jackson had ever seen pounded the desk with her fists. A short, timid-looking man stood beside her.

"Are you going to find my son or not?" she screamed. "Never mind your bloody papers and forms. I want someone out there looking for him. He's been missing all day, hasn't he, Frank?"

The little man at her side opened his mouth, but she did not give him time to speak.

"Are you goin' to get someone out looking for him or not? He is only fourteen, you know."

The desk sergeant held up his hands, palms out. "I do have to write down the details before we can do anything. You said he had red hair..."

Jackson stopped mid-stride as he overheard those words. It was only too obvious where the woman's son was. She must be one of the few people in the town who hadn't yet heard about the murder - and he would have to tell her.

He apologised to the woman and interrupted the sergeant, drawing him into the back office. He explained the situation to the desk sergeant and informed him he would deal with the woman.

"I had a feeling it was her kid as soon as she came in to report him missing," the sergeant said. "Only she was so worked up I wasn't getting any sense out of her."

"Leave her to me. Just tell Sergeant Abercrombie where I am, please."

"Gladly, her name's Mrs Churcher," the sergeant replied, relieved to get the woman off his hands.

Jackson went back to the front office.

"You've got a bloody nerve," the woman shrieked. "Interrupting me when I'm making a report. Is something more important than my missing son, then? I will be writing to my MP, you know, you can be sure of that."

"I'm sorry, Mrs Churcher. Would you like to come this way?"

He led the ginger-haired woman into one of the interview rooms. The small, timid-looking man, who Jackson still hadn't heard speak, followed them. Jackson judged the woman to be in her mid-thirties, the man somewhat younger and certainly too young to be the father of a fourteen-year-old boy.

Mrs Churcher needed to turn sideways to get through the door of the interview room. She was big in both directions, not fat, just powerfully built. She dwarfed the man and Jackson thought in any other circumstances seeing them together would be laughable.

"Are you Mr Churcher?" Jackson asked the man who opened his mouth but was again beaten to it by the woman.

"Yes, he is. Now what are you going to do about finding my Brian?" she demanded before Jackson had time to invite them to sit down or to do so himself. He did so now and sat facing the couple, a small desk between them.

"Mrs Churcher, I'm afraid there's no easy way to say this. We discovered the dead body of a boy this evening."

"What!"

"We'll need the body to be identified, but I'm afraid your description appears to match it. I'm sorry."

She looked at her spouse who seemed even more nervous than before. "I knew something like this would happen." Then turning back to face Jackson, "He wasn't supposed to go out, you know, was he, Frank? You told him to stay in, didn't you?"

Frank again tried to speak and, once more, wasn't given the chance.

"'Course we'll identify him," the woman continued. "Where is he?"

"He's in the morgue. I'll take you there now if you're sure you're ready."

Jackson led the pair to his car and drove the short distance to the morgue. Frank loitered in the entrance as Jackson led Mrs Churcher inside. She spun back towards the exit.

"No, I can't do it! You'll have to do it, Frank." She put both her fists to the side of her head and staggered towards the exit sobbing uncontrollably.

Frank wiped his hands on the side of his trouser legs and chewed his lip, eyes looking back and forth between his wife and Jackson.

"Do it, Frank! For God's sake, please. I can't." She shook her head and retreated from the room. As she went, she repeated in a much fainter voice, which the men had to strain to hear, "I can't."

Frank, plainly surprised at her demand and tone followed her out.

The woman turned to stare at him, her red-rimmed eyes angry. "God, Frank, you heard what I said. Do it, damn you."

Frank sighed, then stepped back hesitantly into the morgue.

Once away from his wife, Frank found his voice for the first time since Jackson had set eyes on him.

"You'll have to excuse my wife," he said. "I'm afraid Angela has to think she's the one in charge."

Jackson thought she was doing rather a good job of convincing Frank she was in charge. Just thinking she was the boss didn't seem to be the case. But how they ran their marriage was none of his business. He was only concerned with what they could tell him about their son. It would require a longer chat with them after the formal identification of the body, but he'd wait as long as he could, giving the news time to sink in.

Now, more to make conversation than anything else, he said, "You look rather young to be Brian's father?"

"I'm not. I'm his step-dad."

Jackson stopped. "You should have told me. Where's his real dad? He has to be told about this."

"You'll need a medium, then. He died four years ago."

"Oh!" Jackson sighed, embarrassed he hadn't considered the possibility of such a young man as Brian's father must have been having died.

"Are you ready to do this?"

"I suppose so."

Jackson pulled open the drawer and raised the sheet to reveal the deceased boy's face. Frank stared down at it and pursed his lips. He nodded and turned away.

"That's him. That's Brian all right." He went out to join his wife, leaving Jackson to replace the shroud and close the drawer.

Jackson felt better once the dead boy was out of sight again. He had seen plenty of deaths in his job, deaths from construction accidents, from traffic, drowning, suicides, murders — death was ever present; it was in the street and around the corner; most people just didn't notice. But dead children always affected him the worst.

He left the place to find Mr and Mrs Churcher waiting outside. She sat on a public bench, and Jackson offered his hand to help her. She shook him off and stood up. Without another word, she marched after her husband towards the car. Jackson drove them home. They got out of the Mondeo and went into their house in silence, leaving Jackson to reflect how differently people reacted to death.

He left them to grieve and went back to the police station to see if there had been any progress in the incident room.

There hadn't.

* * *

The following morning, Jake woke to his radio alarm announcing it was Friday. He had been awake most of the night worrying about whether he should tell the police he'd been walking on the canal bank yesterday afternoon. What was Brian going to do? He had to find out. Jake got out of bed and, still half-asleep, started to dress. Almost all his school uniform had been put on before he remembered there was no school. He took it off again and turned up the radio as the music faded to make way for the early news bulletin.

'A young teenager found dead near the Sanders Canal last night has been identified as fourteen-year-old Brian Churcher...'

"Mum!" Jake screamed, then, still in his underwear, flew screaming from the bedroom. He found his mother in the kitchen.

He flung his arms around her, and she embraced him. "What is it, Jake? You've had a bad dream, that's all."

It was a long time since the twelve-year-old had needed her cuddles and she enjoyed the contact but could see how upset he was.

"Mum," he blubbered. "It's Brian, he's been killed." He was crying now. "It was just on the radio. That kid they found dead last night. It was Brian!"

Although he had worried all night about what he should do, it had never for a moment crossed Jake's mind that Brian himself could be the victim.

"It's my fault," he blurted, "I left him there by himself."

* * *

Jackson entered the incident room and to his surprise found Harry Abercrombie hadn't already arrived. Harry always got there before him. He was consistently so immaculately dressed that Jackson thought he must get ready for work as soon as he'd had supper.

Detective Constable Gloria Waters was the only other member of the team to have turned up so far.

"Harry not here yet, that's unusual," Jackson said to her.

"He's here. He's interviewing a kid downstairs," she answered, shattering his dream of having, for once, beaten his sergeant to his desk. But the kid being interviewed must be connected with the case. All Abercrombie's other cases, like Jackson's, had been put on hold to give the murder investigation priority.

"Did the kid see something?" he asked Gloria.

"No. It's the other boy. The one who was with the victim."

"Thank God!" said Jackson. "He's alive then. I'll get down there straight away."

He went downstairs to the interview room where he found a small fair-haired boy in tears. A woman who Jackson took to be the child's mother had her arms around his shoulders. Abercrombie was sitting on the other side of the boy having disposed of the psychological barrier of the desk between them.

The child rested his head against his mother but looked up at Jackson with frightened eyes. Jackson could tell the crying was genuine enough, but was the weeping because of grief over his friend, or were they tears of guilt?

Chapter 3

Harry Abercrombie glanced up as Jackson entered the interview room.

At six foot two inches, the man towered over the tiny boy beside him. "This is my boss," he told the youngster, looking down at him. "He's in charge. You need to tell him everything."

Turning to Jackson, he said, "This is Jake Swift and his mum. Jake was with Brian yesterday, but says he left him before anything happened."

"Hi, Jake," Jackson said, pulling a chair to the side of the desk. The room was small, designed for one-to-one interviews and, with Abercrombie's idea of not sitting behind the desk to put the boy more at ease, the four occupants of the room were forced into proximity to each other.

A window overlooking the police station car park dominated the sparsely furnished room. Apart from the desk and chairs, the only other item in the office was the tape-recording equipment. It was a room designed to be practical rather than comfortable.

"There's nothing to be frightened of. We need to ask you a few questions, that's all," Jackson said as he took his seat.

"Don't I have to have a defender with me?" the boy asked, still weeping, but he raised his head letting Jackson see his full face. A lightly freckled face fringed with blond hair.

"A solicitor, you mean. No, you're not under arrest or anything like that. We simply want you to tell us what happened. Your mum's the only person you need with you." He gave the woman a brief glance as he spoke. She did not respond, and Jackson wondered if she had already primed her son on what to say. Fleetingly, he considered how he would feel if Karen or Daniel confessed to murder. He quickly dismissed the thought.

Abercrombie had arranged for drinks, and these arrived. After a brief interval, while everyone was given the drink they wanted, Jackson continued, "Now, Jake, tell us what you did yesterday with Brian. Start with when you first met him."

The boy had almost ceased crying, but not entirely. Now and then, a tear rolled down his cheek as he related his story.

"I called for Brian after lunch, and we went for a walk. He was supposed to be grounded, but he sneaked out. We walked down the canal bank."

He broke down.

"It's my fault. I left him by himself."

Abercrombie, who was nearer to Jake than Jackson, put his arm around the boy. "I told you before. It isn't your fault. Don't work yourself up. Take a drink."

He reached for the Coke, brought in for Jake, and offered it to him. Jake sipped it, gradually recovering.

"Are you all right, love?" his mother asked, concerned her son was being put under pressure but knowing he had to tell the police what had happened.

"Yeah," the youngster answered. "We had a fight, and I left him."

"You had a fight?" Abercrombie asked the question.

"Yes."

"A big fight?"

"No. Brian hit me once, and I ran off."

"Where did he hit you?"

"In the face, just once."

"Why did he do that?"

"We argued."

"What about?"

"I can't tell you."

"Why not?"

"I promised."

"But it wasn't a big fight?"

"No."

"You didn't fight back?"

"No. He's bigger than me, he'd have killed me - I mean he'd have beat me up."

"I know what you meant, it's all right, Jake." Abercrombie looked at Jackson to indicate he should now continue with the interview.

"Weren't you angry with Brian for hitting you?" Jackson asked.

"At first, yeah, 'course I was, but then I knew it was my fault. I annoyed him."

"No one has the right to hit you, Jake. But are you saying you provoked him?"

"What does p-provoked mean?"

"Provoked? It means you gave him a reason to want to hit you."

"Yeah, then. I deserved it."

"You didn't get upset with him for hitting you?"

"I didn't kill him!" Jake shouted, suddenly realising what Jackson was getting at. He clutched his mother's arm as his eyes widened. "Mum! They think I killed Brian."

Abercrombie tried again to console the boy. This time, Jake drew away from him. Abercrombie was now one of the enemy.

"You don't really believe he did it, do you?" It was the parent speaking. "You've seen the size of him? I mean, he's twelve, but no one would think it to look at him."

"We have to cover everything, Mrs Swift," Jackson responded, then to Jake, "Would you like to have a break?"

Jake shook his head; he needed to get this over with. It was like visiting the dentist. You went in, had the treatment and got it out of the way. But Brian would never need to see a dentist ever again.

"Can I see your fingernails, Jake?"

"My nails!" said Jake surprised, but held out his hands for Jackson to inspect. Jackson looked down at the tiny hands and saw the fingernails were bitten down to the quick.

"You've got a bad habit there, biting your nails."

"I only do it when I'm worried. Last night I was worried."

Jackson turned to the mother. "Does Jake usually keep his fingernails short, Mrs Swift?"

"Reasonably. Why?"

"It doesn't matter. Did you see anyone else on the canal, Jake?"

"Yeah, a man with a dog, and a bloke on a bike. Brian talked to him. I told him not to. I bet it was him who murdered him."

"This man was on a motorbike?"

"No. A push bike. A blue mountain bike. An Eagle, fifteen gears, I think."

"It's great you remembered all that," Jackson praised. "Now can you recall what the man looked like? The one on the bike, I mean."

"Yeah, he had a beard, a black one. He was little, not tall I mean, but he had strong muscles."

"Anything else about him? I mean something he couldn't change. He could shave the beard off, you see?"

"Yeah, I see. I can't remember anything, though. He had no tattoos or anything like that if that's what you mean. He pretended to strangle Brian."

"What!"

"He put his hands round Brian's throat. Only playing, though. He didn't hurt him. Not then, anyway."

Jackson and Abercrombie looked at each other. They were both aware of what the other was thinking. Forensic would use film to lift the man's fingerprints from Brian's neck but, if they arrested the bloke and matched the prints to him, he would use this playful banter as an excuse for them being there.

"Well, thanks for coming to see us. Your mum can take you home now. We might need to see you again but if we do, we'll arrange it with your parents. And don't fuss about it being your fault anymore. The only person whose fault it was is the one who did it. If it wasn't you, and I'm not suggesting it was, you've nothing to worry about."

He left Abercrombie to show them out and made his way back to his office where Abercrombie joined him again a few minutes later and sat at the desk opposite Jackson.

"Well, it sounds like we only need to find the black bearded man and we have our killer."

"No. We need to find a white man with a black beard."

"'Course," Abercrombie laughed at his own mistake but quickly became serious again. Child murders were not a humorous matter.

"Anyway," Jackson said, "There's nothing so far to prove he's our culprit. Could have been an innocent conversation. I agree he's the most likely suspect, though."

"Do you think he did that deliberately? Put his hands round the kid's neck to destroy the fingerprint evidence, I mean?"

Jackson stroked his moustache.

"I did wonder. But why only one kid? He didn't know the boys would fight and split up. Surely, he wouldn't plan to kill just one of 'em and leave the other alive to identify him."

"Shouldn't we be protecting Jake, then?"

"Oh, I'm positive he's safe now. The killer will be aware he's already described him to us."

"What was all that with the fingernails?" Abercrombie asked. "You don't genuinely think the lad could have done it, do you?"

"As I told the mother, we need to examine all possibilities. The murderer had small hands with long fingernails. That could fit a child."

"Jake did say our bearded fellow was small."

"Yes, I've not forgotten that. But don't forget he could be covering himself."

"Yeah, but he's a lot smaller than the victim. He was frightened of him to some extent, or he wouldn't have run off when he hit him. He'd have fought back."

"We've only got his word that he didn't. Or that he didn't go back again. The kid certainly feels guilty. Is the guilt merely because he left Brian alone as he claims, or is there more to it than that? And size doesn't always come into it, especially if he was angry enough."

"That's true, I suppose." Abercrombie rose from his seat. "I'll get his statement into the computer."

He left Jackson alone to ponder.

Jackson was troubled. Things were taking longer than expected. With the clues they had, the bike; the bearded man; there should have been further progress by now. The bearded man must have heard the news by this time. Why hadn't he come forward? The fact he hadn't could only mean he had something to hide.

In one way, Jackson was glad of that. It meant he was probably wrong about Jake. Despite his remarks to Abercrombie, Jackson didn't want to believe Jake murdered his friend, but he had to accept everything fitted, even the fingernails had only been bitten short since the slaying. It wasn't unknown for a child to kill another child - children with sometimes less of a motive than Jake.

A bigger boy struck Jake. It probably wasn't the first time it had happened. What if he'd decided he'd had enough of being bullied and done something about it?

Jackson had some sympathy with the victims of bullies. He'd been in that situation himself. The memory made him look at the old school photograph he kept in his desk drawer.

A group of smiling kids looked out at him from the picture. He sat second from the end on the front row. They were all clad in the clothing of the late sixties, which looked comical by today's standards.

In the background was the imposing castle-like building that was his home during the school terms of his childhood.

He too was smiling in the photograph, but he could remember how hard it was to force that smile. The two kids sitting on either side of him were his biggest, but not his only, tormentors.

In those days, when he was about eleven, he recalled, he used to scream loud whenever he was threatened, hoping this tactic would make the bullies leave him alone. It never worked. At that age, he didn't understand his attackers loved to hear him shriek in terror and so tormented him even more. Now, it embarrassed him to think about those times.

He eventually learned to stick up for himself, but not for some while after this photograph was taken. He had also learned to resent bullying of any kind. That was partially what made him join the police. To see justice done against the thugs who picked on weaker people.

He threw the photograph back in the drawer, reminding himself again that neither of his kids would ever be sent to boarding school, and turned his mind back to Jake.

Was it conceivable Jake could kill his friend to retaliate for being thumped in the face? Probably not deliberately, but Jackson remembered how often he had fantasised about executing the other kids who made his life hell at school. He had controlled his fantasies. Supposing Jake hadn't?

Abercrombie came back into the room. He had checked the description Jake gave of the suspect with the one Leonard Mason had given, who confirmed the man was short.

"Doesn't prove anything in itself," Jackson said, "But it does mean Jake was at least telling the truth about that."

* * *

Feeling strange without his beard, in a small cul-de-sac in the middle of town, David Ewan sat at his piano softly playing a tune. Ewan, though not competent enough to perform in public, was a sufficiently good enough piano player for his own entertainment. Playing on the keyboard helped him to think and, having no bike, he hadn't much else to do, anyhow.

He wished he'd taken a different route for his ride yesterday, and he'd never set eyes on those youngsters. Why didn't he ignore them? He'd moved here to get away from all that, and now it was going to start all over again.

No one knew him around here. The police would be looking for a bearded man with a bike. He now had neither. But he would still be their number one suspect. Why didn't he leave the kids alone?

* * *

The following morning turned out to be yet another warm day. The heat wave had been around too long for most people. Tempers were flaring. Dogs and cats were seeking shade, looking distressed. It was the sort of weather when smart people tried not to disturb dogs.

Jackson and Abercrombie climbed out of Jackson's Mondeo and found number twenty-six Duke Street, the address of the Churcher's. The blue curtains were closed out of respect for Brian and the short pathway leading to the front door was covered with floral tributes from his friends and neighbours. Despite the early hour of day, they were already wilting. A constable stood at the doorway keeping away the press and sightseers with nothing better to do than visit the home of a murder victim, having no regard for the feelings of the grieving parents.

The two detectives pushed their way through this morbid crowd. The uniformed police officer acknowledged them and let them through.

Inside the house, a female police officer was sitting with the parents. Angela sat forward in a large armchair. She was crying. The news had become reality, Jackson thought.

Frank was sitting opposite her looking more composed but, Jackson remembered, Brian wasn't Frank's own child.

The home was spacious for a family of three. It looked tidy, yet lived in. An assortment of ornamental elephants paraded along the mantelpiece.

"I'm going to have to ask you some questions about Brian. Are you feeling up to it, now?" Jackson asked.

"Go ahead, the sooner you catch this killer, the better."

It was Frank who had replied, surprising Jackson by speaking in the presence of his more dominant spouse.

Apparently, Angela had given him permission to do this, as she couldn't yet face it herself.

"First, do you know if anybody would have a reason for wanting to kill him?"

"Why does anyone kill a child?"

"Well, he didn't, for example, witness a crime where he could identify someone?"

"If he did, he never told us."

"What was Brian like, I mean was he well-behaved?"

"He had his moments like all teenagers."

Angela joined in the conversation. "He was always good for me. He resented Frank because he wasn't his real dad. You had problems with him, didn't you, Frank? We took months to persuade him to change his surname. It used to be Cunningham."

"Angela, you'll make them think I killed him myself," Frank said, then to Jackson, "It wasn't anything more than the usual father and son issues, you know, teenage rebellion and all that."

"You mentioned he wasn't supposed to be out yesterday. Why was that?"

"He was grounded."

"What for?"

"I can't remember."

"You grounded your stepson, and you can't remember why?"

"Well, it was something trivial. I was annoyed because he'd disobeyed and gone out without permission."

"And neither of you saw him go out?"

"My wife is at work during the day. I must have been asleep."

Jackson hesitated before going on, wondering how to approach the delicate subject he needed to ask about. He decided it was best to be direct.

"One thing I have to ask you both, Mr and Mrs Churcher, were you aware Brian had been sexually abused?"

"Well, that's why they killed him then, isn't it?" Frank said.

"No. I didn't mean yesterday. I meant in the past."

"What!" Angela became alert again.

"You didn't know?"

"'Course not, or we'd have reported it, wouldn't we?" Angela sounded indignant.

"That doesn't always happen," Jackson responded.

"So, whoever was abusing him murdered him to keep him quiet?" Frank said.

"We don't know yet."

"You can tell these days, can't you? With DNA and all that stuff?"

"Sometimes. But we need a suspect to do the tests on."

"If you caught someone, can you make them give you a sample or can they refuse?"

"They could refuse unless we charged them, but then it would make them look guilty."

"Must have been one of his teachers or his youth club leader. He doesn't know any other adults."

"No male relatives?"

"You're not suggesting one of the family did this to him?"

"I'm afraid most cases like this do take place within the family."

"Well, it's not me!"

"No one has accused you, Mr Churcher."

Jackson glanced at Frank's hands only to find the fingernails had been neatly trimmed.

At that point, Abercrombie's mobile phone buzzed. He had been taking notes, having some difficulty in the darkened room. Now he moved into the hallway to answer the phone. When he came back, he glanced at the Churchers, then at Jackson. "We need to go," he said.

Jackson apologised to the Churchers and followed Abercrombie outside.

"We'll soon have our murderer - the bike's been found," the sergeant explained to Jackson once they were in the car. "It was thrown in the canal. Some kids fishing down there discovered it."

"So, he's disposed of the bike. That certainly makes him seem guilty. They are sure it's the same bike?"

"It matches the kid's description. There can't be too many like it, and it's a bit of a coincidence for a similar bike to turn up in the same canal."

"Right. If he's dumped the bike, though, he'll have shaved off his beard too. Pity bikes don't have registration numbers, like cars."

"No, but they have frame numbers. We'll be able to trace the shop that sold it."

"Good thinking. Let's hope our suspect bought it new then."

"By the way, didn't you notice Frank seemed a bit edgy when you brought up the abuse?"

"Yes, I did. He's almost certainly the one that's been molesting the kid all right. Doesn't mean he killed him, though. Especially now we know our cyclist can't be ruled out."

"Aren't you going to arrest him then? Frank, I mean?"

"We'll bring him in eventually, but let's just let them grieve for their son for a while. After all, he can't hurt the kid anymore, can he?"

"Right." Abercrombie wasn't too happy about this. He liked to do things by the book, but he conceded Jackson's point.

"Besides, we've no solid evidence," Jackson said, knowing Abercrombie's views. "You know as well as I do that all that stuff about DNA was rubbish. It could only prove Frank had contact with the boy, and since they lived together it would hardly be a surprise. Only a semen sample could show Frank was responsible, and unless he's violated the kid very recently, I think we're too late for that."

"The boy's not going to tell us anything, is he? So, Churcher will get away with it?"

"Not if I can help it. As I said, we'll bring him in and question him about it later. He might even confess. He thinks we can get him with the DNA, remember. We won't tell him otherwise. Let's concentrate on catching Brian's murderer first, that's more important than finding his abuser."

"Yes," Harry conceded. "Though it's unusual for it not to be the same person."

He leant his head back, resting it on the car headrest, taking advantage of Jackson doing the driving. Despite his lower rank, he was the oldest by about five years. He hadn't been passed over for promotion. He just preferred not to climb above the position of detective sergeant. The higher your status, the more bogged down with paperwork you got. Harry didn't join the police to do paperwork.

When they arrived at the police station, the bike had already been brought in and taken to the evidence area. Seeing Jackson and Abercrombie enter the incident room, Gloria handed Jackson a slip of paper on which were written letters and numbers.

"The frame number, Sir," she said. "I've already checked it. It was sold by a shop in Tonbridge, Kent."

"Kent?"

"Yes."

"Do they know who they sold it to?"

"No."

"I thought that would be too simple," Jackson said, glancing at Abercrombie.

"But the customer paid by credit card and they still have their copy of the transaction slip. They're phoning back when they find it."

"Well done, Gloria. So, we just need to find out who owns the credit card."

"Well, not quite, sir. The original buyer might not be the current owner, or he might not have used his own card."

"Yes, I know, but we've got a starting point. Get on to it as quick as possible. I want this all wrapped up by tomorrow so I can enjoy my daughter's birthday party."

Chapter 4

It was Saturday, which didn't help Gloria Waters in her task of trying to find the owner of the credit card.

The few people working on the helplines at the finance company were not senior enough to give out the information. Only when she pointed out the urgency of the request did someone reluctantly agree to contact a high-ranking manager at home. Gloria thought it would have been simpler to call the President of the United States.

Even when the promised phone call came from the official, he refused to give Gloria the credit card details over the phone. Gloria understood this. She couldn't confirm her identity over the telephone and was aware the credit card people had to uphold their client's confidentiality. Giving the manager the police station's number so he could ring back after checking it wasn't acceptable to him either. Because it was a murder investigation, he told Gloria he would waive needing a court order to hand over the information to the police. He would, however, only agree give it to an officer in person.

Gloria considered this unreasonable but could do nothing about it. She called her colleagues in the Kent police force then could only sit and wait until they called back. Another delay.

* * *

David Ewan felt more confident now two days had passed with no one from the police knocking on the door. Sat at his piano, he wondered if he should practice more. It was possible for him to make some cash by teaching kids to play. He certainly needed it. He had money saved from his last job, but that was being depleted fast. The cost of travelling here was greater than expected, then there was the expense of the extra security measures he had fitted in the house. How much could he charge for keyboard lessons? Then again, maybe having kids here alone would be a bit risky.

Perhaps it had been a mistake not to get married. Living by yourself had benefits, but also problems. It might not be too late. But he would miss those advantages like being able to do as he wanted whenever he wished, staying out or coming home as the desire took him. He'd remain single.

*　*　*

In the office, Jackson paced the room as Abercrombie sat at his own desk. Gloria Waters stood by the door.

"What's taking them so bloody long?" Jackson ranted to Gloria after she told them about the issues with the credit card company.

"I believe they need to wait for a senior member of staff to travel from home, sir," Gloria responded. "No one else can release the information."

"That's ridiculous. Their client might be a murderer."

"I know."

The phone buzzed. Abercrombie picked it up.

"The Churchers' are in reception," he said after listening.

"That's all we need! All right, Harry, let's see what they want."

They left, and Gloria returned to the incident room, glad of a reprieve from Jackson's frustration.

At the reception desk, Jackson and Abercrombie found Angela with Frank in tow. She seemed to have recovered a bit since they'd seen her earlier and had re-established her dominance over her diminutive husband who stood a pace behind.

Jackson led them both into the interview room and asked Abercrombie to fetch coffees.

"I'm sorry I wasn't much use this morning," Angela said. "I was too upset to talk. Only now I'm able to think properly again, I want to tell you I'm not satisfied. It's been two days, and you still haven't caught my boy's murderer. Frank thinks you're being too slow too, don't you Frank?"

True to form, Frank didn't get the chance to reply for himself as she went on. "I mean you have a good description and you know he's got a bike. How hard can he be to find?"

"We are doing all we can, Mrs Churcher."

"Well, it's not good enough, is it Frank?"

Just as, for once, it seemed as if Angela was going to pause long enough for Frank to answer, Abercrombie returned with the drinks. These were poured and served before Jackson said, "We have found what we think is the bike."

"So then, what are you waiting for?" Angela asked. "You can get fingerprints from it."

"No. I'm afraid it's not that simple. The bike's been under water for a while. It was dumped in the canal."

Angela went quiet as she considered this and, taking advantage of her silence, Frank found a voice.

"That proves he did it then, doesn't it?"

"It looks like it," Jackson answered. "Unfortunately, we still don't know who he is, though."

Angela had been silent long enough. "And this is the bloke who's been molesting my child? I'll bloody well kill him."

Abercrombie couldn't let that pass.

"The person who killed Brian might not be the same one that abused him," he said.

"It's most probable, though, isn't it? Why else would he murder him, except to keep him quiet?"

"There's lots of reasons kids are murdered besides sexual motives."

"That's not likely, though, is it?" Frank got another sentence into the discussion.

"That is the most likely motive," Abercrombie agreed, having to bite his tongue to stop him from telling Frank of their suspicions about him.

"Tell him what you told me, Frank," said Angela. "Frank thinks he knows who did it. Don't you, Frank? It was the leader at the Youth Club Brian went to. He rides a bike, doesn't he, Frank? What's his name? Steve, no Dave, that's it."

"What makes you say that?" Jackson asked, looking at Frank.

"Brian was always talking about him, saying what such a great bloke he was," said Angela, again before Frank had time to speak.

Jackson could see the only way he would get anything useful out of Frank was to interview him alone. Turning to Harry, he said, "Would you stay here and talk to Mrs Churcher? I'll speak to Mr Churcher by himself."

Harry nodded and, taking their coffees with them, Jackson led Frank from the area into a second interview room.

"Now," Jackson said, once they were settled down. "Is that true, what your wife was saying about the Youth Club Leader?"

"Yes. Brian thought the sun shone if you'll pardon the phrase, and he's known him for quite a while. He'll be the one who's been shaggin' him."

"That's a serious allegation, Mr Churcher."

"Who else could it be?"

"And if you're right, you think your stepson did what this, Dave did you say, wanted willingly?"

"Probably, yes. Always was a weird kid."

"If that's true, why would the man need to kill him?"

"I don't know! Maybe Brian changed his mind or threatened to tell someone. Perhaps he was blackmailing the bloke. I don't know. You're the detective. You find out."

"Rest assured, Mr Churcher. If what you're saying is correct, we will find out. Do you know this Dave's second name?"

"No."

"Which Youth Club was it? We'll find him."

"Don't know what it's called. They meet at St. Luke's church hall."

"St. Luke's Youth Club?"

"Might be."

"So, it isn't a council run club with full-time leaders. This Dave will be a volunteer?"

"I wouldn't know about that."

"Does Dave have a beard?"

"I've never seen him. Brian never mentioned one, but it's not the sort of thing kids' talk about, is it?"

"No, it's not."

* * *

In the other room, Harry Abercrombie looked across at Angela who was wearing a black dress and couldn't help wondering where she got her clothes. Such a large size would never be stocked in the shops.

"Tell me more about Brian," he asked. "Knowing some background might help us."

In truth, he considered they had already learned everything they needed to know about her son, but letting Angela tell the boy's life story would comfort her and stop her asking questions about why Frank had been taken out of the room.

"He was a good boy," she said. "He got into trouble a year or two ago, shoplifting and that, but that was because he was upset when his dad died."

"And you said he didn't get on with his stepdad?"

"Oh, he was all right. It's just that Frank's not used to kids. I'm his first wife, you know. Brian resented me marrying him, though. He had to share me, you see. He was only eleven then."

"And his hobbies? Apart from attending the Youth Club?"

"He went fishing sometimes. Played a lot with that other boy, Jake. Oh, and he has, I mean had, a computer."

"A computer? Where is that now?"

"Still up in his bedroom. Don't know what'll happen to it. Neither Frank nor I understand computers."

"We might want to look at that if it's all right?"

"I suppose so. Why?"

"It's possible Brian made notes on it. Like a diary. It might tell us something useful."

"I wouldn't think so. Brian was never one for writing things in diaries. I'm sure he only played games on it."

"Well, you never know."

* * *

As they compared notes later, it interested Jackson to learn about Brian's computer. Like Abercrombie, he thought there was the possibility of Brian storing something on it, even if the boy's mother considered it unlikely. It was the kind of place a kid would hide what he didn't want others to see; especially if his parents had no interest in the machine. Jackson had little understanding of computers himself, but there were plenty of people on the team, including Abercrombie, who did. He dialled the incident room and asked for someone to arrange for the machine to be collected from Duke Street.

His next call was to the vicar of St. Luke's to inquire if there was a Youth Leader attached to the church by the name of Dave.

"We have two David's," the vicar answered, "David Parkinson and David Glover."

"Which of them rides a push-bike?"

"I'm not aware that either of them do. They both own cars."

"I'll need to see them both, then," Jackson replied, disappointed one of them couldn't be ruled out straight away.

He scribbled down the addresses of both David's as the vicar gave them to him, thanked the clergyman and hung up.

It was now early afternoon, and neither himself nor Abercrombie had yet had lunch. He was about to suggest they did this when Gloria came into the office.

"I've got it," she said excitedly. "The credit card was issued to a David Ewan. He used to live in Tonbridge but moved into this area recently. I've even tracked down his new address."

"Great. Well done," Jackson praised. "Wait a minute, did you say David?"

"Yes."

"Let me see the address." He took the slip of paper from her and compared the address with the two the vicar had given him. They didn't match.

"Damn! We now have three Dave's to interview," he grumbled.

"But this one is the owner of the bike," Abercrombie consoled. "He's not likely to have sold it if he's not been in the neighbourhood long, and even if he has, it would be a coincidence for him to sell it to another Dave."

"That's true," Jackson said, "But you never know. David is a common name, and if he's just moved here, he might have been short of money and sold the bike. We'll need to get all three Dave's brought in for questioning. No arrests, voluntary interviews only for the moment."

* * *

The three David's were all located and brought into the police station at roughly the same time. The two Youth Club leaders, who obviously knew each other, were seen first.

Jackson was aware he could save time by asking Abercrombie to question one of the men while he saw the other but preferred to do all the interviews himself whenever possible. Now he and Harry sat facing David Glover. They had chosen him for the initial interview because his height alone, almost as tall as Abercrombie, ruled him out as the short person they were looking for. They questioned him, anyway, just to be sure.

"You're not under arrest or anything like that, David, you don't mind if I call you David?"

"No, but it's Dave."

"Okay, Dave. We want to ask a few questions about Brian Churcher, the local boy who was murdered. Did you know him?"

"I hear he was a member of our Youth Club, but there are a lot of members. I don't know all the kids by name."

"So, you didn't have a particular relationship with Brian?"

"I don't even know which boy he was. I'd probably recognise him by sight if he came into the club, but I don't recall the name."

"For our records, can you tell us where you were on Thursday, late afternoon to early evening?"

"At home, planning a project for the Youth Club kids."

"Was anyone with you?"

"Not all the time. My wife was there until she went shopping. I didn't know I was going to need an alibi."

"Do you own a bike, Dave?"

"No."

Jackson saw no point in continuing.

"All right, Dave. You're free to go. If you remember anything about the boy, please get in touch. Sergeant Abercrombie will see you out."

Harry got up to show Glover out and came back a minute or so later with David Parkinson.

Parkinson was shorter. Not as short as Frank Churcher, but he had small hands and was short enough for Jake Swift to describe him as 'little'. Of more interest to Jackson was that his fingernails were long and while it wasn't exactly black, more a dark brown, he wore a beard.

"Is it Dave or David?" Jackson asked.

"Either. At the Youth Club, the kids call me David, but that's so they can distinguish between Dave Glover and me."

"Then I'll do the same if you don't mind. Did you know the murdered boy, Brian Churcher?"

"Yes. Quite well."

"Do you have a bike, David?"

"Yes. Hardly ever use it, though."

"What colour is it?"

"Blue, as it happens. I know you've been looking for someone with a blue bike, but as I told you, I don't use it much. I can't even remember when I last used it."

"Didn't you think to come forward when you heard we wanted to talk to someone who owned a blue bike and had a beard?"

"You wanted someone with a black beard, mine's brown, and the bike's not been moved for ages."

"You had a special relationship with Brian?"

"I liked him. I sort of took him under my wing when his dad died. He was quite upset about it."

"What would you say if I were to tell you there's been an allegation that you abused him?"

"What!"

"You deny it?"

"'Course I damn well deny it. I'm not that sort of person. I'm married with two kids."

"Being married, even with children, isn't proof of your sexual inclinations, David."

"No, of course not," David responded as he realised the stupidity of his statement. "It's just the shock of you saying what you did. Where's this allegation come from? It can't be from the dead boy, can it?"

"No. But it is true that Brian was abused."

"Not by me, he wasn't. When I said I had a relationship with him, I didn't mean that kind."

"Where were you on Thursday evening?"

"Working. The Youth Club work's only voluntary."

"Where do you work?"

"I'm a delivery man. I drive a van for Horseman's, the confectioners."

"On your own?"

"I'm afraid so."

"And none of your customers would recall you delivering to them?"

"Yes, but I've got plenty of time between deliveries. I can't prove I wasn't on the canal if that's what you're getting at. But I wasn't."

"Okay, you're free to leave for now. You will tell us if you remember anything about Brian that might help us?"

"I can go? So, you're not taking this accusation seriously, then?"

"I'm afraid we might need to investigate that further. For the moment, we're only concerned with finding Brian's killer. Which might or might not be the same person who abused him."

"I can carry on working at the Youth Club?"

"That's a matter between yourself and the vicar though I will have to tell him about the accusation."

"I'll tell him myself."

Again, Abercrombie led the man away and returned with the last of the Dave's. He had been left until last as he was the one Jackson was most interested in, and likely to need to spend the most time with.

David Ewan was almost as diminutive a man as Frank Churcher, but was clean-shaven, and his fingernails were neatly cut. This did not deter Jackson. Ewan could easily have trimmed his nails and shaved off the beard since the murder.

"You know why you've been brought here?" Jackson asked.

"Something about my old bike, they told me."

"Your old bike?"

"Yes, I used to have a blue bike, like the one you've been looking for. But it was stolen a few days ago."

"Did you report it?"

"No, there's no point is there, you never find them, and it wasn't insured?"

"Where was it taken from?"

"From the front of my house. I'd left it there just for a minute. When I went back, it had gone."

"You're not from round here, are you?"

"No. Kent. I've just moved here."

"Because of work?"

"No. I haven't got a job. I wanted a change."

"Isn't that unusual? You moved all the way from Kent to Greater Manchester without having any work to go to?"

Ewan shrugged.

"What line of work are you in, when you do have a job?" Jackson went on.

"I do labouring on construction sites. Hod carrying, mostly."

Jackson thought Ewan was a bit on the short side for that kind of work, but then he realised despite his lack of height, the man did have quite muscular arms and looked strong enough for such a task. He knew it was also reasonably well-paid work and meant it was possible Ewan had substantial savings and most likely claimed Job-Seekers Allowance as well. That would explain how he could afford to uproot from one part of the country to another.

"Did you know the murdered boy?" he asked.

"No. I know nobody here. I've only been here a week or so. I haven't even met the postman yet."

"Have you ever had a beard, Dave?"

"Yes, but not since I've been here."

"And looking at the colour of your hair, it would be a black beard?"

"Yes, but I shaved it off before leaving Kent."

"Why?"

Another shrug. "Just wanted a change. It was when this hot weather started."

"How long did you say you've been here?" Abercrombie interrupted.

"About a week. Last Sunday, in fact."

"The heatwave only started on Tuesday."

"Well, it was warm in Kent."

"Before the heat wave, the whole country had a cold and wet spell," Jackson said. "I remember because my wife and I were discussing holidays. We can check the records, anyway."

Ewan didn't reply for a moment. Sweating, he leaned back as far as his chair would allow. "All right," he said eventually, "You'll find out soon enough now you've found me. I am the one who was riding the bike, but I didn't kill the kid."

"We will find out everything, as you say," Abercrombie came back into the conversation. "So, supposing you tell us why you really moved from Kent. Moving so far away from your home to a place where you don't know anyone because you want a change of scenery just isn't logical. You must see that?"

"Yes. All right. Your colleagues will tell you anyway now they know where I am. I have a record for child molesting. I moved here to make a fresh start."

And to start with fresh kids, Jackson thought.

"David Ewan, I'm arresting you on suspicion of murdering Brian Churcher. You don't have to say anything..."

Chapter 5

Jake Swift was still worried. He was helping his dad to get rid of the weeds in their front garden when a grey Ford Mondeo pulled up at the gate and the two detectives he had seen at the police station got out. This disturbed him even more. They still thought he'd killed Brian!

"Mr Swift?" Jackson asked as he opened the gate and spoke to the man he assumed to be Jake's father.

"Yes."

"I'm Detective Inspector Jackson, and this is Sergeant Abercrombie. We've already met Jake. Could we have a word with you both, in private?"

"H-have you come to arrest me?" Jake asked through quivering lips as his eyes widened.

"No. I promise, we want to talk, that's all."

Looking relieved, the boy went into the house with the adults.

* * *

It was well furnished inside, everything in place. The living room walls decorated in shades of green. A deep-pile blue carpet softened their tread as they were shown into the room. The coverings on the suite were in a lighter shade of blue. Two highly polished wooden coffee tables dominated the area. A dark oak TV cabinet took up the space along one wall. A grandfather clock in the corner chimed as they entered. The decor wasn't to Jackson's personal taste; he preferred a less opulent style.

Mr Swift invited them to sit on the settee and they did so, sinking into the luxurious padding.

Jake's mother was also in the room and offered tea, but they declined this.

"We need to ask Jake a few more questions. Is that all right, Jake?" Jackson asked.

"I've already told you everything." Jake had remained standing and was now at the same eye-level as Jackson. He trembled slightly, cheeks pale despite the heat of the day.

"Not quite everything. You didn't tell us what your quarrel with Brian was about?"

"I told you, I can't. I promised. It was like you said, I p-proked him."

"Provoked," Jackson corrected. "You know Brian's dead, don't you? Promises made to dead people don't count."

Jake looked unsure about this but held his ground. "No, I can't say."

"Well, it might not be important, but we need to find out as much as we can about Brian. You understand that, don't you?"

Jake nodded but stayed silent.

"What I really need to ask, Jake, is whether you would recognise the man who spoke to you again, even if he didn't have his beard anymore? Do you think you could do that?"

"I think so. Why? Do you think I'm making it up?"

"No, I don't believe you're making it up. You see, you weren't the only one to see the man, so we know he was there. We just need to prove it was him who killed Brian."

"What if you can't prove it? You'll think it was me then, won't you?"

"If we thought that, we'd need to prove you did it, like we're trying to do now with the man."

Jake's father rose from the armchair he had occupied.

"Wait a minute -"

"It's all right, Mr Swift," Jackson interrupted him. "We're not suggesting your son had anything to do with the murder. In fact, we're fairly sure we've already arrested the culprit."

A great weight seemed to lift from Jake as he heard those words.

"So, I'm not a suspect anymore?"

Abercrombie now spoke. "You've never truly been a suspect, Jake," he reassured the boy. "We would like you to come down to the police station, though, to identify the man. If it's all right with your mum and dad?"

"Will he see me?"

"No. But you needn't worry. Even if he does, he's going to prison for a long time so he won't be able to hurt you."

* * *

At the hastily arranged identity parade, Jake had no trouble in identifying Ewan as the person who had spoken to them during their walk. He was sure the man could see him through the one-way mirror and, afraid, put his arms around his father for comfort. An immature act for a twelve-year-old, Jackson thought, but then how many twelve-year-olds had looked into the face of a person who had killed their friend?

He got someone from uniform to take the boy and his father home and then had Ewan brought back to the interview room.

Jackson felt good. He would soon get a confession from Ewan, charge him, and go home to enjoy the rest of the weekend with his family.

Abercrombie again sat in on the interview. He started the tape recorder and took his place beside Jackson.

Ewan, who had not requested a solicitor, sat opposite them.

"Before we continue," Jackson said, "I need to remind you that you are still under caution. Also, you can still use the services of a solicitor. I recommend it, actually. Are you certain you don't want me to call the duty solicitor?"

"No. I've not done anything wrong, so I don't need a solicitor."

"If you're sure?"

"It's my choice, isn't it?"

"It is."

"Well then."

"Okay, if that's what you want. First, I need to tell you we have a witness who has identified you as the person who talked to the murdered boy shortly before his death."

"I've never denied speaking to him."

Jackson realised that was true. They hadn't needed Jake's identification. Being seen speaking to the boys didn't prove Ewan had anything to do with the killing. This wasn't going to be as straightforward as he had first supposed.

"Why didn't you come forward to be eliminated then? You must have known we were searching for you?"

"With my record? I knew you'd jump to the conclusion I'd killed the kid, like you have now."

"If you're innocent what does it matter? You won't be found guilty without evidence."

"That's a joke. Have you never heard of the Guildford Four or the Bridgewater case?"

Jackson had, and been outraged by those events.

"Those cases weren't typical of the British Justice System," he said.

Ewan leaned forward and placed his palms flat down on the desk. "You might believe that. I don't. People have been hanged and later found to be innocent." He relaxed and sat back in his chair again. "Besides, there is something else. You will find what you'll consider evidence. You're going to find my fingerprints on the boy's neck. I put my hands round his throat, just playing."

"Funny kind of play, wasn't it?" Abercrombie now joined in.

"It was only a bit of fun."

"I think you did it on purpose. You knew you were going to strangle him, so you made sure your prints were already on his neck. Isn't that how it happened?"

"No, I never saw those kids again."

"Why did you stop to talk to the boys in the first place?" Jackson asked, taking back the lead.

"I was just trying to be friendly."

"With children? Even though you came here to put your past behind you? A past involving crimes against kids?"

"I wasn't going to touch them. I wanted to be friends, that's all."

"You don't honestly expect us to believe that?"

"It's the truth."

"You've already admitted being attracted to kids. You're saying you didn't have any feelings towards these two boys?"

"I can control myself now. All right, I did fancy the little one, but I could see straight away he wasn't interested, and even if he had been, I've reformed. I don't do that kind of stuff anymore. I've had treatment."

But did the treatment work, Jackson wondered? As Ewan tried to stroke the beard he forgot was no longer there, Jackson went on. "I'll tell you what I believe happened. You met the boys, as you said. You saw the smaller boy wasn't going to co-operate, so you concentrated on the older one and put your hands round his neck telling him you were just playing, fooling around. Whether you did that on purpose like Sergeant Abercrombie thinks, or you intended to kill both boys, I don't know. Either way, you were interrupted. Another adult, a man walking his dog, came onto the scene.

"You rode off on your bike and waited further up the canal for the kids. Unfortunately for you, they had a fight or a squabble of some kind, and one of them ran off. That meant you could only get hold of the one remaining kid. You most likely waited somewhere and ambushed him. He wouldn't do what you wanted - we know he wasn't interfered with at the time - so you strangled him."

"No. None of that's true. I've told you what happened."

"But my version sounds more likely. What do you think, Sergeant Abercrombie?"

"It sounds right to me," Harry replied. "Only, perhaps you did just intend to catch the one kid. It would be a lot easier to handle a boy by himself. Maybe you engineered the argument they had, knowing it would make them split up?"

"How could I do that?"

"Come on, you're a mature man and they're two kids. It would be simple enough for you to manipulate a situation causing them to fall out with each other?"

"What were they arguing about?"

"We don't know."

"Well, whatever it was, it was nothing to do with me. They did have a bit of a quarrel while I was talking to them. The little one was telling the other he shouldn't speak to me."

"He was right, wasn't he?"

"They had nothing to fear from me."

"Nothing to fear! You're a convicted paedophile."

"My time's been served."

"Yes. When did you do that time?" Jackson asked, wondering why the Kent police hadn't notified them of Ewan's whereabouts.

"I know what you're thinking. That I was supposed to register. Well, it was before that rule came out. I was released six years ago."

"And you've kept out of trouble since then?"

"Yes."

No, thought Abercrombie, you've not been caught since. He didn't, however, think he'd better voice that opinion.

* * *

Angela Churcher had heard the news of Ewan's arrest and now came lumbering over the threshold of the police station and waddled to the front desk. This time without her husband.

"Where is he?" she demanded, thumping on the reception counter. "The bastard who killed my kid. I'll pull his balls off."

The desk sergeant came round to her side of the counter and tried to restrain her. She easily overpowered him and shook him away.

"Let me at him," she ranted. "He murdered my son. Surely I'm entitled to punish him for that?"

Jackson, summoned by the commotion, appeared in the reception area and Angela recognised him.

"Oh, Mr Jackson. You've caught him, haven't you? Let me have him, just for a minute that's all. He throttled my son. Let me do the same to him, please?"

"Calm down, Mrs Churcher. Rest assured, if he's guilty he'll be punished."

"If he's guilty? How can he not be guilty?"

"Everyone is entitled to a fair trial."

"Brian never got a fair trial, did he?"

She was quieter now, and Jackson asked for a cup of tea to be given to her, then a lift home. He went back to his office and told Abercrombie what had happened.

By this time, Ewan had been returned to his cell with no progress being made. Jackson was concerned the case would not be wrapped up as fast as he had hoped. He needed to make sure, whatever happened, he would be at Karen's birthday party tomorrow, but the maximum time they could hold Ewan without charge was ticking away. He couldn't afford to take tomorrow off.

"Not one bit of hard evidence," he complained to Abercrombie.

"Plenty of circumstantial, though. He did it all right."

"But the motive's a bit weak, isn't it? I mean why kill the kid when he hadn't actually done anything to him?"

"He might have been afraid the boy would still report he'd approached him."

"So why didn't he abuse him anyway, by force? If he was going to kill him, he might as well have had his way with him?"

"You think Ewan's innocent?"

"I didn't say that, but we need to consider he might be telling the truth."

"No. Not after dumping the bike, hoping we wouldn't find him."

"He has a plausible explanation for that?"

"Yes, after he's had two days to figure out a story."

Jackson turned the fan on his desk to its highest position as he mopped sweat from his forehead. He couldn't help noticing again how Abercrombie managed to look so smart even in this intolerable heat, though for once he had discarded the light grey jacket of the suit he usually wore and now sat in his shirtsleeves. Jackson wondered how long it would be before he removed the tie too. His own had never been worn that week.

As a matter of routine, when Ewan was arrested, Abercrombie had gone with uniform to search his home and Jackson now inquired, "Anything incriminating at the house?"

"Nothing of any interest, really. Sparsely furnished, though from the number of locks on the door, you'd have thought he had the crown jewels in there. There was a piano. That was a bit of a surprise. Ewan doesn't seem like a person who plays the piano."

"Does he play, or does the piano belong to someone else?"

"We never asked him. No one else lives in the house, though. Does it matter?"

"You don't play a keyboard instrument, do you Harry?"

"I don't play any instrument at all. I've no ear for music."

"A pianist plays the keys with the end of his fingertips."

"So?"

"He'd need to keep his fingernails short."

"Oh, I see. That's not enough to rule him out, though, even if he is the one who plays the darned thing."

"No, it isn't, but it is a point in his favour."

"He disposed of the bike. Shaved his beard off. He's confessed to being a child molester. Surely that clinches it?"

"Being a child molester doesn't make him a murderer. He's never killed before."

"There's always a first time."

"I know, Harry, but something isn't quite right, here. It's purely a hunch, but I think we might have the wrong person."

Abercrombie paused for a moment before responding. "I don't think so. We just need to get more evidence, and we will. What bothers me though is that if I'm wrong and you're right, the real killer's still free. That brings the other kid back into the frame."

"I've thought about that too. I don't believe the boy did it, but we can't rule him out yet. There are the two Dave's from the youth club too, David Parkinson fits, he's small and has long fingernails."

"And a beard, but Jake's positively identified Ewan as the guy who talked to them."

"I know, and Ewan's admitted it was him, anyway. But supposing he's telling the truth, and it was an entirely different person who killed Brian? Talking to the kids, and even his inappropriate behaviour doesn't automatically mean he killed the boy."

"Ewan's not a fellow who speaks the truth. He lied to us from the beginning about the bike, remember?"

"Yes. It doesn't mean the rest of his story's a lie, though."

Both men went quiet for a few moments, then Abercrombie continued, "I still think you're wrong."

"There is a flaw, you know, in your theory about him deliberately putting his fingerprints on the boy's neck."

"What's that, then?"

"If forensic didn't find any other prints. It would still incriminate Ewan."

"He'd say the real killer wore gloves."

"The kid's face was scratched. That's not likely to happen if his attacker had gloves on."

"So we need to find out whether there are other prints on the dead boy's throat and that'll prove Ewan's guilt or innocence. I'll get on to forensic straight away."

He picked up the phone, but Jackson held up his hand to stop him.

"Don't you think they'd already have told us if they'd found anything?"

"It's weekend. They might not have completed their tests."

"They have. Not a single useable print on the lad's neck."

"What! Not even Ewan's?"

"No."

"So he must have washed Brian's neck afterwards or something. Probably used the canal water, the bastard. But he couldn't clean his clothing. He dragged him into the bushes, remember?"

"Forensic thought of that. There's plenty of prints there, a whole hotchpotch of different people's. Everyone in Staffington must have handled the kid's jacket at some time or other."

"But if Ewan's prints are among them-"

"It will take them too long to isolate all the prints. And it wouldn't prove anything. Ewan's admitted to having physical contact with the lad, remember."

Harry thought for a moment. He could see Ewan would get away with it if they weren't careful.

"That brings us back to the theory of him handling the boy on purpose, then," he said. "You're right about other prints not being found on the neck. He's thought of that and cleaned his own prints off, but realised there'd be prints on the clothing too. He knew it was likely a kid's jacket would get left lying around all over the place, and plenty of people would handle it, so he didn't worry about his prints being added when he moved the body."

"It's a theory," Jackson conceded, "but only a theory, Harry."

Chapter 6

In the incident room, Jackson and Abercrombie faced the rest of the team. Besides Gloria Waters, there was Alan Hook, a stocky bushy-haired young man who always seemed to be sweating. Next to him sat Kevin Gibson, dressed in a shabby dark-blue jumper and looking less like a detective than anyone could imagine. Sitting at the back were three people from uniform, two men and a woman, who had been seconded to the inquiry.

Affixed to the wall behind Jackson was a whiteboard, divided into columns. In the first column, the names of all the suspects seen up to now were written in bright red. In the second, was their alibis. The third column remained blank but was headed 'comments'.

All the team had listened to the taped interviews and pooled their information.

"I want to recap on what we know so far," Jackson started the briefing. Then turning to the whiteboard, he indicated the first, and chief suspect, David Ewan.

"Ewan is a convicted child molester," he went on. "Now I realise some of you would love to hang him for that alone - but it doesn't mean he's a murderer. It's true Ewan tried to hide from us. He changed his appearance as much as he could and dumped the blue bike he owned. However, he claims he did that because he assumed he would be pre-judged because of his history. He admits speaking to the boys not long before Brian was killed. He even confesses to having physical contact with him but says it was just playful banter. Any comments?"

"Playful banter? He put his hands round the boy's throat, for God's sake!" this from Hook.

"Haven't you ever seen a parent pretending to strangle a child in fun when they get on their nerves, Alan?" Jackson stroked his moustache.

"Yeah, but this is different, Ewan wasn't Brian's parent, was he?"

Jackson continued to rub at his facial hair as he answered. "No, but he still might have been being playful, as he claims."

"I wouldn't want a total stranger to put his hands on my child's neck, Sir," Gloria added her contribution. "I mean, it's not like ruffling his hair, is it?"

"I'm sure you wouldn't, Gloria, but that doesn't mean it couldn't happen. Can you say you know what's happening to your child right now? I'm sure my son, Daniel, doesn't tell us everything he's been up to when he's out by himself. All kids come home with bruises they can't explain. The minute they stop hurting, they've forgotten about them and can't remember how they got them. It's the same with something like this. If Brian hadn't been murdered and had got home, I very much doubt he'd even have remembered the incident, let alone told his parents about it."

Nobody spoke for a moment or so; then Harry Abercrombie joined the conversation. "One issue we've got with Ewan is the motive," he said. "Brian wasn't sexually interfered with at the time he was killed though he has been in the past. Has anyone got any views about why Ewan would want to kill him?"

"Because he wouldn't let him have his way with him," one of the uniformed police officers spoke from the back of the room.

"Inspector Jackson and I talked about that. If that were so, why didn't he force him to?"

"Not big enough. He's not much bigger than the kid."

"But he is an adult. And he would need to be strong enough to strangle the boy. He does keep himself fit - that's why he was cycling."

"Might it have been accidental?" Gibson asked. "I mean couldn't he have been threatening to strangle Brian to force him to perform some kind of sex with him and went too far?"

Harry looked at Jackson.

"It's possible, Kevin, but I don't consider it's likely. If he'd merely wanted to hurt the boy, it's more probable he'd twist his arm or something."

"Perhaps he didn't intend to hurt him. Just frighten him," Gibson proposed.

"It's a theory," Jackson responded.

"I think it's a pretty good theory," Harry said.

"But none of it's hard evidence," Jackson said. "Can anyone think of anything else?"

"Ewan's interfered with kids before, hasn't he? It's got to be him," Hook said.

"You're not listening, Alan. I said being a molester of kids doesn't automatically make Ewan a murderer of them."

"I still think it makes him a damn good suspect."

"Which is why he's in custody and at the top of the list," Jackson pointed to the name. "But there still isn't any real evidence, is there?"

Nobody answered.

"Okay, let's go down to the next name," Jackson continued. "Leonard Mason, the finder of the body. We don't know of anything that would connect him to the murder, other than being in the area at the time. It's true he reported finding the body, but if he is the murderer, he could have done that to cover himself. Anyone anything to say about Mason?"

"I was the first officer at the scene," the WPC said. "Leonard Mason was deeply disturbed by what he'd discovered. I don't think he did it."

"Neither do I, but does anything definitely rule him out?"

"His age," Gibson said.

"His age?"

"He's elderly. He'd be no match against a fourteen-year-old boy fighting for his life."

"Perhaps. But Mason had a dog with him. Brian might have been afraid of it."

"It's only a small mongrel, and a young playful one at that," Gibson said.

"If Brian wasn't used to dogs, and I didn't see one at his house, he might still have been nervous of it." Jackson wrote the word 'dog' in the comments column against Mason's name. "I don't think Mason had anything to do with it, though. But we can't cross his name out yet. Let's move on."

The next name on the list was the one that had been bothering each member of the team, that of Jake Swift.

"You don't really believe the other child did this, do you, Sir?" Gloria asked.

"I know none of you want to think so, Gloria. I don't either, but let's look at the facts. The boys were together to start with. We know they argued. Jake won't tell us what about. At some stage, Brian hit Jake and, according to Jake, he left Brian because of that. We've only got his word for it. Also, we don't know if Jake got so annoyed at being hit that he went back later and attacked Brian."

"But he's much smaller," said Gloria.

"I know, but anything can happen if someone truly loses their temper."

"Is the boy prone to temper tantrums?" Hook asked.

"Not that we're aware of, but he's been a bit jumpy at times when we've interviewed him. Then, he has just lost his best friend."

There was another uncomfortable silence before Harry said, "Nobody really thinks the kid did it, though, do they?"

"We need to treat him the same as any other suspect," said Jackson. "That is, we can't rule him out until something turns up to show he didn't do it."

It went quiet again while the team thought about this. None of them wanted to admit to themselves that children had been known to kill other children. Abercrombie was again the first to speak.

"It's got to be Ewan."

"Then prove it, Harry," Jackson answered.

"You know I can't. Not yet, anyway."

"And likewise, you can't prove it wasn't Jake, can you?"

"He's a nice kid," Gloria said.

"You might like the boy, Gloria, but that doesn't confirm he didn't slay his friend."

"I know. I was only saying."

Jackson saw he was outnumbered in even considering Jake as a suspect. He decided to move on.

"Let's leave Jake for now," he said, "and we'll go on to David Glover. Youth Club Leader. He claims he didn't know Brian though he went to the same Youth Club."

"Must be a big Youth Club," Gibson remarked.

"It is. I spoke to the vicar. They meet three nights a week. Not all the same kids attend each night, but they have about eighty members. It's very informal, so it is possible for a leader not to know every kid by name."

"Isn't Glover bigger than the man we're looking for? Don't we want someone with small hands?" the WPC asked.

"Forensic think so, but they might be wrong. After all, Neil was only going off his initial impressions at the scene, visual evidence, position of the bruises and such, nothing scientific, but I agree he was probably correct. We do now know there aren't any fingerprints they could lift."

"So we can't rule out Glover either, then? Not doing very well, are we?" the WPC said.

"Except that as far as we are aware he had no motive." Jackson glanced at his wristwatch. "Time's getting on, so let's go on to our final suspect, David Parkinson. There's a lot of Davids in this case. Now, what's interesting about Mr Parkinson is he is smallish, has long fingernails, and more significantly, Brian's stepfather claims Parkinson was the one who was abusing Brian."

"Isn't that grounds to arrest him?" One of the uniformed policemen spoke up.

"Just on Mr Churcher's word? I don't think so. We'll need his evidence to be corroborated somehow. Anyway, for now, let's focus on Brian's murderer. It might or might not be the same person as his abuser. If it's true Parkinson was abusing Brian, then he had the motivation to kill him if he considered the boy was going to blow the whistle. It's even possible the kid could have been blackmailing him."

"There's no evidence of that, though," said Harry.

"Not yet, no."

"Gloria's been looking at the boy's computer," Gibson stated. "That's where any threatening messages or anything would be, ain't it?"

"Have you found anything like that, Gloria?" Jackson asked.

"No. There's just games and typical kid's stuff on it. The computer has a word processor, but there are no documents on it."

"He'd need to keep it secret, though wouldn't he? He wouldn't want his parents to see it. Can't you use passwords to stop people seeing stuff you don't want them to see?" asked Jackson, who wasn't into computers, but had been told this by his daughter.

"Yes, but any documents would still show up in a listing of files. You just wouldn't be able to access them without the password."

Gloria had already lost Jackson with the technical terms. He looked to Harry Abercrombie for confirmation.

"That's right," Harry said. "I'll show you later."

"I'd appreciate that, thanks. Well, I'm going to end the briefing. I'm aware we've made little progress, but everyone's up to date now. Anyone anything to say before we close?"

"What about the stepfather himself?" Harry asked. "You know we got the impression when we spoke to him he was the man who had been abusing Brian."

"Yes, but that was before he told us about Parkinson."

"You don't think there's a possibility Churcher himself murdered his stepson?"

"It isn't impossible, but there isn't sufficient evidence to arrest him at present."

"Or to rule out Ewan," Gibson said.

There was silence. Jackson turned back to the board and added Frank Churcher to the list of names. He turned again to face the team.

"Okay, then. All of you go and get some tea, then everyone back here in a couple of hours. I'd like to finish this off tonight if we can." Jackson dismissed the team.

As they filtered out of the room, Jackson watched them leave. He knew they'd all be back long before the two hours he'd stipulated. They were all determined to bring Brian's killer to justice. He wanted to see the culprit dealt with himself too, but he had to be sure the right person was punished.

* * *

Jake was lying down on his bed. After coming back from the police station, he'd gone to his bedroom to think about things. He had no doubt he'd correctly identified the man who had talked to them.

He looked different without the beard, but it was him, he was certain it was.

Why did he have the feeling the policeman, Jackson, he remembered the name, still blamed him for the murder? They'd caught the killer now, hadn't they?

But they wouldn't have let him come home if they still suspected he'd had anything to do with the murder. They'd have put him in prison by now. He knew he was too young for that, but he'd have been sent to whatever the equivalent was for kids.

Then Jake realised suddenly it wasn't Inspector Jackson who blamed him for the murder. It was himself.

If he hadn't left Brian, it wouldn't have happened. They might have been attacked, but it would have been two against one – together they'd have had a chance.

He prayed to ask forgiveness for what he'd done. Jake had always believed in God, but now he got no comfort from his prayers and began to wonder if anyone was there to hear them.

Perhaps none of this had ever happened. It was all a dream, no, not a dream, a nightmare. Any time now, he would wake up, and everything would be all right again. He'd go fishing with Brian.

It wasn't going to be that easy. He had to stop kidding himself. Brian was dead. He was dead because of him. God was no help at all.

At that point in his thoughts, the family cat, Freedom, bounced onto the bed, startling him.

The pet purred softly into his ear, and he stroked it in response finding a strange comfort in the closeness of the cat as it rubbed its head against his chin.

The creature seemed to sense his sorrow as it nuzzled against him. As he continued to stroke it, Jake wondered if it was a coincidence the cat had jumped onto the bed just when he needed its affection. Perhaps God had listened to his prayers after all and sent Freedom to comfort him.

* * *

When only Abercrombie and himself remained in the incident room, Jackson leaned against one of the desks. "They all think it's Ewan, don't they?"

"I do too," Harry responded. "Hiding the bike and all that? Him having a record just clinches it."

"Well, proving he did it would certainly get the case over with. I'll see you later." He left Abercrombie to finish writing up his notes from the briefing.

Jackson had another reason for wanting things cleared up quickly.

He went home to snatch what little time he could with his wife and kids, again assuring Karen he would be at her party even though he wasn't as confident now that he would be able to keep the promise.

To earn a few Brownie points with his daughter, he sat and watched her play with her birthday present, her new computer. Suddenly he realised he didn't need to pretend to be interested; he could genuinely be interested and save Harry some time too.

"What's all this about passwords?" he asked Karen. "How do they work?"

"You can put a password into the computer so no one else can get into it," she said.

"Yes, I know that much. Haven't I heard that it can be done with a particular program though?"

"Some. But I think you mean documents. Yes, you can protect a document from being opened by anyone else by inputting a password when you save it."

"Can you show me? Remember what a dunce I am with computers, though."

Karen typed the first few lines of a nursery rhyme; she saved the document using the password facility.

"Now, only those who know the password can open the file."

"You mean that row of stars?"

"No," she laughed. "The stars came on so you couldn't tell what I was writing. The password is a real word. When I type it to open the file, it will show as stars again so you can't read it, but it has to be exactly the same word. Even the case has to be the same."

"And no one would know the document was there?"

"Not unless they searched for it in a file manager."

"A what?"

"I'll teach you." She made a few mouse clicks and produced a list of file names on her monitor. Pointing to the title of the document she had created she said, "There it is, but if I double click on it, like this," she did so, "it would still ask me for the password before it opened the file, see?"

Jackson saw, or thought he saw. Nevertheless, he was disappointed now realising what Gloria meant and seeing she was right. Brian had no secret password protected documents on his computer. Then Jackson remembered what Gloria had been asked to look for and found he wasn't disappointed after all. The concept of a fourteen-year-old blackmailer, even a dead one, wasn't pleasant, and he was glad no threatening note had been discovered on the boy's computer.

A diary would be useful, though, especially if it referred to his abuser. That might just lead to his killer. If it wasn't Ewan.

Chapter 7

A chanting crowd had gathered outside the police station by the time Jackson returned. He knew it would happen. The word of Ewan's arrest would have spread around the town, and the good citizens of Staffington wanted revenge for the killing of one of the town's children. Most people in the mob doubtless never met the boy, but he was a member of their community, and the public were not happy with his assassin.

Despite the lateness of the afternoon, the sun was yet warm, and Jackson thought folk would be better off finding shade somewhere and leaving the police to get on with their job. He left the car and made his way towards the door. Some people in the throng recognised him.

"What are you going to do to the bastard? Fetch him out here and leave him to us."

Jackson ignored the heckling and pushed through the pack into the police station.

"They'd lynch him if they could," he said to Abercrombie as he entered the office and found the sergeant already at his desk.

"I know. What beats me is how they got to know so soon, before we've released anything to the press."

"Word gets around. Brian's mum found out quick enough didn't she?"

"Yes, but how?" Abercrombie spread his hands as if expecting the answer to appear in the air.

"Cops not keeping their mouths shut. Especially if reporters offer to pay them."

"D'you want me to look into that?"

"No, that would be a waste of manpower. We can't spare time as it is. We'll have another crack at Ewan. You can lead."

"Do you still consider he's not the killer?"

"I never said that. Let's say I'm not entirely convinced, but if it was him we can't hold him without charge much longer, so let's get on with questioning him."

An officer brought the suspect from his cell and escorted him to the interview room.

Because of the heat, even though it was now early evening, the window of the room was open slightly, and the noise of the crowd outside drifted through the imposing window bars to Ewan's ears.

"Hang the bastard."

"Fetch him out here. We'll sort him out."

"Prison's too good for him."

Jackson closed the window. The voices could still be heard, but were now more muted. He started the tape machine then sat next to Abercrombie and nodded he was ready.

"I must remind you you're under caution," Harry began. "Do you still wish to waive your right to a solicitor?"

"Yes."

"You understand that's strongly against our advice?"

"As if you care."

"We do care," Jackson interrupted. "We want everything to be fair."

"And you honestly think I'd get a fair trial with my record?"

"That's all the more reason for using the services of a solicitor."

Ewan leaned towards the desk. "There isn't a lawyer in the world who would believe me any more than you do. Listen to those people outside? They're not going to wait for a trial, are they? They've already found me guilty. And you asked me why I didn't come forward?"

He had a point, Jackson comprehended. The public had definitely prejudged Ewan.

"That wouldn't happen in a court, not with a proper judge and jury to see fair play," he said.

"I asked you before, what about the Guildford Four?"

"That, and the Bridgewater case were two isolated cases. All right, there has been a few mistakes, but miscarriages of justice don't occur very often."

"I can give you the names of at least six people who were hanged and later found to be innocent."

"No one will hang you these days."

"No! You're just going to lock me away for twenty years of my life. I think I'd rather be hanged."

Jackson had no answer to that, and Abercrombie resumed the interviewing.

"All this talk about fair trials is a load of bullshit," he said. "You did kill the boy, didn't you?"

"No! I know you want a confession to solve all your problems, but I didn't do it."

Abercrombie leaned forward and banged his fist on the desk. "Rubbish! If you're so innocent, you'd have come to us straight away to clear yourself."

"I've already told you why I didn't."

"Yes, you have. But I don't believe you. It's a bit of a coincidence, isn't it, you pretend to strangle the boy then we discover that's exactly how he died? Throttled."

"That's what it must be. Coincidence." Ewan sat back in his chair and folded his arms.

"Let's go back to when you were bantering with the kid," Abercrombie continued. "You see, we still find that bit hard to understand. You pretending to strangle him, I mean. Someone suggested that if you were trying to be friendly, you'd have just ruffled his hair or something. Don't you agree that's correct?"

Ewan shrugged.

"Answer the question, please, Mr Ewan."

"That's just what I did. I didn't know the kid actually was going to get himself strangled."

"Didn't you?" Abercrombie absently twirled his pen in his fingers.

"'Course I didn't."

"So you still claim you had nothing to do with his murder?"

"I had absolutely nothing to do with his murder."

"Perhaps it wasn't murder. Maybe you didn't intend to kill him. It would be easier if you told us everything. You might be able to plead manslaughter."

"I didn't kill the kid."

"You must appreciate we've got overwhelming evidence against you. Why don't you confess?"

"I told you. I didn't do it."

"There's no point in you continuing to repeat yourself. It won't change anything. Washing your fingerprints off the boy's neck isn't going to help you, by the way. The forensic people will still be able to lift prints, eventually."

"And that's your evidence? You already know I put my hands on his neck!"

"Yes. But if you're not the killer, the real murderer did so too."

"Well, what are you waiting for then, all you have to do is eliminate mine?"

"But there aren't any others, Mr Ewan."

"What!"

"There's no one else's prints, but then you'd know that, wouldn't you?"

"Why would I know?"

"Because you cleaned your own fingerprints off, knowing we wouldn't find anyone else's either."

"I keep telling you. It wasn't me."

"And I keep telling you, I don't believe you."

"That's your problem."

"No. It's yours. You see, you need to convince us you didn't do it."

"That's not true, and you know it. It's you who has to prove I did it, which you won't."

Abercrombie hesitated. What Ewan said was correct, and he recalled the guy already had experience with the law. He looked at Jackson, but the inspector did not speak, so he went on. "Supposing we believed you and let you go? What do you guess will happen as soon as you walk out of here into that crowd outside?"

"You'll have to protect me."

"That won't be easy."

"It's your problem. That's your job."

"Yes, but it would be easier if you admitted the crime so we can keep you in custody. You'd be safer in a cell."

"I will not admit to something I didn't do, even though I'm sure you're going to charge me eventually. The court will find me guilty although I'm innocent, because of my history."

"The jury won't be told of your record," Jackson cut in.

"You think they're not going to find out? That's a laugh."

"Look, Dave, you clearly don't trust the British Justice System, but in most instances it does work, I assure you."

"You might be sure of that, I'm not. I don't trust the courts any more than I trust you."

"You don't trust me?"

"Nothing personal. I meant I don't trust any police officer."

Jackson couldn't think of a reply to that. He had to admit there were indeed some officers who would bend the rules to get a conviction, but they were in the minority. Ewan's sweeping generalisation didn't apply to the majority of hard-working, dedicated police officers of all ranks within the force. There was no point in saying this to Ewan, who obviously wasn't going to accept whatever Jackson told him.

He rested back in his chair and let Abercrombie resume the interview.

"You know we never let a child killer get away with it?" Abercrombie said. "We're determined to catch this murderer no matter how long it takes. So why don't you save everybody a lot of time and tell us what happened?"

"I thought you said you'd got evidence?"

"We have. By your own admission, you were in the area at the time, and spoke to the boys. You failed to come forward when you were aware we were looking for you. You got rid of the bicycle, destroying evidence, and you've shaved off your beard trying to make yourself look different. I'd say that was quite extensive evidence."

"All circumstantial. I didn't come forward because I knew I'd be your primary suspect. You'd find out about my record and connect this crime with my past. There's no smoke without fire, that's what you think, isn't it?"

"You said it."

"But it is what you think. Which proves I was correct about not coming here willingly."

"We're not getting anywhere with this interview, are we? I'm going to wrap up here for now. Someone will take you back to your cell where you can consider matters. I hope you'll decide it's best to come clean."

"I haven't anything to come clean about."

He was escorted to his cell, and Jackson and Abercrombie reconvened in their office to discuss the interview.

Some of the people outside, bored with the lack of action, had returned to their homes and the babble had receded a little now. Jackson looked out of the window to watch the few remaining demonstrators. He was astonished to see Angela and Frank Churcher among them. He'd ordered Angela to be taken home after her outburst earlier in the day. What good did she expect to do by coming back here again?

He turned to face Abercrombie.

"You were a bit hasty, Harry, telling Ewan we could identify his fingerprints?"

"It was a bluff," Abercrombie agreed. "But I wasn't actually lying. It is possible forensic might be able to enhance whatever prints they've managed to lift."

"It's a long shot, though. They're only going to get partial prints at best."

"A partial print would be sufficient to identify him."

"We don't need to identify him. Remember he's already admitted to having his hands around Brian's neck."

"Oh, yeah. So finding his prints won't help."

"No, but finding someone else's would."

"Eh, how?"

"It would prove Ewan isn't responsible."

"You still think he's innocent?"

"I believe some of his points are valid. I'm still not suggesting he's innocent, just that it's not as cut and dried as we supposed."

They moved down to the incident room to let the other members of the team listen to the tape of Ewan's interview. No one made any remark, and everyone went back to his or her desk terminal, sifting through the information about the case now stored on the computer.

Brian's own computer still sat on Gloria's desk, and Jackson went over to her.

"Anything else found on that?" he asked, pointing to the youth's machine.

"No," she answered. "As I mentioned at the briefing, it's just games and such. He must have used the word processor, though, because he's set up personalised options. Most people wouldn't bother to do that if they weren't going to use it."

"But he hasn't anything stored there?"

"No."

"Course, if he were blackmailing someone, he'd have quite a bit of cash stashed away somewhere, or things he'd bought with the money."

"His parents would know it, though, wouldn't they?"

Abercrombie had come over to join Jackson and had overheard the last bit of the conversation.

"I wouldn't be too sure about that," he said. "What about all the kids who take drugs without their parents knowing?"

"Drugs are easier to hide, though. Oh, my God, you don't think the lad was taking drugs?" Jackson asked.

"No. Not taking them. The post mortem would show if he were, but he could have been selling them."

"If he was, Jake is the one most likely to know about it, isn't he?" Jackson responded.

Gloria coughed. "That means putting more pressure on the boy."

"I'm aware of that, but it can't be helped," Jackson answered. "That might be something to do with their argument. It would explain why Jake is reluctant to talk about it."

"Can I make a suggestion, Sir?" Abercrombie said. "Before we see Jake again, let's speak to Brian's parents. It might be possible they did know if Brian had extra cash."

"Yes, and we can do that now. They're outside," Jackson remembered. He had the Churchers' brought into the police station and settled them down in the interview room. He and Abercrombie took seats on the opposite side of the table.

"Why did you come back here, Mrs Churcher? I had you taken home?"

"I came back to apologise for my tantrum. When I got here, all those people were outside, weren't they, Frank? So we joined in."

"You don't need to apologise, Mrs Churcher."

"Please, call me Angela. I do owe you an apology. When I got home, I realised what I'd done. I'm not usually like that, am I Frank?"

For once, Angela gave Frank the opportunity to reply, and he took advantage.

"No." Then to Jackson, "You've got your man, Inspector. What happens now?"

"Well, first we have to prove he did it."

"He did it, there's no doubt. He dumped that blue bike, didn't he? What more evidence do you need?"

"It's not enough, Frank. It is all right if I call you Frank, seeing that your wife wants me to call her Angela?"

Frank nodded.

"He disposed of the bike because he was sure we'd suspect him, but it doesn't prove he's guilty," Jackson continued.

"'Course he's guilty. He must be the one who's been abusing him."

"You said that was the youth club leader?"

"I thought it was. Obviously, I must have been wrong, or maybe both of 'em have been defiling him, I don't know."

"Our suspect has only been in this area a short time. Brian's abuse has been going on much longer than that."

"How long?" asked Angela, who had managed to remain silent for a few minutes.

"We're not sure exactly, Angela. Definitely more than a few weeks."

"It's that youth club bloke, then," said Frank.

"So why would the suspect we now have here need to kill him?"

"Perhaps they were in it together, or the youth club bloke paid him to do it. He did it all right, I can feel it in my bones."

"Unfortunately, Frank, feelings don't count as evidence. If I could lock up someone every time I had a hunch they'd done something illegal, my life would be a lot easier, but we can't do that."

Frank turned to his unusually quiet wife. "He did it all right. They'll soon get the proof they need, don't worry."

"There are a couple more things I'd like to ask you about Brian," Jackson said, changing the subject.

"Go ahead," Angela found her voice again.

"Did either of you notice he was spending more money than usual?"

"What do you mean?"

"Well, I assume you gave him pocket money. Was he buying things you knew he couldn't afford?"

"Such as?"

"Anything. Computer games, for example."

"Not that I know of. Did you see anything, Frank?"

"No. He bought a box of disks last week, that's all."

"Disks?"

"CDs. Things you can store stuff on," Abercrombie informed Jackson. "They're not particularly expensive."

"Nothing else?"

"No. Not that I saw, anyway."

"And he didn't seem to have more cash on him than normal?"

"He didn't flash it around if that's what you mean?" said Frank.

"What's all this about?" Angela asked. "What's it matter how much money he'd got, he's dead?"

"It doesn't matter. It's just something we're working on."

"It does matter," Angela stormed. "You think Brian's been nickin' money from somewhere, don't you?"

"I didn't say that."

"You didn't have to. Why else would you ask about his money? Well, he wasn't like that. He was a good kid. And even if he was nickin' I don't care. I just want you to get that bloke put away." She pointed towards the door as if to indicate the 'bloke' was in the next room.

"We want to do that too, Angela, but we have to make certain it's the right bloke first. I'm sure you want that too."

"It's the right bloke," said Frank.

Chapter 8

Mr and Mrs Churcher had been taken home. It was dark now, and the crowd outside had dispersed.

"They'll be back in the morning, though," Jackson said to Abercrombie as they made their way to the incident room together.

"I can imagine the headlines. It'll be something like 'The Blue Bike Murderer is detained'. Shouldn't we get Ewan moved to another station for his safety?"

"It isn't really convenient, and it wouldn't take folk long to find out where he is, anyhow."

"A secret location somewhere?"

"Let's see what happens in the morning. With luck, it'll rain and keep people away."

"Not much chance of that, there's been no rain for weeks."

"I know."

They reached the incident room where the rest of the team were winding up for the night.

Jackson brought them up to date and told them about the theory Abercrombie had raised about Brian possibly being involved in the drug scene.

"Not as a user," he said, "but there's a possibility he was dealing."

"At fourteen?" Gloria asked. She had been present when drugs were first mentioned but hadn't seriously considered it.

"It's not impossible," Hook said. "They get passed around in schools."

"Is there any definite evidence of this, sir?" Gloria questioned.

"Not really. It's just a theory, that's all. Another possible motive to think about."

"Has his room been searched?" asked Gibson. "In case it's right. He could have drugs stashed away there, or somewhere in the house where his parents wouldn't bother to look."

"I wouldn't be too sure about that. Frank Churcher strikes me as the sort of character who'd use drugs himself if he could get hold of them." Jackson answered. "Anyway, we've no grounds to do a search."

"The parents might let us look in Brian's room without a warrant," Gibson suggested. "We could say we needed to find out more about his interests and background. They didn't object to the computer being taken."

"Okay, we'll ask them, but not tonight, it's late. Let's all get a good night's sleep." Then, turning to Abercrombie, "We'll visit Jake again tomorrow, too."

* * *

Jackson rose early the following day. As he dressed, he heard the first rumblings of thunder, signalling the end of the heat wave. The weather forecasters had got it wrong again. The noise woke Sheila, and she was surprised to discover her husband up and getting ready for work.

"Tom, didn't you book today off? Karen's party, remember?"

"I'll be home in time. I can't take the whole day off, Love. We've still got a murderer to catch."

"I thought you had caught him."

"We have someone locked up. We're not certain it's the right person and, even if it is, we need to prove it."

"You will be back for her party? You did promise."

"I know. I'll be back, don't worry."

Sheila decided, as she was awake, she might as well get out of bed herself. She did so and went to the window, where she opened the bright-red curtains. She was greeted with a grey overcast sky. In the distance, the still rumbling thunder threatened to bring long-awaited rain.

"It's much cooler, anyway," she said. "Thank goodness for that."

"Yes," replied Jackson, hoping the bad weather would be enough to keep the sightseers away.

It wasn't.

When he arrived at the police station, he found the crowd already gathering, chanting as they came. He wondered if Abercrombie had been correct and they should have moved Ewan during the night.

Abercrombie himself, as usual, was in the office as immaculate as ever, waiting for Jackson.

"'Morning," he said. "Looks like we will get the rain you wanted, but it's not kept that morbid lot away." He was discreet enough not to mention he had proposed moving Ewan.

"No. You were right. We should have moved him."

"We can still do it."

"I'll see what the boss says. Unless we find more evidence, we'll have to release Ewan soon, anyhow. I would like this wrapped up today, Harry. The sooner, the better. I've got to be home this afternoon."

"Yes, your kid's party, I remember. It's all right, though, I'll stay here. You take the afternoon off."

"I appreciate that, but you know I'd prefer to be present myself if anything happens."

"Yeah, but you're only on the end of a phone. If something significant crops up, I can always call you. Though your kid wouldn't be too happy."

"All right, let's see what transpires. I did promise her I'd be there."

"Silly thing that, making promises."

"Don't I know it."

Jackson didn't want to disturb his superintendent too early on a Sunday morning, so he waited until he'd consumed two mugs of coffee before phoning him.

The rain had arrived now, but the people outside were brave enough to get wet and stood their ground.

Jackson made the phone call to the superintendent and explained the situation.

"It would've been better to move him last night. Don't y' think?" Superintendent Peter Everett said, his broad Lancashire accent ringing gruffly into Jackson's ear.

"With hindsight, yes it was a mistake," admitted Jackson.

"All right, what do you want to do?"

"Now I'm seeking your advice, Sir."

Jackson knew he was really requesting permission to transfer Ewan, but it did no harm to butter up the boss and let him believe he was giving support to his men.

"You should move him, I s'pose. This time, make sure no one outside your team knows where he is. Okay?"

"That rules out a police station, then."

"Yes. You find somewhere, and I'll authorise it. You all right with that?"

Jackson was all right with that. He'd manipulated Everett into agreeing to what he wanted. Now all he needed to do was find a suitable location to hold their prisoner.

He informed the team.

"Where?" asked Kevin Gibson. "We can hardly put him in a church hall. He'd go out the fire escape and we'd have a murderer running loose."

"We're not certain he is a murderer yet, Kevin," Jackson cautioned. "But I agree we need somewhere more secure, anyone any ideas?"

"Remand Centre," suggested Hook.

"Without charge?"

"It's for his own safety. He'd need to agree, but what's he got to lose?"

"Harry?"

"I think it's a good idea. I'll ask if he'll agree to it, shall I?"

"Yes, please, do that."

Abercrombie went to ask Ewan for his permission and Jackson remained in the incident room with the team to discuss any thoughts that had occurred to any of them overnight. Everyone had been considering the case, but no one had any fresh information or theories to put forward, so Jackson made his way back to his office to wait for Abercrombie.

"He doesn't mind," Abercrombie told him when he returned. "I've asked Gloria to contact them and ask if they can take him."

"Good. We'll leave her to deal with that. We need to go and talk to Jake."

"Will he be up yet?"

"If he isn't we'll wake him. A growing kid shouldn't be lying in bed this late on a Sunday morning, rain or no rain."

* * *

Jake wasn't in bed. To both Jackson and Abercrombie's surprise, his mother told them he'd gone to church.

"I didn't realise Jake was a churchgoer, Mrs Swift."

"You never asked. He goes most Sunday mornings. There's a group of them about his age go together. Does it matter?"

"Not really. We need to speak to him, though. Is it all right if we wait?"

"You're not going to upset him again, are you?"

"We'll try not to."

"Well, you can wait if you like, but it'll be half an hour yet before he's home."

"That's okay."

They both sat on the spacious settee and settled down to wait.

"Was Brian one of this group of boys that went to church?" Abercrombie asked.

"Sometimes, but they're not all boys. There's a few girls too. I think that's why the lads go, to be honest."

"And this is the same church that has the youth club?"

"Aye, they're all members."

"And the youth club leaders go too?" Jackson asked.

"I don't believe they have to. Some of 'em do, though. There's one called David, who goes regularly."

Both the men looked at each other.

"You don't know his last name, do you?" Jackson inquired.

"No. Jake never calls him anything except David or Dave."

"They might be two different men."

"They may well be, I've never seen them. I've just heard Jake talk about this Dave or David a few times, that's all."

Mrs Swift offered drinks to the policemen, but both rejected these having already consumed several mugs of coffee at the office. The mention of it, however, caused Abercrombie to need to answer the call of nature, and he asked to use the facilities. Mrs Swift directed him to the room upstairs.

When he came back a few minutes later, he said, "Mrs Swift, I couldn't help seeing through the open bedroom door there's a computer up there. Does it belong to Jake?"

"Yes."

"Did he ever let Brian use it?" Abercrombie asked, glancing at Jackson.

"They played on it together sometimes, but Brian had a computer of his own."

"We may need to borrow Jakes," Jackson said.

"Why?"

"To see if there's anything on it that might help us."

"There's no porn or anything. His dad sees to that."

"We're not looking for porn."

Mr Swift had been in bed, but hearing the voices of the visitors and becoming curious, now entered the room.

Unshaven and sleepy-eyed, he looked at the callers.

"You again?" he said. "I understood you'd finished with Jake."

"There are a few more points that cropped up we need to talk to him about," Jackson said.

"Well, I hope you're not going to have him believing you think he's a murderer again. He's still having nightmares, you know."

"We'll be as gentle as possible, I promise you."

"I don't understand why you need to see him at all. You've got your killer, haven't you?"

"We don't know."

"What!"

"We have a suspect. That's all he is, a suspect."

"But it must be him. He disposed of that blue bike, didn't he? Why would he do that if he wasn't guilty?"

"Wanting to hide from the police doesn't always imply guilt, Mr Swift."

"Hold on. You're not suggesting he's innocent and you're going to try to pin it on Jake again? I'm not letting you speak to him without a solicitor present."

"Calm down, please. We're not accusing Jake of anything. We need information, that's all?"

"As long as that's all it is."

"Your wife tells me you're good with computers?" Abercrombie intervened.

"I'm no expert, but I know a bit, what about it?"

"Do you know what your son uses his computer for?"

"Games, homework, typical kids stuff."

"Would he use it to write letters, and things like that?"

"I don't know who he'd write to, but he could. He has a word processor on the machine. Anyway, don't they all use email nowadays?"

"Emails too," Abercrombie said. "And are you aware of everything he has stored on it?"

"If you know anything about computers yourself, you'll realise that's virtually impossible. He may well have saved thousands of documents either on the machine itself or on CD. Besides, I respect his privacy."

So Mrs Swift was mistaken about her husband monitoring Jake's computer activities, Jackson thought. It didn't matter. He couldn't see a twelve-year-old boy being seriously involved in illegal porn. All he was concerned about was whether Brian had created blackmail letters on Jake's machine to make certain his parents never came across them.

"Would you mind if I have a quick look at the computer?" Abercrombie continued.

"Well, I'm not sure about that. I told you I respect his privacy."

"This is a murder investigation, Mr Swift. I believe Brian sometimes used Jake's computer. He might have left something on it which will show us who killed him."

"Doubt it. They just played games on it. Still, I don't suppose it'll do any harm. Come on, then."

Abercrombie followed him upstairs. Jackson, who had always been baffled by computers, stayed with Mrs Swift.

A few minutes later, Abercrombie returned with Jake's father. Jackson could see from the expression on his sergeant's face he had seen nothing of interest to him, but he asked anyway.

"Nothing?"

"No," Abercrombie replied. "Nothing on the computer anyhow. There is a lot of disks, though. We'll need to take them with us and go through them one by one."

"Disks?"

"CD's. A sort of portable storage system," Abercrombie reminded Jackson.

"And letters and stuff can be put on these?"

"Oh, yes."

"Would Brian have used any of these, what did you say, disks?"

"Probably," said Abercrombie realising what Jackson was getting at. "In fact, the stepfather mentioned he'd bought some recently, and I bet uniform didn't bother to look for any. They were only asked to collect the computer."

"Yes, I remember now. See to it as soon as we get back, will you?"

Jake arrived home at that point. The rain was now almost torrential, and the boy was saturated. He came into the room, water dripping from his tousled hair onto the carpet. He looked at the two detectives and frowned.

"Don't worry," said Jackson, noting his concern. "We just need to ask you a couple more things about Brian. Go and dry yourself off first."

Jake turned and went out of the room without saying a word.

The four adults waited for the boy to come back.

"He must be having a shower," Mrs Swift explained when Jake still hadn't reappeared ten minutes later. "Ask him to hurry up, Bill."

Mr Swift trotted up the stairs then galloped down them again.

"He's not here, he's gone!"

"What!" shouted Mrs Swift.

"He must have run out the back door."

"Damn!" Jackson yelled.

"If anything happens to him, I'm holding you responsible," Mr Swift rounded on him. "You've scared him off."

"He had nothing to be scared of."

"He plainly didn't know that!"

"Calm down, both of you. We'll find him." Abercrombie tried to soothe the situation. "Where is he likely to go?"

"Dave or David, whatever he's called. The youth club leader," screamed Mrs Swift.

Chapter 9

The rain showed no sign of abating. After weeks of dry, hot weather, it seemed all the moisture in the sky was being released at once.

Jake didn't care. He was already drenched and couldn't get any wetter.

After being dry for so long, the roads were now dangerously greasy with the continuous rain, and traffic moved cautiously alongside the boy as he ran splashing through deep puddles, on the way to sanctuary.

* * *

Jackson and Abercrombie left the Swift's home and, having contacted the police station for Parkinson's and Glover's addresses, were driving towards Parkinson's house.

The rain had eased off a little, but it had now made the roads slippery. Abercrombie drove carefully, despite their hurry to find Jake.

"There isn't any rush, is there?" he asked. "The boy's safe enough, apart from getting wet. It's just going to delay us questioning him, that's all."

"Think about it, Harry," Jackson replied. "Suppose my hunch about Ewan being innocent is correct. It would mean there's still a killer out there somewhere. If it isn't Jake himself, who's the most likely suspect?"

"I see," said Abercrombie. "Parkinson. If the allegation about him abusing Brian is true, he might have been at it with Jake too."

"Right. And even if he hasn't, Jake's still a dangerous witness to him."

"And the lad could be heading straight for him."

"Indeed. And we can't phone him. His mother told me he never takes his phone to church and it was still on charge, she checked,"

Abercrombie increased his pressure on the accelerator.

* * *

Jake reached his destination and pounded on the front door.

David Parkinson was about to sit down to lunch with his family when the frantic knocking startled them all.

"Who can that be in this weather?" David's wife said as she put the final additions to the dining table.

"I'll go," David said. "Most likely Jehovah's Witnesses."

"Not in this weather, surely. Even they're not so dedicated."

David went to answer the door and was startled to find Jake on the doorstep, soaked to the skin. He stared at the boy for a second or two unable to believe his eyes.

"Jake. What are you doing here? What's up?"

"The police are after me. They think I killed Brian. You've got to hide me, please."

David hesitated for a moment and looked down into the frightened face. Rivulets of water trickled down it; he couldn't tell whether this was caused by rain, or tears. Perhaps a mixture of both.

"What makes you think they suspect you?"

"They came to my house. They're going to lock me up. I know they are."

"Jake, if you killed Brian, you have to tell the police. They'll understand it was an accident."

"I didn't. Honest."

"You must still go back and tell the police. I can't hide you, Jake. You know that."

"Why not?"

"Because I have my family here. Besides, I'm a suspect too. How would it look if I helped another suspect?"

Jake stared. "They think you did it?"

"Well, they questioned me."

"Did you?"

"Of course I didn't. Did you?"

Jake stamped his foot. "No! You don't believe me either, do you? You're the same as the rest of them. I'm going to kill myself!"

"Jake! Come back," Parkinson shouted as the boy ran from the building. Jake carried on running.

Parkinson called out a brief explanation to his wife then grabbed his raincoat from behind the door, putting it on as he chased after the youngster.

* * *

Jake arrived at the vicarage by the time the rain eased off, but he didn't want to see the vicar.

He waited in the church porch, keeping the vicarage door within his view. The rain stopped altogether before the person he had come to see emerged from that doorway.

"Mark!" he called as quietly as he could, hoping the boy would hear him, but that no one else would.

Seventeen-year-old Mark Chegwin was the son of the Rev. Mike Chegwin. Though he was a vicar's son, most of the parishioners knew Mark wasn't a rigid follower of Christian principles, a constant source of embarrassment and disappointment to his parents.

The slender youth paused as he strode up the church drive.

"Mark!" the whispered voice came from the church porch.

The teen turned back, went into the porch, and found Jake cowering there. Mark knew Jake from the youth club, but he wasn't one of his favourite people, and he was somewhat surprised the small kid should want to attract his attention.

"What d'you want, you little squirt?"

"I have to hide, the cops are after me. Can you get me the key to the youth club?"

The youth club was based under the church. A flight of stone steps just a few yards from where they were now standing led down to a door which opened into the basement. Jake knew the vicar had a key to this entrance.

"Why are the cops after you?"

"They think I killed Brian Churcher."

"Bloody Hell!"

"I didn't do it, honest."

"I could get the key, but why should I help you?" Mark responded. "I'd be in lumber then for harbouring a murderer."

"I'm not a murderer."

"You'd say that even if you did it, wouldn't you?"

"You've got to help me. If you don't, I'll kill myself and it'll make you feel guilty."

"Don't try to blackmail me, you little bastard. I'll squash your balls."

He moved his hand towards Jake as if to carry out the threat but, unruly as he was, even Mark had a conscience and seeing the agonised expression on the smaller boy's face, he relented.

"Do what you want to me. Beat me up if you like. I'll still kill myself afterwards," Jake said, oblivious to just having escaped being put in agony.

"You wouldn't have the guts. Beat it before I do hurt you."

"Please, Mark."

"Get lost."

"I'll do anything you want." Tears had started to flow now.

"Stop babbling, you baby. Look, even if I got you the key, how long d'you think you could stay down there? Look at the state of you. You'd catch pneumonia. If you didn't starve first."

"You can bring me some food."

"What happens tomorrow when the youth club's open and everyone's looking for you?"

"I'll hide in the storeroom."

"And you think no one will smell you in that scruffy condition?"

"I can wash in the toilets."

"You can't wash your clothes or dry them."

"I can. On the radiators."

"You bloody little idiot. Do you think the radiators will be on after all the hot weather we've had?"

"I'll think of something."

"I'm not getting the key for you. Now scarper before I fetch my dad."

This threat made Jake run. He didn't want to see the vicar, or any other grown-up at the moment. He waited until he was safely out of Mark's reach then turned and growled in as low a voice as he could. "They'll have to drag my body out of the canal."

* * *

Mrs Parkinson thought the world was going mad. For the second time during her Sunday lunch, there was a loud rat-a-tat-tat on her front door. Didn't anyone use doorbells anymore, she thought, as she rose from the table? She cautioned her two small boys to behave and went to answer the summons.

"Mrs Parkinson? Is your husband at home?" Jackson asked, showing his ID card.

"No. I'm afraid not."

"Can you tell me where he is?"

"One of the lads from his youth club came to see him. There was some problem. I don't know the details. David went running after him."

"Which way?"

"I didn't see."

"Okay thank you, we'll find him."

"What is it? There's nothing wrong is there?"

"Thanks for your help, Mrs Parkinson," Jackson replied walking away from the door wishing he could give a better answer both to her and himself.

"We'll have to do a full-scale search," he said to Abercrombie. "Just in case. Let's hope we're not too late."

"Yes, but you're going to have to get off. Your kid's party."

"I can't leave now."

"Of course, you can. I'll see to everything here."

"The old man would go berserk if he found out I'd gone home knowing we have a possible murder on our hands." Jackson visualised Everett, red-faced, as he demanded an explanation.

"He can't expect you to live at the station, even during a murder investigation."

Jackson hadn't time to sit and think. If Jake was in any danger, the sooner they began looking for him, the better.

"All right," he said. "You can drop me off at the station to get my car. You will tell me the minute you find Jake, dead or alive?"

"Alive, we hope. Okay," Abercrombie promised. "D'you want Parkinson brought in again?"

"Oh, yes."

"Pity the days are gone when we could torture a confession out of him."

"So you consider Ewan is innocent now?"

"No. I meant for the child molestation. Torture him to get the confession then torture him again for punishment. That's how all child molesters should be dealt with, in my view."

"You're forgetting, though, if Parkinson is the man who was abusing Brian, there wasn't any motive for Ewan to murder him."

When they reached the police station, the mob was still outside, though some of its members had given in to the rain and there were only a few of the more hardy ones remaining.

Jackson was surprised to see any there at all. Surely, the team had got Ewan moved by now.

"Perhaps they have, but the grapevine hasn't found out yet," Abercrombie said.

"Let's hope that's it," Jackson replied. "I'd better come in to find out for sure, though."

"You're better getting straight off. If you come in you might become involved in something and finish up breaking that promise to your daughter."

"Yes, as usual you're right, Harry. Keep me informed."

He got out of Abercrombie's car, went straight to his own and headed for home.

* * *

Harry Abercrombie went into the incident room and discovered the team all making what sounded like hectic phone calls. He waited for one of them to finish and explain what was going on.

Gloria was the first to put her phone down.

"What is it, Gloria, what's happening?"

"It's Ewan. He's escaped."

"What!"

"Sorry, Sarge. We got the place in the remand centre, but he managed to get out of the car on the way there."

"How could that happen?"

"It wasn't a police car. It was a security firm. They thought he was low risk and let him out for a leak."

"They what? Are they ruddy stupid? He's a suspected killer."

"They claim they weren't told that. They assumed he was just a prisoner being transferred to remand."

"Why are those people still outside, then?"

"They haven't been told he's gone. We moved him out the back way and didn't tell anyone. We were planning to make an announcement later, but in the circumstances..."

"Yes, I know. They're going to find out we've bungled and let a suspected murderer loose. They'll be claiming we're incompetent, and they'll be right. Bloody Hell, I'll have to call Jackson back in. His kid will love me."

"One positive thing, though, Sarge. Proves he's guilty, doesn't it?" Alan Hook said as he finished his phone call.

And if so, Abercrombie thought, he might yet go after Jake. Hell, he'd forgotten he had to set up the search for Jake. Now they didn't know if the boy was safe or whether Parkinson, Ewan or both of them wanted to harm him. They had to locate him before any of them did so.

He quickly explained the situation to the team, and a full-scale search was under way within minutes.

Abercrombie went back to the office and contemplated whether to call Jackson. He knew the guv'nor would not forgive him if he didn't tell him what had happened. On the other hand, once he was aware of the position, Jackson would desert his family birthday celebration and come rushing into the police station. Would he be able to do anything that wasn't already being done? No, Abercrombie decided, he wouldn't. He'd let his boss enjoy the party a while longer, at least until they found little Jake's body. Hopefully, that wouldn't happen because they'd find him alive, in which case, the interview with him could wait until Karen's party was over.

* * *

Jackson was not enjoying the party. He was in no mood for the screaming kids who filled his living room. He sat in an armchair, slouched back, twirling his moustache, his long face not helping the party atmosphere.

"For God's sake, Tom, cheer up," Sheila told him. "It's a birthday party, not a funeral."

"Sorry, Dear, I can't help it. I'm worried I will have to go to another funeral soon. Another child's."

"You've found another dead kid?"

"Not yet, but we might if my officers don't find him before he's killed."

"You want to be back there leading them, don't you?"

"I won't break my promise to Karen."

"Karen will understand. Besides, you're hardly a bundle of fun in that mood. You're putting everybody off enjoying themselves. Karen'll want you to leave."

"You sure?"

"Just go. I'll explain to her."

"No. The least I can do is tell her myself. I'll talk to Daniel first. Where is he?"

"Probably sulking up in his bedroom. It's not his sort of party. These kids are too old for him."

Jackson went upstairs. Daniel wasn't in his bedroom, but he found him in Karen's room sitting at her computer.

"Hi, son, does your sister know you're using that?"

"Yeah, she lets me do my homework on it."

"You put it on a disc, do you?" Jackson asked, recalling the discussion at the Swift's house.

"Sometimes. Other times I print it off."

"And what are these 'discs'?"

Daniel took a CD out of Karen's box and showed it to his father. Jackson had seen computer discs before but now reflected on how small they were. They could be hidden almost anywhere.

"How much stuff can you put on one of these?"

"About seven hundred megs."

"What's that mean?" Jackson asked, embarrassed he had to ask an eight-year-old for an explanation.

"A lot."

"Thanks. He would ask someone older."

"'S okay," said the child, simply.

"I'm going to have to go back to work, Daniel. I'll spend more time with you another day, okay?"

"Okay," said the boy uninterestedly. He was well used to his father not being around.

Jackson then went to find his daughter. Although it was nowhere near Halloween, she had organised some of her friends into bobbing for apples as others boogied away to the loud music coming from the entertainment system.

"Karen, can I have a word?" he had to shout to make himself heard above the screaming and music, which wasn't to his taste.

"What's up, Dad?" Karen shouted back. "Too noisy for you? Mum said it's all right."

"I don't want to talk about the music. Come into the hall a minute so we can hear ourselves speak."

She followed him into the hallway, and Jackson closed the door to muffle the noise.

"Are you going to tell me off? At my own birthday party?"

"You're not being told off. Karen, you're making this hard for me."

"What?"

"I have to go back to work. I'm sorry."

"All right," she said and went straight back into the living room.

But it wasn't all right, and Jackson knew it.

He found his car keys and got into his Mondeo. Karen would have to sulk. Preventing Jake Swift's death was more important than even his own girl's happiness.

Chapter 10

"Here he comes, Inspector Plod." The crowd jeered as Jackson made his way through them to the police station.

"Ever thought of joining the Keystone Cops?" Another voice rang out.

Unaware of the reason for the taunts, Jackson knew there was trouble. The hairs on the back of his neck rose as he went quickly to the incident room and was greeted with apparent chaos.

"What the hell's going on?" he yelled.

Harry Abercrombie turned, surprised to see him. "Come into the office, Tom, I'll explain."

They both went to the office and remained standing as Abercrombie told Jackson what had happened.

"Why the hell didn't you contact me?" Jackson stormed.

"I had it all under control. I didn't see any need to disturb you."

"Under control! An escaped prisoner? A missing boy? Heads will roll for this, Harry."

"It's not us. It's the security firm."

"The public won't see it like that. We're the ones responsible."

"I know. One positive thing, though. It proves his guilt, doesn't it?" Abercrombie echoed Hook's words.

"It makes matters worse for him, yes. That won't be any consolation if he finds Jake and kills him. Has the Superintendent been informed?"

"Yes. Once the crowd outside got wind of the escape, I decided I'd better phone Everett before he heard it on the news. He's coming in."

"That's all I need! What about Parkinson?"

"He's in the cells. He was caught going back to his house and detained."

"What's he said about Jake?"

"I've not questioned him yet. I was busy coordinating the searches. Now you're here I expect you'll prefer to do the interview?"

Jackson went to his desk and sat down "No. I'd better wait for Peter Everett. What manpower have you got?"

"Practically the whole shift. 'Course we've had to divide the resources between searching for Ewan and the boy."

"Let's hope they don't find them together. Get Hook to take over the search co-ordination then you and Gloria interview Parkinson. If there's the slightest suspicion he's done anything to Jake, you know what to do."

"Right."

* * *

Abercrombie went back to the incident room to collect Gloria; glad Jackson had decided to take the flak from Everett. Whatever Jackson thought of his officers, and Abercrombie knew it wasn't much at present, he would defend them to his superiors.

Gloria Waters was glad to get out of the incident room. She went with Abercrombie to the interview room where the custody officer was already waiting with Parkinson and the duty solicitor, Robert Bramhall. Abercrombie had met Bramhall before and they were far from being friends.

Once the two CID officers settled down, the custody officer left them to it.

"I've got to remind you again, Mr Parkinson, you're still under caution. You realise why you've been arrested?" Abercrombie began the interview.

"Yes, it's all rubbish. I didn't kill Brian, and I didn't hurt Jake. I understand your chief suspect's done a runner. Doesn't that prove he did it?"

"It may well mean there's a good chance he murdered Brian, yes," Abercrombie agreed. "What about the allegations of abusing him? That wasn't Ewan. He hasn't been in the neighbourhood long enough."

"Well, it wasn't me."

"I believe it was. Not only that. I think you were at it with Jake, too."

A cough from Bramhall.

"I wasn't. I'm not that way inclined."

"Why did you go after Jake?"

"Go after him?"

"When he called at your home this morning. Why did you follow him?"

"I wasn't following him, well, I suppose I tried to, but only because I was worried about him. He told me he was going to kill himself."

"Where is he now?"

"I don't know. I couldn't find him."

"It would suit you for him to be dead, wouldn't it? You'd be sure of him keeping his mouth shut. You followed him all right, either to make certain he carried out the threat to kill himself or to murder him yourself. Isn't that it?"

Another cough from Bramhall.

"That's ridiculous. I'm not a murderer. I like kids."

"You like kids?"

"Yes – not in that way, though. Obviously, I like 'em or I wouldn't be working at the youth club."

Gloria, who had been sitting quietly with her arms folded now unfolded them as she said, "I can accept you're not a murderer. As you said, we're pretty sure now Ewan is the killer so you wouldn't need to murder Jake, would you? Why don't you admit to the sexual offences then we can forget about this more serious business of murder?"

"I didn't do it!"

"If you're not prepared to own up to child molestation, we must presume you've something more serious to hide," Gloria went on. "Perhaps you did kill Jake, not to stop him talking about Brian's murder, but to keep him quiet about what you've been doing to him and Brian. What I'm suggesting is perhaps we have two murderers on our hands. You and Ewan."

Parkinson banged his fist on the table. "No! No! No! You've got it all wrong. I never molested a kid in my life and I didn't see Jake again after he ran from my front door."

"I hope for your sake when we find him, he's still alive."

Bramhall decided it was time to do more than just cough.

"Are you going to charge my client with anything?" he asked.

"Not at the moment, Mr Bramhall," Abercrombie responded.

"Then I suggest you stop making these wild allegations. My client has given you a perfectly reasonable explanation for his actions."

"And if we find the boy, he'll be able to confirm what your client has told us. If he's alive."

"I hope he's alive too," Parkinson said. "I've told you he said he was going to kill himself."

"Yes, you did," Abercrombie said. "That'd be a great alibi for you, wouldn't it? You make it look like a suicide and assume we'll forget all about it."

"No! I'm as worried about the kid as you are."

"Worried we'll find your fingerprints on his throat."

"No, that's not what I meant at all. Look, these sexual allegations, there's tests you can do isn't there?"

"Not this late. We'd need the clothes you were wearing at the time of the alleged offences before they'd been washed."

"What about a sperm sample?"

"We'd require a match from the kid. We can't get one now from Brian, and you'd need to have had recent sex with Jake for anything from him to be of any use. Did you?"

"'Course I didn't. As I keep telling you, I'm not like that. I'll take a lie-detector test if you want."

"That would take too long to set up and they're not reliable anyway. Okay, D.C Waters will escort you back to your cell for now."

"How much longer do I have to stay here? I've got a family, you know."

"Until we find Jake Swift. It would be quicker for you to tell us where he is."

Bramhall intervened again, "You've no right to say that. You know you can't keep my client here without charge."

"And you know we can hold him while we conduct further inquiries. This is a murder investigation. We can apply to keep your client here for extra time if we need to." He looked at Parkinson. "Where is the boy?"

"I have no idea where he is."

Gloria took him back to his cell then went to meet Abercrombie in the incident room to discuss the interview. She noticed raised voices from Jackson's office as she walked along the corridor. The Superintendent had arrived, she realised.

Abercrombie was waiting for her.

"Well, what do you think?"

"He offered to take the polygraph test. Would he do that if he had anything to hide?"

"If he was aware the tests were unreliable and couldn't be used in court."

"And the sperm sample?" Gloria sat at one of the desks.

"He'd know we wouldn't be able to do that this late. Most people do."

"So you think all that was a bluff?"

"I don't know. I'm only saying it could be."

"Something doesn't add up, though, does it, Sarge? If Ewan hadn't fled, we'd be treating Parkinson now as our primary suspect."

"Yes, so?"

"Ewan killed Brian. We're pretty confident of that now. So, if Parkinson wanted to do away with Jake and pin it on Ewan, he'd have to know Ewan was free. At that time, he couldn't have known."

Abercrombie paused for a moment. "Yes, I see what you mean, but perhaps he wasn't interested in putting the blame on Ewan. He simply wanted Jake silenced."

"With Brian's murder so recent, anyone wanting to kill his friend would try to make us believe both crimes were connected, wouldn't they?"

"Maybe the first murder just put the idea into his head."

"But Parkinson didn't know Jake was going to knock on his door."

"You could be right. As Jackson would say, 'it's a theory'."

"What is?"

"That Parkinson's innocent."

* * *

In Jackson's office, Superintendent Peter Everett paced the room.

"How the hell was a suspected murderer allowed to escape? Tell me, how?" he stormed.

"It wasn't our people," Jackson answered. He sat at his desk appearing much calmer than Everett. "It was the security company that let him go."

"Why were they used in the first place? Why couldn't one of our patrols take him?"

"It is Sunday, sir. They would have been short staffed."

"I suppose so. You'd have been better off keeping Ewan here, where he was secure. I don't know why you didn't do that. There's going to be hell to pay now, isn't there?" Everett seemed to have forgotten it was himself who gave permission for the suspect to be moved.

Jackson ignored the comment.

"It was a mistake. We thought it best at the time."

"And what about the boy? How did you scare him so much that he ran away?"

"Jake's a nervous little kid. Whenever we go near him, he seems to get the idea we think he killed Brian."

"Has he any reason to think that?"

"We had to consider him. We know the boys argued and he won't tell us what it was about. So we had to treat him as a potential suspect for a time."

"For a time? So you don't believe it now?"

"We never really seriously thought he did it, we just needed to be sure. Anyway, it seems now as if Ewan is our man."

"Yes, and you've lost him. How am I going to explain that to the commissioner, let alone the press?"

"Look, Sir. If you have to give me a rollicking, can it wait until tomorrow? I have urgent work to do as you know?"

"Yes, I know that. All right, I'll let you get on with it. I want a full report about this on my desk first thing. You got that, Jackson?"

Jackson nodded as Everett left the room. He hadn't once mentioned to the Superintendent that he had not been present himself at the time of Ewan's escape. His absence did not excuse his responsibility.

Having seen Everett leave, Abercrombie entered the office with the tape of Parkinson's interview. Jackson listened to it then asked, "have the team heard this?"

"Yes," Abercrombie confirmed. "No one came up with anything, though Gloria figures there is something weird in that Parkinson didn't know when he followed the boy that Ewan had escaped."

"No, he didn't, did he?"

"You agree then, there might be two murderers?"

"You're speaking as if Jake's dead."

"Sorry. There isn't a body, true. But Jake hasn't been seen since Parkinson went after him. He still hasn't gone home."

"Let's be optimistic, Harry. If there's no body, there has to be a good chance the boy's still alive."

"I hope so. The trouble is, even if Parkinson didn't hurt him, there's this threat to kill himself. And there's Ewan."

Jackson thought for a minute.

"Ewan won't stay in this area, he's too easily recognisable. Anyway, what reason has he got to kill Jake?"

"The kid's a witness."

"Only to the fact Ewan was on the canal bank that day. He's admitted to that, anyhow."

"Yes, I see what you mean. I still can't help feeling uneasy. He might go after him for revenge or something."

"He might," Jackson agreed. "Except it would lead us straight back to him, not to mention giving us more evidence against him."

"He's nothing to lose, though, has he?"

"Get the boy found, fast."

* * *

The phone buzzed on Jackson's desk and he was told the Churchers had arrived in reception.

He knew they would come, or at least that Angela would. He'd been expecting her ever since the local radio station broadcast news of the escape in its hourly bulletin.

Abercrombie wasn't in the office so Jackson went down alone to see them. He'd been wondering for some while what he would say to them. Now the time had arrived he still had no idea how he would explain why their son's alleged killer was free again.

The Churchers followed Jackson into the interview room and sat in their usual places.

"You've let him go, haven't you? He killed Brian and you let him go," Angela ranted.

"We didn't let him go. He escaped. I'm sorry, Angela. We'll get him back, don't worry."

"You should have let me have him. I'd have seen he confessed for you, all right."

"You know we couldn't do that."

Angela stayed quiet and Frank once again took advantage of her silence to enter the discussion.

"You don't need a confession now, though, do you? I said it was him all along, didn't I? I kept telling Angela I knew it was him."

"Yes, you did, Frank." Jackson felt like saying Frank also insisted Parkinson was the killer but this was not the time.

"What will happen now?" Angela asked. "When you catch him I mean. You've got enough evidence now, surely?"

"Well, escaping from custody is a crime in itself, of course, but we still don't have any evidence he killed Brian."

"What! Surely, he wouldn't have escaped if he wasn't guilty?"

That was what everyone was assuming, Jackson thought.

"Escaping by itself doesn't prove he's guilty, Angela."

Frank stood up sending his chair reeling backwards.

"You can't really believe he's innocent, not now?"

"What I believe doesn't matter. We still need evidence."

"Evidence? I don't see what more proof you can want!"

"I agree Ewan escaping makes it look bad for him, but it proves nothing."

"Come on, Angela, let's go. They're all idiots here. We'll talk to those reporters outside."

Angela raised her vast bulk from the chair, gave Jackson a long stare, then started to follow Frank out of the interview room. In the doorway, she hesitated, reached into her handbag and fished out half a dozen small, flat, circular objects.

"You might as well have these. Somebody phoned and asked me to bring them."

Jackson recognised them as computer discs. He was surprised there were so few.

"Is this all of them?" he asked.

"That's all there is."

She threw the discs onto the table and went after Frank. Jackson looked at the discs. He couldn't understand why there were so few. Harry had indicated that Jake had hundreds. Still, Jackson thought, it wouldn't take as long for one of the team to go through them. The discs had labels on which were written names that had no meaning for Jackson. One did take his interest, however, it was marked 'private'.

Chapter 11

Jackson took the computer discs into the incident room and gave them to Gloria.

"Go through these, as fast as you can, especially this one," he said, pointing out the disc marked private. "How long will it take you to find out if they have anything of interest on them?"

"I can check this one disc right now. It'll only take a moment."

She placed the CD into her machine, pressed a few keys and soon had a file directory showing on her monitor. The only file was called 'diary'.

"This is it," Gloria said excitedly. "Not a blackmail note, a journal. This might tell us something useful."

"Look at it then," Jackson prompted, but Gloria was already in the process of opening the document. She turned to Jackson with a disappointed look on her face.

"It's password protected."

"Try something."

"Sir, he could have used any word in the dictionary or even one not in the dictionary, an anagram, anything."

"It would be something he'd need to remember, though, wouldn't it?"

"Oh, yes, but not only can it be anything, it also has to be case sensitive. Do you realise how many combinations of each word that gives? It could be all lower case, all upper case, numbers, a mixture. It would take forever to find it."

"Okay, I get the picture, Gloria. Some computer engineer must be able to get into it, though?"

"That's possible, but they might destroy what we're looking for. We're better trying to guess the password."

"How? You said that's practically impossible."

"As you mentioned, he'd need to remember it. Most people use something they identify with. The name of a pet, something like that."

"He didn't have any pets. Try his own name."

Gloria had continually been typing during the conversation.

"I already have. First name, last name, alone and together. No joy."

"Someone mentioned his hobby was fishing."

"There are a lot of different kinds of fish, sir."

"Well, keep trying and get anyone who's not doing anything else to help you."

He turned to leave; disappointed it would not be as straightforward as he'd hoped. Before he reached the door, he spun back to Gloria.

"Why did Brian have so few of those things? His friend seemed to own hundreds."

"It would depend on how they used them. Jake might store less stuff on his hard disc or be more conscientious about making backups. They may also have passed discs on to each other. Some of Jake's discs could belong to Brian."

"So, we need to go through all those too?"

"Possibly, but Brian protected this file with a password, so he's probably done the same with any others he had. Even if we discover the password for this document, the others might be different."

"Great! So, the discs are no use to us?"

"Not unless someone comes up with a word Brian is likely to have used as his password, and he's used the same one consistently."

"You said the names of pets. What about friends?"

"I've already tried 'Jake'."

"Oh!" he left the room.

He went back to his office where Abercrombie was leafing through the case file.

"Any news?" Jackson asked.

"Afraid not. No trace of either the boy or Ewan."

"Ewan's an idiot. What did he want to do a runner for?"

"Because he's guilty."

"We can't be certain of that, even now."

"You're joking! Why else would he need to run?"

"I know. You're probably right, you usually are. But I've still got my hunch."

Abercrombie stared. "You can't think he's innocent now. Who else is there? I mean, there's Parkinson, but surely Ewan's proved his own guilt?"

"I wish I was that sure."

"Well, if you're correct, but I doubt it, Jake will be safe enough, wherever he is."

"You're forgetting he told Parkinson he was going to kill himself."

"We've only got Parkinson's word for that."

"Don't you see? If Parkinson was lying, then you might be right about him following the boy to kill him. What other reason would he need to lie? If he wasn't lying, then Jake's in danger from himself!"

"Oh, shit!"

* * *

Jackson felt his stomach tightening as darkness approached with no progress in finding either Jake or Ewan.

A severe storm warning had been issued bringing a high risk of flooding and Jackson hoped this, when it arrived, would force the boy home. Of course, to go home, he had to be alive.

Jackson remembered how rough the weather had been when Jake ran from his home. There had been little improvement since. The rain slackened for a while but later returned in a series of heavy downpours. Wherever Jake was if he hadn't found shelter, he'd be saturated.

As Jackson pondered this, he asked himself where a twelve-year-old boy needing help and shelter would go. Not to the police; he was running from them. Not to his parents; the police were certain to find him there. Where had he turned for help? David Parkinson. Irrespective of what Parkinson might have done to the boy since then, it was a fact Jake went to him for help. That help was refused, but Parkinson was the first person Jake thought of. Would Brian have done the same? The name of a friend.

He picked up his phone and dialled Gloria's extension.

"Got anywhere with that password, Gloria?"

"No. It's hopeless."

"Try a combination of Dave or David Parkinson."

"Right."

He replaced the receiver and tried to work out in his head how many combinations there could be of the name. D parkinson, d Parkinson, Dave, dave, DAVE. At that point, he gave up as the enormity of what Gloria had told him dawned on him. He had planned to go into the incident room after a few minutes but now decided it was only fair to give Gloria a little longer.

However, within a minute or two, Harry Abercrombie came bursting into the room.

"We've got it! It was simple after all that, just one letter 'D'."

"D for Dave."

"So it seems. Gloria's printing it off now. You will be interested in what the boy's written."

Gloria appeared with the printout and Jackson took it from her eagerly. He placed it on the desk so he and Abercrombie could read it together.

Not every day had an entry, and those that did had just brief notes:

'17th June - D made me do it again today. He thinks I like it but I don't. It hurts.

20th June - D did it again. I should tell mum but I can't.

24th June - I wish D would stop making me do things.

28th June - If D doesn't stop I'm going to tell mum, I don't think she'll believe me though.

3rd July - D won't stop. I can't tell mum. I hate D.'

It went on in a similar vein until the 20th of August, two days before Brian's death.

"Well, it's pretty certain who 'D' is," said Abercrombie.

"Yes," said Jackson. "Let's get him back in the interview room."

"His solicitor's gone."

"Call him back then."

Abercrombie went to phone the solicitor, leaving Jackson and Gloria to peruse Brian's diary further.

"He doesn't say what Parkinson did to him," said Gloria.

"I know. Neither does he actually say it was Parkinson. With no mention of his name, Parkinson could deny it referred to him. It could just as easily be the other David. David Glover."

"He's not in the frame now, though, is he?"

"That won't matter to Parkinson."

Thunder rumbled. The threatened storm was drawing closer.

* * *

Jackson and Abercrombie sat across the desk from David Parkinson and the solicitor. Robert Bramhall wasn't happy about being called back.

"I understand you have new evidence to discuss with my client," he said. "It better be something worth bringing me back here for. I was looking forward to an evening at home."

You'll be looking forward to your pay cheque for this too, Jackson thought, but he said nothing. He didn't bother to tell Bramhall he should himself at that moment be enjoying a family birthday party.

He showed the computer printout to Parkinson.

"We have printed this from Brian Churcher's computer. I think you'll agree it implies Brian was sexually exploited?"

"It looks that way," Parkinson agreed.

"And by someone he refers to as 'D'?"

"Yes. So?"

"You know what, David, don't you? The 'D' is you, isn't it? D for David."

"Is this your so-called evidence, Inspector?" Bramhall exploded. "D can be for anything. Derek, Damien,

Daniel. I'm sure my client wasn't the only person this boy knew whose name started with a D."

"No, there's Dave Glover for a start," Parkinson added.

"Besides, just because the victim wrote it on his computer doesn't mean it took place," Bramhall went on. "It might all be fantasy."

"No," Abercrombie said. "That's one thing we are sure of, that it happened I mean. We've got medical evidence to show Brian Churcher had been abused."

"Exactly in the way he describes it here?"

"Well, er, no, he doesn't describe it, does he?"

"Precisely."

"But he says who was doing it to him."

Bramhall slammed a hand onto the desk. "No, he doesn't. He states it was someone called D. You have no evidence whatsoever that D refers to my client, do you?"

"We don't," admitted Jackson. "But putting everything together, the allegation, the fact no one has seen Jake since your client chased him, the relationship he admits to having with Brian. What are we going to think?"

"You can think what you like, but you know perfectly well none of that is evidence, just as you know that printout wouldn't be accepted in court. You can't even confirm the boy wrote it. Because you found it on his computer doesn't mean he typed it himself. Any number of people might have had access to the machine."

"His parents know nothing about computers, and he had no siblings."

"So, you're telling me you're positive he never had friends in the house. I propose we end this interview now unless you've anything more substantial than a printout which has an unidentifiable name as a suspect and can't even be confirmed to have been written by the victim. I suggest you release my client. You've got nothing at all to charge him with."

Jackson conceded to end the interview but not to letting Parkinson go. Not yet. If he was responsible in any way for Jake's disappearance, Jackson wanted him where he could reach him fast.

"Bramhall's right, though," he said afterwards to Abercrombie. "Everything he said is correct. The D could mean anything, and we've no way of proving Brian wrote the diary himself or, even if he did, that what he says is true."

"There must be something we can do."

"I'm afraid not. Not as far as the computer stuff is concerned. Unless you know of any way to prove the boy was the sole person who could have composed it, and that D refers to David Parkinson?"

"No," Abercrombie admitted, "that's the problem with computers, you can't give them to a handwriting expert."

"Indeed. Anyway, our priority at the moment has to be finding Jake Swift. Find out what the situation is, will you? If the kid's still alive and hasn't found shelter somewhere, he's going to be in trouble when this storm hits."

"True. He's in hell of a mess, isn't he? If Ewan or Parkinson haven't already got to him, there's the possibility of him drowning in the floods."

"I stand by what I said before. I don't consider we need to worry about Ewan. The boy is in danger, though. If Parkinson hasn't already harmed him, there is, as you say, the floods to think about. That's apart from the threat to kill himself."

"You don't think he meant that seriously? If he said it at all?"

"He's scared. He's lost his best friend, and he thinks we believe he's guilty. Yes, I think he meant it. Whether he'd have the courage to carry it out when it came to the crunch, I'm not sure, but we can't afford to take the chance."

"Right, I'll see if they've found anything."

Jackson heard the rain lashing at the window as Abercrombie left the room. He couldn't recall such a heavy downpour. He was concerned the weather would hamper the search. It certainly wouldn't be safe for any vehicles to be on the roads for a while.

Chapter 12

Jackson's team remained at the police station late into the night. The storm got worse, and fears for Jake's safety increased as midnight passed with no sighting of the boy. Most of the crew, along with Jackson himself, were in the incident room.

"Let's hope he's taken shelter somewhere," Gloria said as they drank coffee.

"The best shelter is home, though," Kevin Gibson responded. "Wouldn't he go there before it became this bad if it was possible?"

"Let's be optimistic," Jackson encouraged. "Perhaps he didn't expect the weather would get as bad as this. He thought it would improve and he'd ride out the storm. When the weather got worse, it was so awful he had to find refuge and couldn't get home. It's only a theory, but it's possible."

The team didn't look convinced. Gloria drummed her fingers on the desk. Alan Hook, pacing like a caged animal, cleared his throat.

"A twelve-year-old kid out in this weather by himself hasn't much of a chance," he said. "Remember how tiny he is."

"There'll be plenty of other kids out besides Jake, though," Gloria said. "It's school holidays. Some of them will be camping."

"That's true," said Jackson. "If they can survive, so can Jake."

"But the kids who go camping are going to be with an adult. If not a parent, a youth leader, scout leader or something," Hook said.

Jackson rocked back in his chair and looked at him. "Not always. It's clear you were never a Scout, Alan. Many of them go only with other kids. Anyway, what can an adult do in this weather any better than the kids?"

"In that case, let's be glad there aren't any Scout Camps in our area."

"Oh, they'll cope. They might have to abandon the tents, but in most campsites there are huts and such for emergencies. We only need to worry about Jake. Let the campers sort themselves out."

At that moment, Abercrombie rushed into the room. Everyone stopped talking and stared at him.

"The drains can't take the downpour," he said. "We're going to have extensive flooding on our hands, on top of what we expected, I mean."

Everybody looked at Abercrombie as if waiting for him to announce the solution.

"They will have to take officers off the search," Jackson said. "They'll need to help folks who are trapped."

"Jake might be one of those trapped people," said Gloria.

"Well, if he is, let's hope the rescue squads locate him. It's an alternative to the search."

"What about Ewan?" Gibson asked.

"He'll be well out of the district by now. We'll call off the local hunt for him. Uniform will need all the manpower they can get now."

* * *

David Ewan couldn't believe how easy it had been to escape. They had let him answer the call of nature and, to give him some privacy, left him unsupervised for a moment or two. That moment or two was all he needed. He bolted from behind the bush, and it had been a simple matter to give his guards the slip. He wasn't sure what to do now, though. Home was out of the question. There'd be no chance now of convincing anyone he was innocent if they caught him. Pity that, after all the expense of installing the extra security into the house.

He hid in the woods to work out his plans, knowing it wouldn't be long before a massive search for him was underway. He had to find a better hiding place.

It looked as if bad weather was on the way. That would stop them from using helicopters. Dogs might be an issue, though.

That damned kid had got him into this mess. He wished he could find the boy. He'd make him suffer for a while. The lad deserved punishing.

But he had no idea where the youngster lived so he'd have to let him get away with it. For a few minutes, he fantasised about what he would do to the boy if he found him. Then he realised he hadn't got time for daydreaming. He had to be away from here before they sent those dogs.

The sky became darker still, and he knew shelter would be even more of a priority than flight for the moment. He spotted a church in the distance and made his way towards it. Church buildings often had basements which made good shelters as well as hideouts.

* * *

"Come back, kid," Mark Chegwin called after Jake. "I never said I wouldn't help you."

Jake skidded to a standstill and turned around. He didn't look too sure about trusting Mark.

"Come here," Mark repeated in a quiet voice.

Jake hesitated, then deciding Mark was his only chance, ambled towards the older boy.

"I'll let you into the youth club," Mark promised, "but I can't give you the key. I'll have to put it back in case my dad misses it. I'll need to lock you in."

Jake thought about this. He didn't like the idea of Mark locking him up, but at least the police would never find him there.

"All right," he agreed. "As long as you can get me some food."

"I'll see what I can do. Wait there."

Mark went back into the vicarage, and Jake waited in the porch. He could leave now; it would be his last chance. Once Mark got back, he'd be a prisoner. He was still standing there trembling when Mark returned. This was it. He'd allow the bigger boy to imprison him.

"Come on." Mark led him to the heavy oak door of the basement and unlocked it. He ushered Jake into the familiar room of the youth club, then closed and locked the door.

Jake was alone. He knew his surroundings well but had never been here by himself before. As he looked around the big building, he felt entombed and thought he would never see daylight again.

He realised that idea was irrational. The windows let in quite a bit of light despite their low level.

He needed to get out of his wet clothes. He undressed and put his garments on the radiators aware, as Mark had told him, they would be cold. It was better than nothing and better than to go on wearing them and catching pneumonia or something.

Shivering, he went to the washroom where he used all the paper towels in an attempt to dry himself off. With his skin still quite damp, he went into a storeroom where they kept clothes for jumble sales. It was empty. Not even so much as a towel to dry himself properly. He sank to the ground, the stone floor cold against his skin. He sat there and wept.

Some time later, he was still crying when he heard someone unlocking the door to the basement. He froze for an instant then sprang to his feet and scampered into the farthest corner of the room. He relaxed when he heard Mark's voice call him.

"Jake, where are you?"

"Here," Jake responded and emerged from his hiding place. Embarrassed, he tried to cover his nakedness with his hands as the older boy approached him.

Mark chuckled at this. "What's the matter, kid, don't you do P.E at school and have to undress?"

"Yeah, but in front of kids my age," Jake answered.

"We're all t' same, you know. Anyway, you'll need to move your hands if you want to eat this."

He held out a cheese sandwich. It wasn't wrapped or plated, just in his bare hand, but Jake wasn't concerned about hygiene. He realised he hadn't eaten all day. He gingerly moved one hand to take the snack.

"Thanks."

"It's all right. I couldn't get you anything to drink, though, you'll have to make do with water."

"That's okay. Thanks."

"There is a price to pay, you know. You said you'd do anything, remember?"

"What do you want me to do?"

"You'll see. Nothing too difficult."

He went away, leaving Jake to wonder what the cost of his cheese sandwich would be. Mark knew he hadn't any money and wouldn't be able to get any. It must be some chore then he'd have to do. It was true he'd said he would do anything. Well, he wouldn't mind cleaning Mark's trainers or whatever it was he wanted. If Mark kept feeding him, it would be worth it.

He went to the washroom and filled his mouth with water to wash the food down. It had only been a sandwich, but he felt much better for it. Then he went to look at his clothes; he didn't want the embarrassment of Mark seeing him naked again. They were still soaking wet.

For a moment, he considered whether to put them on anyhow, then decided against it. Sitting in wet clothes would be less comfortable than letting Mark see him in his birthday suit again.

He hoped the clothes would have dried by morning, even though he had no idea where he would go. He knew he needed to be well gone from here by the time the youth club opened - and he couldn't run away naked.

Worried, he went back to the storeroom and sat down again. He wouldn't cry again, he told himself. There was no point in it. It didn't help and didn't make the slightest difference. Perhaps he should try prayer instead; after all, he was below a church.

He thought an hour had passed before he heard the key in the lock again. Hoping it was Mark with more food, but unable to be sure, he again scampered into his corner. He heard Mark's voice and relaxed for a moment, then stiffened. Who was Mark talking to?

Expecting Mark to walk in with his father - or the police, Jake shrank back as far as he could into the corner.

Mark did walk into the room, but it wasn't the police or his father who accompanied him. It was another boy about Mark's age, though much tubbier. What struck Jake most about the newcomer was his teeth were rotten.

"Hi, Jake," Mark said as they both approached him. "Time to pay the price. Turn round."

Jake saw the stranger unzip his jeans as Mark spoke.

"N-no, n-not that, p-please, Mark."

"You said you'd do anything," Mark replied in a stern tone. "Now stop whining and turn, or I'll hit you."

Jake turned.

When it was over, he twisted back to face the older boys. Tears streamed down his face, and his anus was sore. His terrified, tear flooded face pleaded for mercy as he waited for Mark to take his turn. Then he saw the unknown youth hand Mark a ten-pound note and realised Mark was selling his body. He also knew there would be others.

He'd come in here as a willing prisoner, and now, Mark was using him to increase his income. He knew Mark wouldn't let him out now.

The two older boys left the building. Jake heard Mark snigger as they went. He knew he had to get out of there, wet clothes or not, before Mark came back with another customer.

The fire escape! That was the answer. He started to dress. His clothes were still wringing wet but had stopped dripping. He had trouble dressing as the clothing stuck to his skin. It didn't matter, he decided. Anything was better than going through that disgusting ordeal again. He tried to rush, hoping to be gone before Mark returned. The quicker he attempted to dress, the more tangled his clothes got. He realised this and tried to take his time a bit more but was still in too big of a hurry to make swift progress. He could hear the rain had started again, even harder than before. It would have been a waste of time for his clothes to have dried.

Eventually, he was dressed. The wet clothes clung to him as he made his way to the fire escape. He pushed the bar. Nothing happened.

"What's going on?" he asked himself. Mark must have realised he could get out this way and somehow blocked it. He thrust harder. This time, the door moved a little, and a gush of water came rushing through it. Jake was ankle-deep before he got the door shut again.

He knew what had happened, and it was nothing to do with Mark. Litter had clogged the drains. The leaders were always telling the kids not to drop their rubbish in the bay surrounding the church. This was the reason. Jake made a mental note never to drop litter anywhere again. Then he realised he might never get out of here to drop litter or do anything else. Trapped! A prisoner. And Mark would soon be back with the next pervert.

Jake slid to the floor and buried his face in his hands. Forgetting his reasoning that crying was of no use, he let the tears flow again.

Chapter 13

David Ewan headed towards the tower of the church he had seen. He recognised that church, and it wasn't too far from his home. The police would guess he'd fled the area by now and wouldn't consider searching for him around there. Perhaps he might even risk going to his house after all. If he covered his scent and threw the hounds off the trail until he reached the building, he could assume a new identity and blend in with the locals. He would be safe.

He would hide in the church for a while, though, in case the police were still watching the house.

The heavy rain was a problem. It was getting worse, and the trees provided little protection. He had to hope the wood would become denser as he went on.

But as he made his way forward, the torrent became relentless, lashing at his face and driving him back. He stumbled over a tree root and fell, sliding down a grassy slope. A clump of bushes suddenly checked his slide. The fall made him realise it was getting too dark to move through the woods safely; he'd have to stay here until morning and put up with the rain. Cursing, he dragged himself to his feet. Then when he looked closer at the shrubs that broke his fall, he discovered they surrounded the entrance to a naturally formed pothole. He crawled into this and found it to be more or less dry. It would make a perfect place to stay for a time. Even the dogs weren't likely to be out searching in this weather. Even if they were, the rain would put them off the scent for a while.

He found the driest spot available and attempted to get some sleep.

* * *

Jake couldn't believe how quick the water was rising. It was already above his ankles and ascending at an alarming rate. He stood spellbound as it came to his knees with no sign of abating. The boy realised it would soon be over his head and started to pile up tables and chairs. He clambered onto the makeshift tower and stared into the still-rising water. If he'd stayed on the ground, it would be up to his neck by now, and he feared that even his tower wouldn't be high enough.

***

Jackson strolled from his office to the incident room. He found Abercrombie talking with the other members of the unit.

"Harry, the schools start back tomorrow," he said. "Gloria and I will visit Brian's school to see if anybody there knows why anyone would want to murder him. Jake's at the same school, so while we're there, we can ask his pals where he might have gone."

"I was hoping we'd find him before that," Abercrombie replied.

"We're not going to find the lad tonight. The weather's getting worse. It's too dangerous to carry on searching, especially in the dark." He stumbled and had to place his hand against the wall to support himself.

"You're tired. Why don't you go home for a while and get some sleep?" said Abercrombie.

"I can't go home now. I will put my head down on the desk for a while, though." He returned to his office, sat down at his desk and rested his head. Sleep, he knew, would not be possible, but if he rested his eyes for a while, he thought he would be all right. He closed his eyes and within no time sank into a deep sleep.

***

Jake stood on top of his tower of furniture and peered into the water. He was still horrified at the speed at which it climbed. He knew it would soon be too dark to see the surface of the water and hoped it would stop rising before that happened. Then he realised it didn't make any difference whether it was light or dark; he could do nothing about it.

It was becoming too much for the youngster. Even at his elevated level, the water had now reached his feet. Deep enough for him to drown. All he needed to do was slide into the water, and all his problems would be over. He'd be with Brian, and they'd be friends again. Yes, he decided, he was going to jump.

***

The storm had forced Mark Chegwin home. He went to his bedroom, disappointed about not being able to continue his new fundraising scheme. His parents didn't bother to ask where he'd been. They'd given up doing that as a waste of time when Mark was fourteen.

Mark needed to feed the kid in the basement, but he wasn't going out in that weather again. The kid would have to wait.

* * *

Jake stood on his precarious tower as he attempted to pluck up the courage to slide down into what he knew would be a watery grave. Something in his mind seemed to tell him it would be a sin to take his own life. Somebody sometime, he couldn't remember who, must have told him that. His mother, perhaps, or maybe the vicar. He was certain whoever it was didn't expect he would ever be under this extreme pressure.

Should he allow himself to fall into the water or let nature take its course and see what happened?

Then, the decision was made for him as the entire shaky contraption he was standing on collapsed sideways, tossing him into the cold, murky liquid below.

* * *

Mark looked out of his bedroom window and found the rain had slackened. He went downstairs to the kitchen and hurriedly prepared another cheese sandwich to feed to Jake. After making sure his parents were busy watching TV, he took the youth club key from its hook in his father's study, put the snack into a paper bag, slipped on his coat and made his way towards the church.

When he got to the steps leading to the basement, he stared in disbelief. The whole of the sunken walkway surrounding the church was full of water. The basement would be flooded, and Jake would be trapped!

The drains. Mark knew almost at once what the problem was, but what could he do? He daren't ask his father for help; that would mean having to give embarrassing explanations. Dropping the sandwich, he ran to the rear of the vicarage where his mother kept the pole she used to prop up the clothesline. Grabbing this, he rushed back and prodded at the drains. A gurgling noise told him he had, for now, cleared the grid covering the drain and the water started going down, though slowly. He hoped it would be in time to save Jake from drowning. A dead body being found when the youth club opened would be as hard to explain as telling the truth now.

He couldn't stick around to make sure the water receded entirely; it was taking too long, and he didn't want to be missed. So, he returned the clothes prop and went back inside the vicarage, hoping there would be no further rain tonight.

* * *

Jake thrashed his arms and legs in panic as he sank below the water's surface. His head re-surfaced as he realised it was deep enough for him to swim. It was too dark to see where he was going, and his waterlogged clothing made progress slow. He tried to find something to stand on. Groping his way forward, he hoped to come across a table from the remains of his collapsed tower. He did collide with what he assumed to be a table leg and feeling the object with his hands confirmed he had found a table. But it was upside down which would give no height advantage. In desperation, he attempted to turn it over but soon discovered this would be too difficult. Continuing in the same direction, he did, at last, find a table, or what he thought might be a table. This time, the right way up, and he scrambled onto it, relieved to find it raised most of his body from the water.

Looking down, Jake couldn't see the surface of the water any longer. He could feel it was well over his knees. Was it still rising? He couldn't be sure. He was scared. A few minutes ago, he'd wanted to die. Now, he wanted to live.

He prayed. Then he cried.

Chapter 14

At first light, David Ewan cautiously peered from his hiding-place. The rain had ceased, and a return of the hot weather looked likely. As far as Ewan was concerned, this was a change for the worse. They'd be resuming the search for him any time now. He hoped they would assume he had used the darkness to get well away from this area. His fingers and toes were numb from lack of activity during the night. He tried to massage them to get his circulation going before setting off once more toward the church. The rain had been much heavier than he thought, and large pools of water appeared everywhere, compelling him to make several detours. He cursed the English climate as he made slow progress towards his destination, knowing he needed to reach it before the police got their helicopter, with its thermal camera, into the sky. No one stood any chance of being undetected with that thing flying around.

* * *

In the vicarage, Mark Chegwin, yet in bed, lay awake fretting about what to do about the kid in the basement. He hoped the boy was all right after the storm. If so, he'd just be able to let him go, but he'd need to make certain the kid told no one what happened. Mark had no respect for his parents, but he needed a roof over his head. Something he guessed he might no longer have if his father, the vicar, found out what he had done. But how could he keep the lad quiet? Threatening him would be no use. The kid had guts. He'd already proved that. He'd just have to punch the kid on the nose. That, coupled with a threat of worse to come, should make sure the lad kept silent. Then Mark considered the other possibility—that the kid had drowned. How the hell could he explain that? As he fretted about this, Mark gradually realised it wouldn't be too much of a problem. While he didn't want to go into the basement and find Jake's lifeless body, it would mean there was no chance of his actions ever being discovered. No one knew he had locked Jake in the basement. There were other keys to the youth club. All he needed to do was lock the door again and wait for someone to find Jake when the club opened that evening. He could pretend to know nothing of how or why Jake was in the youth club. Then he remembered his punter. He knew. But if the youth said anything, his own deeds would come to light. He'd find him, anyhow, and give him a thumping to keep him quiet. Just in case.

* * *

Jackson lifted his head from the desk and realised it was daylight. Why hadn't they wakened him? He went to the men's room and splashed cold water onto his face and finger-combed his hair. Although he realised he must have slept at his desk through the night, he didn't feel any less tired. He noticed the rain had stopped at last though it would already have done the damage. Through the window, he saw a crowd of people gathered in the car park. What did they want? They must have heard by now that Ewan was no longer here. Bracing himself for news of flood damage he knew would be waiting for him, he made his way to the incident room. He found Abercrombie, as usual, immaculate in his grey suit. How did he do it? Abercrombie's appearance made Jackson conscious he had not yet shaved, or even washed properly.

"Why didn't you wake me?" he asked.

"I thought you could do with the rest. You looked shattered. To be honest, you still do."

"I'll go home and get an hour in my bed later. What's the situation?"

"The flood has done a lot of damage. There was over a month's worth of rainfall in one night. People need to be evacuated and taken to higher ground. Social Services are looking after them, but some of our staff are helping out too."

"I meant about Jake?"

"Oh, sorry. No, nothing."

"What are those people doing outside?"

"Volunteers. They've come to help us find the boy. I was just about to address them, but I suppose you'll want to do that now?"

"No. You carry on. I'll come with you, though."

They went into the car park. It was cooler after the rain, but Jackson glanced up at a break in the clouds and wondered if the heatwave would return. As he looked down again, to his surprise, he saw Angela and Frank Churcher amongst the volunteers. There was, though, no sign of Jake's parents.

"Too upset to come," Abercrombie whispered in response to his question. Then he addressed the small crowd.

"First, thank you all for coming. I'm aware many of you have troubles of your own because of the flooding. You all know why you're here. We need to find the child you've been given a picture of."

Uniformed police officers moved through the crowd distributing photographs of Jake as Abercrombie spoke.

"The boy has been missing since yesterday morning," Abercrombie continued. "So, we don't know what condition he's in or whether he's safe. Be prepared for anything.

"We will divide you into teams with a police officer in charge of each team. Each team will be given a specific area to search. Any questions?"

"Have you caught that murderer yet?" This was Angela.

"Don't worry, Angela," Jackson now stepped in. "He can't run forever. Wherever he is, we'll catch him."

"Then what?"

"He'll be sent for trial, of course."

"What's he need a trial for?" Someone called out from the crowd. "He wouldn't run if he weren't guilty, would he?"

"In this country, no one is guilty until it's been proven."

"Rubbish! He's proved it himself."

"Let's concentrate on finding Jake Swift, shall we?"

Most of the crowd appreciated the sense of this and calmed down. A sergeant from uniform divided them into teams. Jackson and Abercrombie left them to it and made their way back inside the police station.

"They've made up their minds Ewan's guilty," said Jackson.

"You can't blame them, can you?"

"That proves Ewan's point, though. He'd never get a fair hearing."

"You can't still consider he's innocent. Not now?"

"I'd hate to send the wrong person to prison, and I still have that bit of doubt."

"But you won't send him to prison, will you. It'll be the judge and jury. So even if he's innocent, you have nothing to feel guilty about. It won't be your mistake."

"But the court will take our evidence into account when they make that decision. Yes, Harry, I think I have reason to feel guilty. At least, if the wrong man is convicted, I will. To say nothing of the real murderer going free - or the reputation of the police force."

"You look terrible," said Abercrombie, changing the subject. "Why don't you go home for a while? We can always call you back in if we need to."

"I'll wait until nearer lunchtime and go home to get a bite to eat and a bit of sleep. It'll give me a chance to see my kids. They'll be home from school for lunch."

"A lot of the schools are closed. Either flood-damaged themselves or being used to shelter victims."

"Oh, I wanted to visit Brian's school this afternoon. Ask Gloria to find out if it's open."

Abercrombie went off to do this and Jackson returned to his office to attempt to freshen up.

* * *

The search teams moved to their allocated areas around the town. Angela and Frank Churcher were put into a small group sent to investigate the area around the church. The leader of their team was one of the few black police officers in the Division. Once in the church grounds, Constable Vincent Peart split his unit into even smaller groups. This left Angela and Frank on their own. They were designated to search the area immediately surrounding the building itself as other members of the party spread out to check the extensive grounds.

"Make sure you check for any possible way into the church," Peart had told them.

They approached the steps leading down to the basement.

"I'm not going down there," Angela said as she looked at the narrow steps. Frank had to agree they were not built for the use of someone of her bulk. He knew she must already be exhausted. He peered down the steps into the alley where all was quiet. Frank didn't much like the idea of going down himself.

"We don't need to go down. There's no point," he said.

"The policeman told us we had to search everywhere."

"We don't have to take orders from that black bastard. Besides, there can't be anyone there, the door's shut."

"Don't you want to find Jake?"

"I want him to be all right, of course I do. But I don't see it's any of our business. I don't know why you dragged me into this."

His wife gave him an icy stare. "I didn't drag you. You said you wanted to come. Anyway, the Swift boy was the last person to see Brian. He could tell us something."

"What's to tell?" Ewan killed him.

"Jackson doesn't seem that sure. Suppose he's right. It might even be Jake who did it."

"That little shrimp! Get the better of Brian? Although now you mention it, he might have surprised him, yeah."

"So, get down those steps, just in case he's in there. We need to find him before anyone else does. We have more chance of making him talk than the police."

"I'll kill the little bastard," Frank turned and made his way shakily down the steps.

* * *

Mark dragged himself from his bed and dressed. He needed to get the kid out of the church before anyone was up and about. He couldn't rouse suspicion by rushing out too quickly, though. It would be difficult enough explaining why he was out of bed so early. Early for him, anyhow. He opened the curtains of his bedroom and stared out towards the church. It stunned him to see people moving around the church. No, not today, not this early! People couldn't come to see the church now! Then he thought about the possibility the people might be looking for Jake. Either way, it would be a disaster if they got into the basement. He was relieved to see the people move away from the youth club area, but also afraid. Why hadn't Jake called out? Did that mean…? No, he wouldn't think about that.

He ran downstairs and, after making sure his father wasn't around the vicinity, went to the office where the keys were kept hanging on a board. His eyes went to where the key to the youth club should have been. It wasn't there! Those people doing the searching… had his father given them the key? Had they already been inside the building and found Jake? If he was alive, why hadn't they brought him out with them? He went back to his bedroom, ashen-faced, and sat on the bed to think.

* * *

Towards lunchtime, Jackson, still tired, took Abercrombie's advice to go home for a short while. Gloria had learned the school he wished to visit was on the higher ground to the north of the town and open as usual. Jackson decided he and Gloria would go there after lunch to see if they could discover any more about Brian's background. It would also be an opportunity to find out if any of his school friends knew where Jake might have gone.

Now, too tired to drive safely, he strolled towards his home, continually checking on what progress the search parties had made whenever he came across them. There had been none. He arrived at his house, and Daniel came running down the garden path to greet him. The boy's face was dirty, which told Jackson he had been at play and not at school. Daniel's school must be one of those that hadn't been able to open after the flood. He scooped his son up in his arms.

Daniel's dirty face sent Jackson's mind back again to his own hated school days, where one of the tortures he suffered several times was to have his face rubbed in the mud. He preferred this to some of the more painful punishments his peers gave him, until the day they didn't bother to check there weren't any stones embedded in the mud. His face was badly scratched and impossible for his housemaster not to notice. The housemaster, a tall, slim gentleman called Mr Powell, insisted Jackson named the culprits. Jackson refused, knowing he would get a beating if he snitched on the bullies. This, however, was in the days of the cane and in the absence of identification from Jackson or a confession from his attackers, he watched horrified as the whole of his group, innocent as well as guilty, were each whacked in turn. Despite his silence, he got the beating anyway. That didn't trouble him too much. What worried him was that his one friend in the school was among those punished, and he had done nothing to prevent it. It was quite some time before that friend spoke to him again. Now, he wondered again if Ewan was also innocent like that friend. Like him, he would be punished for something he hadn't done and, like then, Jackson would be a party to it.

He went into the house, still carrying Daniel. He looked into his son's grubby face and felt relieved that school bullying was a thing of the past. Or was it? He knew that neither Daniel nor Karen would tell him or Sheila if anyone was bullying them. Not from fear, like his own silence had been, but because they would think tale-telling was wrong. He'd have a chat with his children soon.

Chapter 15

Sheila, Jackson's wife, greeted him as he entered the house carrying Daniel.

"You look dreadful," she said.

"I know," he responded putting down his son who scampered off to play. "I'm going to get my head down for a bit. Is Karen here?"

"No. She's still at school. She'll be home for lunch soon. Daniel's school is closed because of the floods."

"So I see. Well, I'll go and lie down. Call me when lunch is ready."

* * *

The rainwater was up to Jake's waist and still rising. He had stopped crying, mesmerised by the speed at which the water level ascended his body. It already covered whatever he had found to stand on. As he stared, shocked, at the fast-climbing water, it seemed to stop rising. Was it his imagination? He felt tears rolling down his cheeks again; he didn't know if they were tears of fear or relief.

The water was definitely not getting deeper. Once he realised this, a surge of relief ran through him. He thought he saw the flood level going down, though extremely slow. For a moment, he supposed it might be wishful thinking, but as he watched, he saw it really was going down. Now, he only needed to wait until he could open the door and get out of here. He shouldn't have to cope with all this; he was just a kid.

Then, it became all too much for him. He felt a moment of dizziness before there was total darkness and oblivion took over.

* * *

Jackson woke up feeling better. He hadn't slept long but combined with the nap he'd snatched at his desk; it was enough to refresh him. The lack of sleep would catch up with him again, but he hoped that would be after they found Jake.

He wasn't concerned so much about Ewan, confident by now he would be out of the area and, for the moment, someone else's problem. He washed, shaved, trimmed his moustache and went downstairs. Daniel, now clean, already sat at the dinner table waiting for his lunch. Karen came in from school while Jackson arrived at the living room.

"Am I forgiven?" he asked his daughter as their eyes met.

"There's nothing to forgive. I understand catching a murderer is more important than my party. I'm not a kid anymore."

Did she understand, he wondered, or was this all an act? Karen's silence during the meal did nothing to lessen his fears.

Daniel, on the other hand, hardly stopped talking long enough to put food into his mouth.

Have you caught the killer yet, Dad? Is he dangerous, Dad? When will you lock him up...? And so it continued; the excited eight-year-old not bothering to wait for answers.

"Leave your father alone," Sheila reprimanded gently. "He's tired. Let him have his lunch."

The boy looked at his mother for an instant as he wolfed down a mouthful of food, then his eyes went back to his father. "How many men have you got, Dad?"

"Daniel!" Sheila warned.

"It's all right, Love," Jackson said. "Let him talk, he doesn't see enough of me as it is. He might as well chat with me while he can. I wish you'd change the subject, though, Daniel. We can talk about other things besides my work."

"I like talking about your work."

"I know you do, but I don't only investigate murders."

"That's what you're doing now, though, isn't it?"

"Well, yes. But it isn't nice to talk about it when we're eating."

The boy looked disappointed as he put a forkful of potatoes into his mouth.

As soon as he swallowed the food, Daniel forgot his father's caution. "How did he kill the boy, Dad? Did he cut his throat?"

Karen had had enough. "Shut up, Daniel, or I'll batter you."

Both her parents stared at her. "Karen! That's enough. And this is your last warning, Daniel. Any more talk like that and you'll go to your room."

"Sorry, Mum, but he's bugging me."

"I know, but I never want to hear you threaten to hit him. You know that."

Daniel, sitting opposite Karen and enjoying seeing her rebuked, took the precaution of glancing at his parents to make sure their eyes were still on his sister, then cheekily stuck his tongue out at her as she glared at him.

That was too much for Karen, who, despite her mother's warning, would have cuffed her younger brother there and then if she'd been able to reach him. She threw down her knife and fork and stood up, sending her chair back.

"It's not fair. You always take his side, just because he's the youngest. She stormed out of the room."

"Karen!" Jackson shouted after her. He was ignored and heard his daughter's footsteps stamping up the stairs as she went to her bedroom to sulk.

"This is your fault," Jackson said to his son.

"I didn't do anything," Daniel retorted, his head bowed.

"If you'd been quiet when we told you this wouldn't have happened, Daniel," Sheila said.

Daniel lifted his face, revealing the beginning of a tear starting to flow. "It's not fair, you always stick up for her just because she's a girl."

"Don't be silly," his mother said. "We treat you both the same, and you know that."

Jackson was frustrated. This wasn't what he wanted when he came home to see his family. Daniel had left the table and gone into the front room to do his own sulking, wisely avoiding his bedroom where he would be within the clutches of his big sister. Jackson still felt tired, and after his recent interviews with Jake, he'd had enough of crying children for a while, especially his own.

"I'm sorry," he told Sheila. "I shouldn't have come home."

"Don't be silly," she replied. "They'll get over it. It's a kids' quarrel, that's all."

"Yeah, but it's not only that," he turned to make certain his son couldn't overhear the conversation. "I don't like this fascination Daniel has about murder."

"He'll grow out of it."

"And Karen? I think she really would have beaten him up if we hadn't been here."

"But we were so stop worrying."

"I think you'd better keep them apart for a while."

"She'll be going back to school soon. By the time she gets home, they'll have forgotten all about it. Stop worrying."

"Does she ever hit him?"

"You know all siblings have fights. I'm sure she gives him a slap now and again, but nothing serious. They're quite friendly most of the time. She even lets him use her computer."

"She slaps him?" Jackson's thoughts again went back to his hated days in that boarding school. Was his boy now going through the same sort of torment, and at the hands of his sister?

"I'm sure she does occasionally, and he probably deserves it. It isn't something to make an issue of. He might be small, but he can be a pest sometimes," Sheila said.

"But if she's bullying him…"

"I wouldn't call it bullying. She does nothing worse than give him a good pat on the soft part of his cheek, I'm sure. Look, you'll be lucky to find any brothers or sisters who didn't fight with each other as children, and usually far more seriously than giving their opponent a slap on the face. You're worrying about nothing."

"I hope so, but you know what I think about bullying."

"Yes, I do, and so do the kids. Karen wouldn't dare leave the slightest mark on Daniel. She wouldn't want to go through one of your interrogations."

"I don't interrogate them," Jackson protested. "I just don't want either of them to go through what I did."

"Things have changed since your day. They supervise kids at school much better now. They have all kinds of schemes going to prevent bullying."

"But if Daniel isn't being bullied at school, but here, at home…"

"He isn't. Believe me, I'd know."

"All right, but promise me, if you do find out Karen does anything bad to Daniel, you'll tell me."

"She'd never really hurt him. Stop fretting. You don't want him to grow up a wimp, do you?"

He'd heard that expression before, about twenty years ago. At that time, it had been referring to himself. No, he didn't want his son to grow into a wimp, but neither did he want him to go through the torment he had suffered himself.

"I must go." He kissed Sheila.

She returned the kiss. "Stop worrying about Karen and Daniel, they'll be all right. Go and solve your murder."

* * *

David Ewan emerged cautiously from the woods and surveyed the outskirts of the town. He saw people being escorted into vehicles, which then drove away towards the other side of town. He quickly worked out what was going on. People had been trapped by the floods and were being evacuated. That explained why he'd had such good luck. The police had been too busy to look for him. He took further advantage of the apparent chaos and headed towards the church. As he walked, he noticed groups of people who seemed to be looking for someone. Surely, they weren't still hunting for him around here. No, maybe seeking other flood victims. Nevertheless, he took the precaution of keeping well out of their view, staying as far as possible in the back alleys as he made his way slowly towards his intended hideout.

* * *

Jake woke up groggy. For a moment or so, he thought he was in the middle of some bad dream. As he wiped the sleep from his eyes, he realised he was wet. Surely, he hadn't wet the bed. He hadn't done that for years. Then he became aware that all his clothing was soaking wet, and everything came back to him. The murder. Being trapped in here. Being raped. Why hadn't Mark returned?

The rainwater had been rising, he recalled, and he must have blacked out. For a second or two, he felt sick as he realised he might have drowned. Then he remembered the water was going down before he fainted. How long had he been lying there in these wet clothes? Once again, he undressed and hung his saturated clothes over the cold radiators.

He stood naked and shivering as he tried to decide what to do. The water had now receded and even though there was an inch or so left, he was sure he could get the fire-escape door open. But how could he leave without his clothes? More importantly, where would he go?

He answered that last question in his mind quickly. He'd had enough. Once out of here, he would go home, whatever the consequences. His clothes would take ages to dry enough to wear, though. What could he do? He had to be away from here before Mark came back. He couldn't cope with any more of those filthy sessions. Jake decided to make his getaway now, no matter what state his clothes were in. The worst that might happen was he'd catch pneumonia.

But, as he inspected his garments and found them saturated, he realised it would be foolish to get into them in their present condition. He squeezed as much water as possible out of his underpants and put them on. This, he decided, would be no worse than wearing wet swimming trunks. It would be embarrassing if anyone saw him on the street but better than nothing.

Then someone tried the door. Mark! It was too late. But the door didn't open. Instinctively, Jake ran to his former hiding place in the clothing store.

"There's nobody here. It's locked."

Jake stiffened as the voice reached his ears. An adult voice. It wasn't Mark!

The voice was familiar, but he couldn't quite place it. Then, as he was about to yell out, he recognised the voice; it was that of Brian's father.

He stifled the scream as he recalled what Brian told him his father did to him. If he'd done it to Brian, he might also do it to him. It was bad enough going through it with Mark's customer. Jake didn't want to think about going through the same horrific ordeal with a fully grown person. He backed further into his corner and was relieved to hear the man's footsteps move away from the building.

* * *

David Ewan made slow progress as he had to stop at every corner to make sure it was safe to go on. At last, he got to the church.

He tried the main entrance, finding it locked, as he expected it to be. There would be no chance of gaining entry through the heavy oak door.

He walked around the building searching for other possible entrances. He came to a flight of stone steps and went down them. This looked more promising. At the bottom of the steps, he found himself on some kind of footpath leading round the cellar of the church. There were windows, but they were too high to reach. As he strode along to where he could see a door, his eye caught a polythene bag in which an uneaten sandwich had been discarded. Instinctively, he hesitated. The snack couldn't have been there long, or rats or birds would have consumed it by now. Did that mean someone was inside the church? He proceeded to the door and listened. He heard nothing. Satisfied he was alone, he looked at the entrance, but this was as sturdy as the main door. He didn't even bother to try it and continued walking along the pathway.

He came to another door, one that had no exterior handles and was flush with the wall. This door he took to be a fire-escape, the kind that could only be opened from the inside. It wasn't as thick as the other doors but would still be difficult to force. There had to be an easier way. There always was in these old buildings. He stared at the door as he pondered this.

* * *

Frightened, Jake stayed trembling in his corner for a while after he heard the footsteps move away.

When he thought Brian's father would be well away from the church, he went again to the fire-escape exit, still wearing nothing except his underpants. This time, he was more cautious, half expecting another gush of water to rush in and trap him again.

He opened the door with no problems and was about to move out when a man barred his path and placed his hands on the boy's shoulders.

"Back you go, son," the fellow said as he guided Jake back into the basement and closed the door behind them.

Jake screamed as he looked into the face of the man who had killed his friend.

Chapter 16

Ewan stared at the fire escape door, wondering how to get it open. To his surprise, it opened itself and a young boy, wearing nothing except his underpants, stepped outside.

He took a moment to realise it was the kid from the canal bank. What was he doing here?

Well, however the lad got there; he would make a perfect hostage. He blocked the boy's exit and gently pushed him back inside the building by his shoulders.

"I'm not going to hurt you," Ewan said, keeping hold of the boy.

The child struggled and screamed. "You killed my friend!"

Ewan knew of only one way to deal with a hysterical person. He slapped the boy hard across the face. He was sure this wasn't the correct modern-day treatment, but it worked. The boy, shocked by the sudden blow, stopped struggling. He continued to cry but was now less noisy.

"I didn't kill your pal. It wasn't me."

"Yes, you did!"

Ewan looked down at the semi-naked child. The tousled blond hair; the small freckled face; skin brown from being wet. No one had any idea where they were. He could do anything he wanted to the kid. He'd never have an opportunity like this again.

But he'd had treatment. He didn't do that anymore. Perhaps if the boy were dressed, the temptation wouldn't be so great.

"Where's your clothes?" he demanded.

"They're wet."

"Put them on anyway."

Jake, even more frightened of the man now he had struck him, retrieved his clothes from the radiator and got dressed.

"Are you g-going to k-kill me?" he asked, peering up into the eyes of his captor.

"I don't want to kill you, and I didn't kill your friend either. Whether you believe me or not doesn't matter because I will kill you if I have to, but only if you don't do as I tell you."

Jake didn't answer. He wasn't convinced the man hadn't killed Brian and even more certain he would carry out the threat to kill him.

"What's your name, kid?" the man asked.

"Jake."

"Okay, Jake, you can call me Dave. We might be together for a while."

He looked at the trembling boy. Making him get dressed hadn't done the trick. It was the face; it was too pleasant looking. No, he had to resist somehow. Perhaps if he gave the kid a black eye, making him a little less attractive...

Even as Ewan considered the idea, he realised it wouldn't work. If he battered Jake's face to a pulp, it would make no difference. The temptation would still be there. He steeled himself to resist.

"Do you understand what a hostage is, Jake?"

"Yeah. You'll kill me if the police come to get you."

"Well, I'll just pretend I'm going to kill you. I won't really hurt you."

"You hit me."

"I'm sorry. I had to calm you down."

"You didn't have to hit me."

"I said I'm sorry. It will be easier if we're friends."

Jake looked down at the floor, avoiding eye contact. "I don't want to be friends."

"Have it your way, I don't care. Does anybody know you're here, by the way?"

Jake thought about this. "No," he answered.

But he had hesitated too long, and Ewan remembered the discarded sandwich he had seen outside. Someone was feeding the boy.

"Who knows you're here, Jake?"

"No one, honest." Jake backed away as he spoke. Ewan went after him, and when he reached the youngster, he grabbed Jake's cheek, the one he had just slapped, between his finger and thumb and squeezed hard.

"Who knows you're here?" he repeated.

* * *

Keith Reynolds, the Head Teacher of Greenways Comprehensive School, sat at his desk in his spacious office, which looked much more like a sitting room. Facing him were Tom Jackson and Gloria Waters.

"It's a sad business," Reynolds said. "Brian was quite a popular kid. We held a special assembly in his memory this morning. This being the first day back since the tragedy, some of the children weren't even aware of it."

"Did he have any particular friends, apart from Jake, I mean?" Jackson asked.

"No one in particular. Everyone liked him. His temper got him into trouble now and again. The best thing you can do is talk to the head of year tutors of both boys. Mr Helesby, Jake's year tutor, will be teaching at present. I can get Brian's head of year, Miss Payne, for you now, though, if you like?"

"Right, we'd appreciate that, Mr Reynolds."

Reynolds picked up his phone and asked his secretary to summon Miss Payne to his office.

A few minutes later, somebody tapped on the door and a small frail-looking woman entered the office. Jackson thought she looked well past the age of retirement for teachers and wondered how she could control one class of teenagers, let alone a whole year's intake. Yet even before Reynolds introduced her, he knew by her stern matronly look this was the teacher who had been sent for.

"This is Miss Payne, Brian's head of year," Reynolds said. "I'll go into the outer office to give you some privacy."

He did so, and Miss Payne took the seat he had vacated.

Jackson explained who they were as Reynolds had failed to do so, and Miss Payne nodded she understood.

"What do you want to know?" she asked, glancing through thick spectacles at Jackson and Gloria in turn.

"Tell us what Brian was like," Jackson replied. "Anything we can learn about his background might help."

She removed the spectacles before answering. "Basically, he was a good lad. He did get into trouble a couple of years ago, shoplifting and such. That was about the time his father died, though. He had difficulty coming to terms with that."

"Didn't he have counselling?" Gloria asked.

"Oh, yes. Otherwise, I'm sure he'd have been much worse. But he was only twelve at the time. I didn't know him that well then, but I think like many kids when they lose a parent, he felt guilty about it."

"Guilty?" Jackson queried.

"Oh, yes. They get the idea into their heads it's somehow their fault. They believe they are being punished for something they've done."

"I can understand that with small children," said Jackson, "but surely at twelve, they'd be able to reason better?"

"When someone close to you dies, it affects people in different ways. Even adults can't always come to terms with it."

Jackson remembered the number of suicides there had been after their partners died and conceded the point. He changed the subject.

"I'm informed he was a popular boy?" he said.

"On the whole, yes. Although he did have his share of scraps. We got used to seeing him wandering around with a black eye rather often."

Gloria, who had been busy scribbling notes, now glanced up. "Black eye!" she repeated. "Did he arrive at school with them?"

"I'm quite certain he got most of them on the playground here," Miss Payne replied. "As I'm sure you've heard, Brian had a temper. He'd lash out at other kids, including those bigger than him. You couldn't expect them not to retaliate."

"I thought you had schemes in place these days to prevent bullying?" Jackson queried.

"We do. But we can't be everywhere at once, and not every case gets reported."

Jackson made a mental note to check Daniel for bruises next time he was in the bath.

Miss Payne polished the lenses of her spectacles and replaced them before continuing. "Besides, it wasn't really bullying. I know I shouldn't be defending the bigger kids for thumping Brian, but as I said, he lashed out at them first."

"Yet, you say he was popular?" Gloria asked.

"Oh, he was. His temper never bothered anybody. He knew when he was in the wrong and always took the blame. He was respected for that, both by the kids and teachers. Sometimes, I think he even took the blame when the incident wasn't his fault."

"You mean he bought his popularity?" asked Jackson.

"Oh, no. What I said might sound like that, but it was just his personality."

"What about his friends?" Gloria asked. "Apart from Jake."

"There was no one special. All the students liked him," Miss Payne answered, confirming the headmaster's statement.

"Nobody you consider we should speak to?" Jackson emphasised.

"No, I don't think so. There's certainly no one here who would know who killed Brian. Many of the children didn't even know about it until this morning's assembly. They'd heard a boy had been murdered, of course, but they hadn't realised it was Brian."

"Yes, so Mr Reynolds told us. Well, we won't take any more of your time, Miss Payne. Perhaps you would ask your secretary if Jake's Head of Year is free yet?"

"Of course." She got up and left the room.

* * *

"Let go, you're hurting me. Please!" Jake squealed as Ewan continued to squeeze his cheek firmly.

"Tell me who knows you're here then."

"All right. Let go first, please."

Ewan released his grip but remained close to the boy, preventing any chance of escape.

"Who is it?" he demanded.

"The vicar's son," Jake replied as he rubbed his face.

Another kid, Ewan thought. That wouldn't be so bad. He'd just grab that one too. Two hostages would be even better.

"When is he coming back?" he asked his prisoner.

"I don't know," answered the frightened boy, truthfully.

Ewan raised his hand as if to slap Jake again.

"I don't know. Honest," Jake repeated as he flinched from the expected blow. It never came. Ewan seemed to suddenly decide the boy was telling the truth.

"All right, Jake, I told you I don't want to hurt you. I wasn't lying to you. How old's this friend of yours, same as you, about ten?"

"I'm twelve," said Jake, indignantly.

"Sorry, but you've got to admit you're a bit on the small side for twelve. Anyway, how old is your pal?"

"I don't know. He's older."

"How much older?"

"He's big. A teenager."

Ewan wasn't happy on hearing this. A bigger kid might be harder to deal with. Then he studied the small boy before him and realised his perception of any older kid of average size would seem big to him. His helper was probably just a fourteen or fifteen-year-old then. Although Ewan was small himself, he was fit and strong. There shouldn't be a problem. Not in kidnapping the boy, anyhow. The real question was what he would do afterwards.

"I have to use the toilet," Jake interrupted his thoughts.

"All right, but I'm coming with you."

"Okay," said Jake, who by now was too desperate to care.

Ewan put his hand on the back of the boy's neck and followed him into the toilets.

Chapter 17

David Ewan kept a firm grip on the back of Jake's neck as the boy urinated.

Jake was too desperate to be embarrassed, but he was afraid. Having already been abused by Mark's customer, he didn't want to go through the same humiliating ordeal again, especially with a full-grown adult. Somehow, he thought that would be even worse. Knowing if the guy intended to do anything of that nature, he would most likely have kept him in the toilets; he was relieved when David escorted him back into the main hall. He still couldn't be sure, though. He sent up another silent prayer.

"What is this place?" Ewan asked looking around the large hall.

"A youth club," Jake answered.

"When does it open?"

"Tonight."

Ewan let go of the boy. He needed to think. He had to be gone from here before the place opened. But where could he go? His home wasn't too far away. The police would already have looked there for him by now; they wouldn't expect him to return. But, getting there in daylight would be difficult, especially with the kid.

"What are you going to do to me?" Jake asked as if reading his captor's thoughts.

"You're my hostage. I told you." Ewan didn't want to hurt the boy, but he would be a hindrance to his escape. Yet, now the kid knew he was still in the locality, leaving him here wouldn't be possible.

* * *

Jake's year tutor, Arnold Helesby, a man in his early thirties now sat in the chair Miss Payne had vacated.

"Before we talk about Jake," Jackson said. "How well did you know the other boy, Brian Churcher?"

"He was in my class a couple of years ago. I was only a form tutor then, not head of year."

"That would be around the time his father died?"

"Yes, that's right. He had a hard time of it."

Gloria looked up. "I understand he got himself into some trouble?"

"He did some shoplifting, that's true. But most children try something like that when they're about that age."

"So, you don't think his father's death had anything to do with it?"

"It might have caused it or not. Kids test the system at that age. They want to find out how much they can get away with."

"Well, I didn't," Jackson said. He didn't bother to mention any breach of the boarding-school rules, let alone the law, would have earned him a thrashing from his housemaster.

"Not all kids submit to the temptation. In Brian's case, the death of his father wouldn't help, but it doesn't mean he wouldn't have got into trouble, anyway."

Jackson glanced at Gloria indicating she should continue.

"We've been told Brian got himself into a few fights," she said. "Was he that way before his father died?"

"No, actually, he wasn't. He always had a temper, but he seemed able to control it. He had red hair and got annoyed if any of the kids called him Ginger–he didn't like that. But in those days, his reaction was purely verbal."

"So, when did he start getting physical?"

"I can't say exactly, but I first noticed he was acquiring bruises not long before he left my class. I don't think it helped when his mother married again so soon."

"Did you question him about the bruises?"

"Of course, I did, but I never got anything out of him. He wasn't one for telling tales."

"They were definitely given to him by other kids here, though?" Jackson interrupted.

"I had no reason to suspect otherwise. Who else would it be?"

"The person who killed him."

"We're talking two years ago. I understood the person you're searching for isn't local."

"The man we're looking for hasn't yet been charged with his murder. Anyway, we've enough information there about Brian for now. Let's move on to Jake. You know he's gone missing?"

"Yes, I heard. I don't see how I can help, though."

"You probably can't yourself, but perhaps some of his classmates might know where he might go to hide. Does he have any friends here, apart from Brian?"

"Not really. He spent most of his free time with Brian, even though there was quite an age difference. There might be a few boys who are in the same Scout Troop. Brian wasn't a member."

"Jake is in the Scouts? Which Troop?"

"I don't know, but I can ask the boys, or you could ask his parents."

"How do you know he is in the Scouts?"

"Before breaking up for the holidays, he told me they were going to camp."

"Where was the camp?"

"Again, it's something you'd need to ask his parents. If it was local, there's only one Scout Camp round here. That's the one at Westwood."

"Yes, and they have huts there, don't they?"

"I suppose they have."

"Thank you, Mr Helesby. We need to leave quickly." Jackson turned to Gloria. "That's where he'll be hiding. He's most likely got himself trapped. They're searching in the wrong place!"

"But, sir, they might have camped further afield. Shouldn't we find out which Scout Troop it was and where they went camping?"

"It doesn't matter where they camped during the summer. If Jake's in a local Scout Troop, he would know about the campsite at Westwood. Drop me at the station then go to see his parents just to make sure. Find out which Scout Group he's in and who the contact person is."

* * *

Mark Chegwin stared out of his bedroom window towards the church. Everything seemed quiet there now. He subconsciously placed his hands into his trouser pockets and his fingers closed around something metal - the key. His stomach muscles relaxed as he realised that in his haste last night he'd forgotten to take the key out of his pocket.

He went into the kitchen where he found his mother making coffee. "Do you want one, Mark?" she asked, looking surprised to see him.

"No. I was going to make a sandwich. I'm a bit peckish."

"You should get up in time for breakfast. Go on then, make your sandwich."

Mark prepared the snack as slowly as he could, hoping his parent would make the coffee and leave the room before he'd finished.

But his mother was in no hurry either.

He had finished making the sandwich well before the coffee was ready.

To buy more time, he deliberately dropped the freshly made sandwich on the floor, threw it into the waste bin, and had to start again.

But no matter how much he delayed he couldn't make the chore last.

"I'll take it with me," he said.

"Take it where?"

"To my bedroom."

"Mark, you know I don't like you eating in your room."

"I'll be careful, mum. I've got a lot to do."

"You have a lot to do? Since when?"

"I'm tidying my room."

The vicar's wife almost dropped the coffee cups she was taking to the tray. "Did I hear you right?"

"You and Dad want me to turn over a new leaf, don't you?"

"Of course we do. But I didn't think you would ever do it. Okay then, I won't discourage you. Just this once, mind."

Mark put the sandwich on a side-plate and went to his room with it. Then he waited until he heard his mother take the tea tray into the living room. As soon as he thought it was safe, he removed the sandwich from the plate, crept downstairs, slipped into his denim jacket and went quietly out of the front door.

He walked across the churchyard towards the basement. He'd give Jake the sandwich, then before letting him go, give him a few hard warning punches to make sure he never told anyone what had happened.

Reaching the basement door, he unlocked it, opened it and went in. He saw Jake standing against the far wall looking terrified. Well, that would make the job of scaring him easier.

After he'd taken two more strides, Mark felt a strong arm thrown around his neck. Someone kicked the door shut.

Mark struggled, but the more he squirmed, the tighter the grip around his throat became. He dropped both the sandwich and the key and reached up to prise the arm away. It was hopeless.

He couldn't speak, but grunting sounds came from his mouth as he twisted and writhed.

Then, just as he thought he would be strangled to death, his attacker let go.

"Get against the wall, kid."

Mark went to join Jake and turned to look at the scruffy looking man who had attacked him. He was a small man, not even as tall as Mark himself, but he was strong. Mark had felt the power of those arms.

The man picked up the key and locked the door.

Chapter 18

In the car, Jackson used his mobile phone to call Abercrombie as Gloria drove towards the police station.

"Anything yet?" he asked.

"No," Abercrombie responded. "Do you think we should widen the search area?"

"I think you're looking in the wrong place. He might be at the scout camp at Westwood."

"You want me to move the search parties. All of them?"

"Is that a problem?"

"Not really, but I assumed by this time you'd want to scale things down, and Westwood isn't in our area."

"I know it isn't in our area, so do whatever you need to do. I'll authorise any action you take. As for scaling down, we're looking for a twelve-year-old boy, so there'll be no scaling down until we find him, one way or the other."

He disabled his phone and returned it to his pocket. "Get a move on, Gloria," he said, regretting they were in her private car and not a patrol car so they could use the blues and twos.

In fact, he realised the traffic was surprisingly light. Everyone in town must be looking for the boy, or perhaps trapped in their homes by the floods.

They arrived at the police station, and Gloria dropped him off before spinning the vehicle around and heading towards the home of the Swifts.

* * *

Ewan looked at the two boys cowering against the wall. This last captive was older than he had expected. When Jake told him his friend was older than he was, he thought he meant a year or so. It wasn't a major problem; he was still just a kid. But what was he going to do with them? He had to leave this place soon, certainly before it opened for the evening. His home was the obvious place to go now, but how could he get there with these kids in tow? Both lads were quiet, apparently too frightened to speak. Well, that suited him for the present. He needed to think.

* * *

Jackson got to the incident room where he found Abercrombie standing in front of Hook's desk, using his arms to support himself as he spoke to the other detective. Jackson only caught the end of the conversation, but it was enough to tell him his sergeant wasn't happy about being ordered to switch the search area.

"I don't understand what Tom's playing at," Abercrombie was saying. "We've no evidence to show the boy went to the camp. Why would he go there in that weather?"

Hook saw Jackson enter the room and nodded in his direction, hoping Abercrombie would take the hint. It was too late. Jackson had overheard enough to get him annoyed.

"In the office, Harry," he said and turned towards it, the sergeant reluctantly following him.

Jackson sat down at his desk. Abercrombie remained standing, sheepishly awaiting his boss's reprimand.

"I'd appreciate it if you didn't call me Tom in the ranks. It isn't good for discipline," Jackson said.

"Sorry, sir. It was just habit."

"You can drop the sir in here, but not in front of the team. Get yourself out of the habit. Right?"

"Right."

"Now. You don't sound happy about moving the search parties?"

"Well, no. Why would the kid go all the way out there in the pouring rain? Surely, he'd seek shelter closer to home?"

"We've learned he's a member of the Scouts. He's familiar with the camp, Harry. They'll have huts he'd be able to get into."

"In that weather, any campers would have been evacuated, and the place closed down."

"Exactly. Leaving it deserted. Where better for someone to go who wants to hide?"

"I'm not so sure. Why hasn't he gone home? He must be pretty hungry and miserable by now."

"That's why we need to move fast. The boy could have got himself trapped somewhere in those woods." He knew Jake might be dead in the woods, but avoided saying this. Jackson was no longer concerned that Parkinson might have harmed the boy, and was sure Ewan would be nowhere near by this time, but there was still the danger of the storm itself. Jake was small, vulnerable, and out in the woods alone. He could have got into one of the huts and got himself locked in. He might even have been hiding in there when the warden locked up. Jackson hoped that was the case. Trapped inside a hut, Jake would be hungry but safe and able to survive for a while.

"I suppose it's possible," Abercrombie said. "But moving the whole of the search party?"

"You have searched everywhere in town, haven't you?"

"Yes."

"Then there's nothing to lose, is there? All right, if you're concerned, leave one small group here to go on checking in the town, just in case. I'm going to the campsite myself. You stick around here until Gloria reports back with the name of the Scout Group Jake is in. Send someone to see the contact person and then follow me up to Westwood."

"Okay," Abercrombie agreed.

"I suppose you've had to let Parkinson go?"

"There wasn't any choice. We had no grounds to hold him."

"I know."

"He's not the killer, anyhow. It's got to be Ewan."

"Because he's escaped? We've been through all that."

"Not only the escape. There's his history."

"Harry, he has served his time for those past crimes. Haven't you heard of the Christian concept of forgiveness? Once a person's punished, he has the right to a clean slate."

"For that kind of crime, I'm not so sure. There isn't any reliable cure for men like him."

He went back to the incident room and despatched a message to Constable Vincent Peart, requesting him to keep his small unit in the town. The unit that contained Angela and Frank Churcher.

* * *

Ewan had instructed the boys to go into the storeroom and left them there with the threat of a beating if they attempted to leave the room. They sat side by side on the stone floor.

Jake stared down at his still wet and ruined Sunday trousers and for a moment wondered what his mother would say about his damaged clothing. She wouldn't be happy. Still, he was glad he hadn't had the chance to change into his jeans, knowing from experience how much longer they would take to dry out.

"Who is he?" Mark whispered, jolting Jake back to reality. What did it matter about his clothes? He might never get the chance to change them again.

"The murderer," he hissed back. "He's called Dave."

He looked at Mark hopefully. On his own, he could never have hoped to overpower Dave, but if Mark would help....

The expression of fear on Mark's face quickly dispelled any hope Jake had. Mark was a bully; his idea of kindness was to offer his victims the choice of which cheek they wanted to be punched on, and like most bullies, he was a coward when it came to facing someone his own size.

"What's he going to do to us?" Mark asked.

"Use us as hostages."

A gulp from Mark.

"He said he wouldn't really hurt us."

"And you believe him?"

"I don't know."

Ewan walked back into the room, having heard the boys whispering to each other. He couldn't distinguish their words but assumed they were plotting an escape. He wasn't concerned. His plan was formulated now. "Shut up," he said, "otherwise I'll have to shoot you." He appeared to be holding a gun concealed in his pocket.

Shoot us! Jake thought, alarmed. He had seen no gun. Where had it come from? He didn't believe Dave had a gun. He was just bluffing. But what if he wasn't?

"Now," Ewan continued. "We're all going to go for a little walk, you two in front of me. Don't forget, this gun will be pointing at your backs. Stay close enough for you to hear me. And if anyone sees you, you're not with me. Understand?"

Both boys nodded that they understood, and Ewan shepherded them towards the exit.

* * *

Knowing Jake's parents blamed her colleagues for their son's disappearance; Gloria Waters didn't feel comfortable when she rang their doorbell. Her discomfort turned to a mixture of concern and curiosity when she got no response. She was aware they hadn't joined the search party. Why had they left the house with Jake still missing? What if the boy came home?

She knocked on the neighbour's door, again getting no reply.

They'd possibly gone to help with the search, she supposed, as she made her way to the neighbours on the other side. This time, she had better luck. She saw the woman inside through the window as she approached. A toddler sat on the woman's knee, and she lifted the infant onto the floor as she spotted the visitor approaching the door.

With no need for Gloria to knock, the woman opened the door. Gloria showed her I.D card. "I'm sorry to bother you, she said. I'm trying to find your neighbours, Mr and Mrs Swift. Do you have any idea where they are?"

"Haven't they told you?" the woman replied with some surprise.

"Told us?"

"They asked me to watch out for Jake, in case he came back. I can't help with looking for him, you see. I have the little ones to look after. They said they were going to visit that boy's parents to see if they knew anything. You know, the one who got murdered. He was a friend of their boy, you know."

"What!"

"Didn't you know?"

Gloria wasn't sure whether the woman meant about the friendship or their visit to the Churcher's. It didn't matter. She didn't think it was a good idea for the two sets of parents to meet at the moment. Not without someone less involved being present.

"Thanks for your help," she said and went back quickly to her car. She spun toward the Churchers' home.

* * *

Being a cop's kid didn't make a person popular at school. You tried to keep it quiet, but too many people knew and soon, everyone knew. It didn't matter that your dad had a thing about bullying; if anything, it made it worse because you would never dare tell him about whatever happened to you.

Still, as long as you did what the bigger kids wanted, you wouldn't be beaten up. Unfortunately, this might mean you sometimes had to beat up other kids.

The child realised what they were about to do was wrong and felt guilty, but there was no choice.

* * *

Constable Peart wasn't happy about the order to continue searching where they'd looked dozens of times, but he made the best of it. He had already divided his small team into even smaller pairs and decided to leave them as they were, allocating them fresh areas.

One of those pairs now hunted for the boy in the back alleys of the houses surrounding the church.

"We're wasting our time," Angela said. "If Jake were anywhere around here, we'd have found him by now."

"I know," her husband responded, "but we have to keep looking, Angela. We need to find him before the police do."

"Why are you so keen all of a sudden? And what's it matter if the police find him first, as long as he's safe?"

"As you said, we can get him to talk easier than the police can."

He sneezed and pulled his handkerchief from his pocket. With it came Brian's sharp fishing knife, which clattered to the ground.

Angela stared at it in horror. "What are you doing with that?" she shrieked.

"It's only to frighten the kid if we find him. To make him talk."

"No, it isn't. You were going to cut his throat, weren't you?"

Chapter 19

Ewan ushered the two boys through the door and ordered them to walk towards the street. He waited at the top of the steps until they were almost at the church gate, then glanced around. Once sure no one else was in sight, he followed the youths. "Turn left," he mumbled, trusting his voice would carry far enough for them to hear. They turned in the right direction, confirming he was correct. The kids had their backs to him, but he could see the side of their faces and saw their complexions white with fear. That was good. He needed them to be scared. If they made a run for it now, he could do nothing. He hadn't got a gun, but they wouldn't know that, not for certain.

* * *

Gloria pulled up outside the Churchers' home. A blue Toyota was parked in front of her with a man and a woman seated in the front. Gloria had never seen Jake's parents, but this had to be them.

She left her car, relieved the two sets of parents didn't appear to have met each other yet.

She tapped on the window of the Toyota and showed her identity card. The window opened.

"Are you Mr and Mrs Swift?" she asked.

"Yes," the woman replied sharply. "Is this about Jake? Have you found him?"

"No, not so far, I'm sorry. I don't think it's a good idea for you to be here. Besides, someone should be at the house in case Jake gets home."

"Don't lecture us," the man said, angrily. "It's your lot that frightened our boy into running away in the first place."

"Waiting here for the Churchers' won't help Jake," Gloria said.

"Jake played with their kid. They might know some of the places they went to." Mr Swift banged his hand against the steering wheel.

"I'm sure Inspector Jackson has asked them about that."

"We want to ask them ourselves," said Mrs Swift.

"They've lost a child in suspicious circumstances. Your son was the last person to see him alive. I don't think they would want to see you right now."

"Well, we want to see them. And we will wait here until they get home. You can't stop us," Jake's father said.

"No, that's correct, I can't. But if you insist on staying here, I'll have to stay with you."

"Please yourself. It's your time."

Gloria returned to her car and telephoned Jackson's mobile number.

* * *

At the campsite, the search parties combed through the woods; their progress slowed by the thick mud everywhere, sucking their feet into the ground.

The warden of the site had been located, and he unlocked all the buildings. These were thoroughly searched, but there was no trace of the boy. Jackson was frustrated. He had been sure they would find Jake here. Perhaps Gloria had been correct, and he'd gone to a campsite farther afield. What was taking her so long to call the station with the details of where he spent the camping holiday?

He strode across to the woods then hesitated when he saw the thick, sticky mire that oozed from beneath his feet. How his former school chums would have loved to corner him somewhere like this. Even now, he dreaded he would slip and fall face-first into the mud. He could imagine those school chums laughing as he rose, his face blackened, this time without their help. But, no, he thought, they'd laugh all right, but they'd be disappointed they hadn't been the cause, so they'd do something to make him cry.

He'd been about fourteen when the bullying stopped. At the time, he believed his housemaster was a sadistic brute, no better than the bullies; now he realised he should be grateful to the man.

It was during a Sunday afternoon walk with his group that a boy slightly smaller than himself picked a fight with him. To his amazement, the housemaster encouraged the fight rather than stopping it. In fact, thinking about it later, Jackson was almost sure he had engineered it for his benefit.

The other boy started to punch Jackson in the chest. Jackson stood there, taking the blows as he always did without retaliating. The housemaster was close by and would stop the fight before he was hurt too much. Then the punches were switched to his face, despite the fact he was already in tears. The housemaster approached, and Jackson expected to have his punishment ended. But to his bewilderment, Sir just looked on saying nothing until his attacker had landed several more blows on each of his cheeks.

"You're bigger than him. Fight back. I'm not going to stop him."

Jackson's stomach sank as he heard the adult's words. He couldn't fight back. Even if he tried to hit the other kid, the rest of the group would punish him later.

He stood still as yet more punches landed. The other boy now reverted to thumping him in the chest.

"Fight back!" the order came again.

Encouraged by how effortless this was, and apparently having permission from the housemaster, his attacker punched harder, now varying his strikes to Jackson's chest and face. At first, the thumps to the face were restricted to the cheeks, but after a while, the boy threw the odd blow to the bonier parts to cause even more pain. Then he gave Jackson an especially hard punch in the eye.

Even then, the housemaster did not stop the so-called fight. "Hit him back," he said again and was now joined by other youths in the group also egging Jackson on, even though they all knew he would take the beating until either the other lad was bored, or Sir ended it.

This time, they were wrong. The thump to the eye made Jackson see red, not just physically but in his mind. He could never remember having lost his temper before, but now he'd had enough. He screamed, then retaliated and laid into the other boy, pummelling him until he too screamed. After that, he had always stood up for himself and before long, the others left him alone and looked for another scapegoat.

He brought his attention back to the present and remembered what he had been told about bullying at school still being a possibility. He had decided to check Daniel for bruises on his next bath night. Now, he made up his mind he wouldn't leave it that long. He'd inspect him tonight. Assuming he got home this evening.

His mobile phone rang, and he answered it, hoping it was Abercrombie. It was Gloria. Jackson hadn't expected her to call him direct.

She told him about the situation with the Swifts, and he agreed she should stay there.

"Did you ask them about the Scout Troop?" he asked.

"Damn! I forgot."

"Gloria!"

"I'm sorry, I'll ask now. I'll call you back in a minute."

"Okay."

He came away from the woods, which he had not entered fully because of the mud. He hoped the kid wasn't in there; otherwise, there would be little chance of him being unharmed. He went to the warden's den, which had been turned into a temporary office, and waited for Gloria's call.

* * *

Gloria approached the Swift's vehicle again and once more knocked on its window.

Mr Swift opened the driver's window. "I've told you, we're not moving," he said.

"I know," Gloria answered. "This is about something else. We understand your son is a member of a Scout Troop?"

"First I've known about it. Who said that?"

"One of his teachers."

"Then they've made a mistake. Jake was once in the Cubs for a while, but he's never been a Scout."

Gloria imagined Jackson's rising temper when she gave him this news.

"But didn't he go camping during the holidays?"

"Yeah, but that was with the youth club, not the Scouts."

"Where did they camp? Is it possible Jake could have gone back there?"

This time, Jake's mother answered. "I doubt it. They went to Abergelie in North Wales. Even if he could walk that distance, there's nothing for him to go to. They were under canvas, and he didn't enjoy it all that much."

"Thank you." Gloria went back to her car and called Jackson.

* * *

As they walked across the churchyard towards the gate, Mark glanced at the vicarage, for once hoping one of his parents would be looking through a window and be able to work out what was happening. There was no sign of either of them.

Outside the gate, he heard the soft voice of their captor order them to go left. Together with Jake, he did so, unwilling to risk annoying the guy for now.

"He hasn't actually got a gun, has he?" he muttered to Jake in a low tone.

"I don't know. I haven't seen one."

"Why don't we make a dash for it, in different directions? Even if he's got a gun, he'll only have time to shoot one of us."

"It's too dangerous. He's violent. He's hit me once already."

"If he has no gun, he won't be able to catch us."

"What if he has?"

"We won't be any use to him as hostages if we're dead."

The younger boy thought about this for a brief period before answering. "He only needs one hostage."

"Yeah, but even if he does shoot one of us, the other can get away."

Another silence from Jake, then he said, "If he has got a gun, you're the one he'll shoot. You're a bigger target."

"Geeze thanks."

"Shall we do it then?"

"I'm not so sure now."

"Go to the right," Ewan ordered from behind, "and stop chatting. Keep walking."

He watched the boys cautiously as he kept a safe distance behind them. He could hear them talking but was unable to make out the conversation. It worried him. He had assumed they were too scared to talk. What were they saying to each other?

He hoped no one would see them as they approached the cul-de-sac in which his home stood. The bigger boy wasn't too bad. Dressed scruffy but looking like a typical teenager. The younger kid, on the other hand, was a mess. His clothing wet through and his blond, tousled hair, which had been so neat and tidy when they met on the canal, now looked like something out of a nightmare. Anybody who saw him would be unlikely to forget him. Ewan decided if somebody did see them, he would cut his losses and let the boys go. He would walk off in a different direction and look as if he had nothing to do with the youngsters. For a while, the kids would think he was still behind them and, by the time they realised they were free, he would have found another hiding-place.

But so far, so good. They were almost at the turn for the cul-de-sac and had seen no one.

Then, he was taken by surprise as the boys suddenly bolted in different directions. Damn! He wasn't going to lose them that easily now, besides–they knew where he was.

But he couldn't go after them both. Selecting the smaller kid as the easiest to catch, he sprinted after Jake.

Ewan was fit, and Jake was hampered by the weight of his waterlogged clothing, so it didn't take long to catch up with the boy and grab him by the nape of his neck. He pushed him towards a brick wall and shifted his grip from the boy's neck to his arm, twisting it and causing a groan to escape from Jake's lips.

"You'll pay for that, kid," Ewan threatened.

Then he gulped as a weight was thrown onto his shoulders. He twisted to find the other boy had come back and jumped onto his back. Holding Jake with one hand, he reached up and grabbed Mark's head, pulling him over his shoulders and slumping him against the wall beside Jake. "Now we'll start again, shall we?" he said. This time, holding the boys by their arms, he walked them into the cul-de-sac towards his house.

He glanced at the windows of the other houses in the cul-de-sac as they passed; hoping none of his neighbours would be around at this time of day.

But he was unlucky; he spotted one elderly lady, whom he knew by sight but not by name staring out at them from her open upstairs window. Not too much of a problem at her age, he thought, she was bound to be confused.

"Don't worry," he called to her. "I'm the new truant catcher. I caught these two bunking off. I'll take them back to school afterwards." He squeezed both boys' arms to warn them not to say anything.

The woman smiled. Truant catchers were part of life in her day, and the boys' disgruntled appearance gave credibility to the fact they hadn't been in school. Ewan relaxed, then unlocked his front door and pushed the youngsters inside.

* * *

Jackson was annoyed with himself at having wasted time and resources in investigating the Scout Camp.

"Seems you were right again," he said to Abercrombie. They were now back at the police station.

"Anyone can make a mistake, and given the information you had, I'd most likely have done the same," the sergeant answered tactfully.

"The thing is, where do we go from here?"

"What about questioning Dave Glover, the other youth club leader? His name starts with 'D' too?"

"You think Jake could be with him?" Jackson paused and considered this for a moment. "No, he went to Parkinson, remember? Besides, he hasn't got the small hands we're looking for."

"Isn't it odd he hasn't joined the search, though?" Abercrombie asked.

"Hasn't he?"

"No."

"Perhaps he couldn't get time off work. And he did say he didn't know the boys all that well."

"Most of the people searching don't know Jake at all. All they have is the photocopy of the picture we issued. They're still keen to help. And Jake is a member of the club that Glover helps to run."

Jackson rubbed his chin as he pondered on this. "What motive would he have for hurting Jake?"

"If he's the one who killed Brian, Jake might know something about it. Maybe he knew that Glover, not Parkinson, was the one who was abusing Brian."

"It's a theory," Jackson conceded. "Let's have him brought in for further questioning. No arrest at this stage, though. We don't want egg on our faces again."

"What about the search parties?"

"Set them up on the outskirts of town. The boy can't be in the town itself if it's already been searched thoroughly."

"It has. We have to go back to a few houses, though, where we got no replies in the house to house search."

"You checked outbuildings, sheds, garages and such?"

"Yes. If he's anywhere in town, he has to be inside someone's home. That isn't likely, but we are checking in case."

"Get some of the troops to carry on with that, then."

* * *

In the school playground, the child was well aware of what had to be done. The victim had already been chosen. If the child's father knew what was about to take place, he'd probably have a heart attack. It was wrong. All bullying was wrong. But there was no choice. After all, Dad wouldn't want his own child to be beaten up. Besides, it was the unwritten law of the school. All new kids had to be initiated. Of course, the rumours about the initiation ceremony for new kids having their heads thrust down the toilet while someone pulled the chain were untrue. Those new kids didn't know that, though. If they did, most would undoubtedly have preferred it in preference to what was going to happen to them. It would be degrading, and the victim would get a bit wet, but unlike what was going to be done to them, there would be no physical pain.

* * *

Jake and Mark had been bundled into the bathroom of the house. The door had a mortise-type lock, and Ewan locked it from the outside.

"Thanks," Jake said, rubbing his arm where the kidnapper had held it in a vice-like clutch.

"What for?"

"Trying to save me. You could have got away."

"I know. I should have. Then I could have raised the alarm."

"It was brave of you. Coming back."

Mark blushed at the rare compliment.

"Listen, kid. If we ever get out of this, you won't tell anyone about what happened before, will you?"

"You mean about the boy with the bad teeth? I'm not a snitch."

"Good lad. What are we going to do now, though?"

Jake looked longingly at the bathtub. He felt dirty and knew he smelled horrible from the pungent water in which he had been submerged.

"Do you think he'll let me have a bath?"

Despite the desperate situation, Mark couldn't help chuckling. "I know you stink, kid," he said, "but I didn't mean that. What are we going to do about getting out of here?"

Jake looked at the one frosted window. Too tiny for even someone as small as himself to crawl through. Even if that had been possible, he knew they weren't on the ground floor and it would be too far for them to drop.

"That lady who saw us," he said. "She might call the cops."

"I doubt it. She's most likely senile. She was ancient."

"Well, we have to wait 'til he lets us go, then."

"If he lets us go! Didn't you say he was a killer?"

Chapter 20

Dave Glover, the youth club leader, had been located and now sat across the desk from Jackson and Abercrombie.

"You understand you're not under arrest? We need to ask you a few more questions, that's all," Jackson said.

"Okay."

"You told us you didn't know Brian Churcher. What about Jake Swift?"

Glover leaned back and seemed to consider this before replying.

"I don't think so. Is he the kid with the ginger hair?"

"No, that was Brian."

"Oh!"

"Are you now saying you knew Brian?" Abercrombie interrupted.

"No. Well, only by sight."

Jackson produced the printout from Brian's computer and gave it to Glover.

"I want you to look at this," he said.

Glover read the text and glanced up. "What has this got to do with me?"

"Your first name begins with a D."

"So what? Plenty of people have names starting with a D. There's David Parkinson for a start."

"We've already questioned him about it."

"And what did he say? The same thing about me, I suppose."

"Actually, yes, he did."

"Well, it's nothing to do with me. The D could even stand for Dad, couldn't it? Isn't that where you normally start, with the victim's own family?"

"Brian didn't call his stepfather Dad."

Abercrombie shuffled his feet and coughed, causing Jackson to look towards him.

"Can I see you outside for a minute, sir?" Abercrombie asked.

"Interview suspended," Jackson said for the benefit of the tape, then followed his sergeant into the corridor. He closed the door of the interview room and looked into Abercrombie's eyes, wondering what was so important as to interrupt the interview.

"Sir, Brian did call his stepfather Dad. Remember, Angela told us they had difficulty getting him to call Frank, Dad, but he had eventually done so."

"Yeah, but under protest."

"Exactly. But he had to call him something. Don't you see, he couldn't bring himself to use the name Dad in the diary, so he called him D? A sort of code."

"You might be right," Jackson agreed. "We suspected him of being the abuser in the first place. It still doesn't mean he's the killer, though."

"But it moves him up the suspect list a bit, doesn't it?"

"Yes, I suppose it does. I thought you were convinced Ewan is guilty, though?"

"I'm prepared to admit it's possible you are correct and Ewan's run because he's scared."

"Right. Let's have Frank Churcher brought in then."

"The Churchers' are helping on the search. They were with P.C Peart. I'll tell someone to radio him."

"Do that. I'm going to tell Glover he can go for now." He went back into the interview room, and Abercrombie went to the incident room.

Abercrombie radioed to Constable Peart himself; deciding this was quicker than trying to find someone else free to do the task.

"Receiving, Sarge," Peart's voice came clearly from the receiver.

Abercrombie spoke. "We want Frank Churcher at the station, Vince. He's with your party, isn't he?"

"He should be, but we split up. I haven't seen the Churchers' for some while now."

"Well, when you find him bring him here. If possible, without Angela."

"Okay, Sarge."

* * *

Jackson dismissed Glover with a thank you and returned to his office.

Miss Payne's comments about school bullying not being outdated came back into his mind. Daniel would be getting home about now. His son would never tell tales about anyone hurting him. Jackson couldn't delay any longer. He had to be sure. There was no way he could get home at present, though.

He picked up the telephone and dialled his home number.

Sheila answered almost immediately.

"It's me," he said.

"Hello me."

"Stop messing about, Sheila, this is serious."

"What's the matter?"

"Is Daniel home from school, yet?"

"He didn't go to school. The floods, remember."

"Right, I forgot. Is he there?"

"No. He's out playing with his friends."

"Sheila, as soon as he gets home, I want you to strip him and check him for bruises."

"What!"

"Just do it, Sheila. I need to be certain he isn't being hurt."

"You're obsessed with this bullying thing."

Jackson sighed. It wasn't going to be easy to persuade her.

"Sheila, I heard today that bullying in schools still goes on."

"Of course it does. It doesn't mean it happens to the same extent you suffered. You were at a boarding school, remember. Your parents weren't there to see you were unhappy. If anything was worrying Daniel, we'd know."

"I'm not so sure."

"Tom, Daniel's eight-years-old. Do you think I don't check he's cleaned himself properly after his bath? If he had any bruises, I'd notice then."

Looking at the boy during his bath was what Jackson had planned to do himself. He hadn't associated that checking Daniel for cleanliness, as his mother would routinely do, would also make any bruising obvious.

"You check him every time he has a bath or shower?"

"Not every time, but now and again. Certainly, enough to spot if there was any trouble. Stop worrying."

"Okay. Bye, I'll see you later."

He put the phone down feeling some relief, but it didn't last long. Another thought entered his head. If Daniel was free of bruises, what if it was him who was doing the bullying? God, no! That would be even worse than discovering his boy was a victim.

* * *

Young Tim Canning had been cornered. He knew it had to happen eventually though he didn't know what they would do to him. He stood facing the three girls, all at least a year older than him, and waited to find out what the so much talked about, yet secret, initiation ceremony for the first-years would be.

The biggest of the girls took hold of Tim's shoulders and turned him to face the wall they had trapped him against. Then he yelped as one the of girls rubbed something rough against the nape of his neck. It only lasted a second, but it was a moment of pain. As the teenagers released him and ran off, Tim put his hand on his neck and realised they had rubbed it with sandpaper, most likely nicked from the woodwork room.

He heard the girls giggling as they ran to capture their next victim. They waited outside the school gates, ready to waylay someone. Yet, several first-year kids passed without the girls challenging them in any way. Tim realised they must be waiting for a particular kid. They had already chosen their prey. This surprised Tim. He thought they had chased him at random, but it seemed the older kids had some system. His neck was sore, and he wondered how he would explain the abrasion to his parents, knowing that telling the truth would earn him a beating.

* * *

"Your turn next, Karen."

"I know."

"Did you get the sandpaper?"

"Yeah, course I did."

"No backing out."

"I'm not."

The girls waited outside the gate. Karen Jackson, the youngest, was being coached by her older friend, Denise, before she performed her first initiation ceremony.

She hated the thought of having to torment the small boy they had chosen for her and was horrified of what would happen if her father ever found out.

But he didn't understand. He didn't realise what these other girls, probably helped by boyfriends, would do to her if she refused to be part of the gang. He was only interested in protecting Daniel. As if she would let anything happen to her little brother. She was the only one allowed to hit him, and God help anyone else who tried. Daniel didn't need their father's protection. But didn't her dad realise girls got bullied too?

"Get ready. He's coming," Denise interrupted her thinking.

Tim saw the boy approaching too and deduced from the girls' actions as they crouched closer to the wall, that he was going to be their next sufferer. He knew the boy from his previous school.

"Run, Anthony!" he yelled as the boy approached the gate.

Anthony saw the gang at the same time as he heard the shout. They sprang towards him, but before they could grab him, he ran, dodging the girls as he went through the gate into the street. The girls sprinted after him, Karen, being the fittest, in the lead.

"Get him!" shouted Denise as she and the other girl ran out of steam and followed at a more leisurely pace, soon giving up altogether when the boy and Karen went out of sight as they negotiated the back streets.

Karen kept going. The boy was fast, but she was gaining. She had to catch him, or the others would never forgive her. She could let him go and say he'd been too quick for her, but no, they'd just make her get him another time. She might as well get it over with.

The boy ran into a back alley, and she saw him go through an open gate into a back yard. His house? She could still get him before he made it to the door. What she had to do to him wouldn't take a second, and he wouldn't dare shout for his parents. She followed him into the yard where, to her surprise, he didn't head towards the door, but tried to hide behind a dustbin, obviously having thought she hadn't seen him enter the yard.

The bin wasn't big enough to hide him, and she couldn't help smiling as she went to capture him.

"Get off me! Leave me alone," he yelled as he manoeuvred himself around the trashcan out of her reach.

Karen shut the gate to make his escape more difficult then went back to the bin where the boy cowered on the other side. "You might as well get it over with," she said.

"What?"

"Your initiation. You have to have it sometime. Even if you get away now, and you won't, we'll get you another time. It's the school custom."

"I'll tell."

"You mustn't ever do that, for your own sake, honest."

"Leave me alone!" he pleaded again.

"I can't." She reached over the top of the bin to grab him. He stepped out of reach, at the same time thrusting the bin towards her. It tipped over with a loud clattering.

Karen looked towards the house, alarmed. Too late, the back door had already started to open.

* * *

Inside the building, David Ewan was making plans. Staying here, he decided, wasn't a good idea after all. He needed to get away from the area. It was those kids' fault. He couldn't keep them here forever, but how could he depend on them to keep their mouths shut if he let them go?

Besides, there was always the risk the police would come back to check this house again. He decided to wait until dark, then tie the boys up, leave them here and make his way back down south. The kids would escape eventually, but he'd tie them well enough to give himself plenty of time before that happened.

There was a loud clanging in the backyard. Someone had knocked the dustbin over. Police? No, they wouldn't be that clumsy. Probably dogs scavenging. He went to the back door to make sure. As he opened it, he saw a young girl and a slightly younger boy staring at him. They both rushed towards the gate.

He got there before they had time to unlatch it. "What the hell, do you want?" he asked.

"We were just playing," Karen answered, nervously.

More witnesses to his whereabouts. Damn! But then, perhaps more hostages. He took both children by the shoulders and led them to the house. "Inside," he ordered.

"What are you doing?" Karen screamed. "You can't do this!"

She struggled, but the man's grip was too firm, and she knew there was no escape from it.

"Inside," he said again, prodding her in the back to get her into the house.

The boy was crying now. "What are you going to do to us?" he blubbered.

"You were trespassing."

"So," said Karen. "Get the police, then."

"No. I'll punish you myself."

Chapter 21

Angela stared at her spouse, who avoided eye contact as they argued. "I'm right, aren't I?"

"Of course I'm not going to cut the kid's throat. What do you take me for? I only want to frighten him, that's all."

"Why?"

"What do you mean? I told you, to make him tell us what happened to Brian."

"You never liked Brian. Why the sudden interest now he's dead? Why were you so eager to come on this search?"

"It wasn't that I didn't like Brian. He didn't like me. I tried to get on with him, you know that?"

Angela paused for a moment as she pondered things. The knife. Frank's unusual desire to help without her asking. He wanted to get rid of Jake. Why? There could only be one reason; he'd witnessed the crime, or–"You bastard! It was you, wasn't it? You killed my boy!"

"No, Angela. Don't be stupid. Why would I do that?" He backed away, then turned and ran as Angela approached him menacingly.

* * *

Ewan pushed his two new prisoners into the bathroom to join the others.

"You won't get away with this. My dad's a policeman," the girl yelled as he thrust her through the door.

"Is he, now?" he replied, wondering if she was bluffing, but considering whether he could make use of that information if it were true. He locked the door and went back downstairs. He sat in the fireside chair to revise his plans.

* * *

In the Jacksons' house, Sheila was annoyed. Karen hadn't arrived home from school yet, and it was well after teatime. Sheila spent most of the last school year drilling into her daughter she must tell her when she was staying behind for extra-curriculum activities. The first day of the new term and it seemed she had forgotten already.

"I'm hungry, Mum," Daniel's voice interrupted her thoughts.

"Your sister isn't home yet. You know we have to wait so we can eat together."

"Where is she?"

"I don't know. She's late."

"I'll kill her."

The idea of eight-year-old Daniel killing his much bigger sibling made Sheila laugh. "It'd be like David and Goliath," she giggled. "Anyway, you can't because I'm going to do it first."

She turned the heat down on the cooker and topped up the water in the potato pan for the third time.

"If she isn't here in ten minutes, we'll eat anyway," she promised. She was tempted to make Karen go without altogether, but she couldn't be that cruel to her daughter. She would definitely ground her, though.

Fifteen minutes later, there was still no sign of Karen. Sheila fed her son.

* * *

Ewan moved to the settee, a steaming mug of coffee in his hand. What a mess. He thought back to the treatment programme he'd been through. Avoid contact with kids, they'd told him. It was their most emphatic instruction. Well, he'd tried. It wasn't his fault there were four kids locked in his bathroom. He didn't go looking for them. They came to him. It was true he'd spoken to the two lads on the canal bank, but he was just trying to be polite. What the hell was he going to do now?

If the police found him, he would face charges of child abduction as well as the murder. Yes, they'd charge him with the murder now, of that he was sure.

He decided to stick to his original plan. Wait until dark, then tie up all four kids and make his getaway. They'd identify him once they escaped, but it didn't matter anymore. He needed to be as far away from here as possible by the time they did so.

It would take them a few hours to work the ropes loose; he'd make certain of that. He could tie knots. They might take until morning to get loose. In which case, he supposed, he'd better feed them first. He didn't want them to starve to death and be accused of their murders too.

He wasn't going to do the cooking, though; one of them could do it. The girl would do.

He went to fetch her from the bathroom. When he opened the door, he found all four of his prisoners seated on the floor, their backs against the tub. The older boy glared at him, hands behind his head, fingers intertwined as if being kidnapped happened to him every day. He didn't speak.

The small boy whose name Ewan didn't yet know, the one he'd caught with the girl in his back yard, sobbed quietly, the girl trying to comfort him.

Jake quivered. Ewan wasn't sure whether this was from fear or cold, remembering he still had on wet clothes. He didn't want the kid dying from pneumonia, but what could he do? There was no clothing in the house that would fit Jake. He'd have to dry the clothes the boy was wearing.

"You look as if you can do with a hot bath," he said to Jake. "I'll dry your clothes while you have one."

Jake glanced at Karen. "I'm not getting undressed with a girl in the room, you perv," he said.

Ewan resisted the temptation to slap Jake across the face again for being insolent. Now wasn't the time to upset the boy further.

"It's all right. I'm taking her out of here for a while. You'll have plenty of time for your bath."

"What are you going to do to her?" Jake asked, his own discomfort forgotten as he tried to protect Karen.

"I'm not going to harm her."

"You'd better not." This time, it was Mark who made the threat.

"And you're in a position to do something about it, are you?" Ewan sneered. Then turning back to Jake. "Don't worry. I won't hurt your girlfriend. Now, you get undressed and in the bath. I'll collect your clothes to dry them in a few minutes."

He turned his attention to the girl. "You, out," he said, pointing to the doorway.

Karen went without protest; realising Jake did need a hot bath. She'd been sickened by the smell coming from him as well as having some concern for his health. He had coughed badly several times since she was shut in with him.

Ewan led her downstairs and into the kitchen. She was frightened but hoped he would keep his promise not to hurt her.

He hadn't taken her into one of the bedrooms, so there was a good chance he wasn't going to rape her - not yet, anyhow.

"Now," Ewan said. "We all need to eat. You'll find some potatoes under the sink. Start peeling them."

"I'm not your slave."

He hadn't expected resistance. What was it with these kids; did they all have a death wish?

He pinched her cheek between finger and thumb and squeezed, recalling how Jake had squealed when he did the same to him.

"All right. I'll do it," Karen screamed, tears streaking her face.

Ewan knew the pinch hurt her. In fact, he enjoyed hurting her. It wasn't his fault he had a sadistic streak running through him, and she refused his order. That surely entitled him to punish her. He hadn't broken his pledge to the boys not to hurt her. They, he was sure, had been thinking of a different kind of harm.

He let go of her cheek, and she promptly went to find the potatoes.

Ewan made sure the back door was secure then went back to the living room to finish his coffee.

He sat on the settee again as he drank. He heard the girl working in the kitchen; sure she would look for a way out but knowing she wouldn't find one. He was really in it up to his neck now. A murder suspect; a child abductor; escaping from custody. They were already going to throw the book at him, what more did he have to lose? There were four kids under his roof. He might as well have his way with at least one of them before he left.

He went back to the bathroom to collect Jake's clothes.

* * *

Sheila Jackson telephoned her daughter's school. Her anger had now been transferred from Karen to the school itself. She had checked there were no after-school activities on a Monday. That only left detention. Sheila was angry they had kept her girl behind without telling her beforehand. Karen wasn't the sort of child who got herself put into detention often. In fact, Sheila couldn't remember another occasion. Surely, the school had an obligation to notify parents when they were going to detain their children.

She got no reply, and her annoyance turned to concern. She had parked her son in front of the TV set and checked to make sure he was all right. Daniel was staring at the screen and didn't even notice her. Sheila went back to the phone and called Karen's friends.

Half an hour later, she was even more worried. Karen wasn't with any of her friends, none of the ones Sheila knew, anyway. All she discovered was that Karen was last seen chasing a boy. Chasing a boy! Karen wasn't old enough to be chasing boys, and wasn't it usually the other way round, anyhow? Grounding her would not be enough.

* * *

Jackson wasn't happy to be told of another missing child that evening. Eleven-year-old Anthony Bowers hadn't returned from school.

"Can't uniform deal with it?" he asked. "It's not as if he's been missing that long and we have plenty on our plate trying to find Jake."

"Most of uniform are already helping with that," Abercrombie replied. "They're not passing the new misper on to us at this stage. They felt they should inform us in case we find this other boy while we're looking for Jake."

Jackson leant back in his chair. "You don't think there's a connection, do you?"

"How can there be? Jake went missing yesterday and this, er, Anthony, only a couple of hours ago. As far as we're aware, the two kids don't know each other."

"We need to make sure of that. We've been assuming Jake hasn't gone home because he's hurt or trapped somewhere, but he may be just hiding, and this other kid might be taking him food or something."

"I'll get someone to look into it, although I don't think it's likely."

"Nor do I, but it's a theory. Let's not take any chances. We can't afford to, there's still a child-killer out there someplace."

"You don't really think—"

"No, I don't. In fact, I hope I'm right about him feeding Jake…"

The phone rang on Jackson's desk. He picked it up and was surprised to hear his wife's voice. She seldom called him at work.

"Tom, Karen hasn't got home from school."

"What! Hasn't she gone to one of her friends and forgotten to tell you?"

"No. I've phoned them all. Nobody has seen her after they came out of school."

"They came out of school together, though?"

"Yes. Apparently she went chasing after some lad, and no one's seen her since then."

"Karen chased a boy?"

"I know it doesn't make sense, but that's what they told me."

"Have you tried ringing her mobile?"

"She was at school. They're not allowed to take their mobiles with them."

"I'm coming home."

He put the receiver down and looked across at Abercrombie.

"We have another missing child," he said. "Mine."

* * *

Jake wasn't too self-conscious about undressing in front of the other two boys. Mark had already seen him naked, and the younger boy whose name Jake now knew was Anthony, was close enough to his own age for it not to bother him. And he needed that bath. He knew himself that he reeked. But while he could tolerate the boys seeing him nude, he didn't want Ewan to see him in his birthday suit. What could he do, though? Ewan was coming to collect his clothes. There was nothing else to wear. The only thing he could think of was to wrap the towel around his waist. He clutched it tight when he heard the door being unlocked.

He was spared any embarrassment. Ewan walked in, picked up the bundle of clothes Jake had discarded, then went out and locked the door again without saying a word.

* * *

For once, Frank Churcher was glad of his wife's excess weight. He'd easily been able to outpace her and was now crouching behind a garden wall.

There was no talking to her in her present state. Angela always was one to hit first and ask questions later. If he didn't convince her he hadn't killed Brian, she'd do more than hit him; he'd be safer with the police.

Holding his breath, he heard her footsteps coming along the street, her own breath panting heavily. He tried to crouch lower.

She passed, and he breathed out slowly in a long sigh of relief. He waited until she was out of sight, then swiftly moved off in the opposite direction. He had to give her time to calm down before facing her.

* * *

Old Mrs Millward went from one surface to another as she did her daily dusting. She was proud of the fact she still did most of her own housework. As she dusted, she wondered if she should ring the police. She had seen that new neighbour of hers take two youngsters into his house earlier, and they didn't go willingly. He'd claimed he was a truant catcher, but they hadn't had those for years. They did have them when she was a girl, a long time ago, but even then they would take children back to school, not to their own home.

Was this some new scheme they'd brought in, she wondered? She didn't bother to follow the news these days so she couldn't be sure. If she phoned the police, and the man was merely doing his job, after all, it would make her look a fool. A lot of people already thought she suffered from senile dementia because of her advanced years. She didn't want to give them something to add to their gossip.

He couldn't do any harm to the boys, could he? She left the duster on the mantelpiece and made herself a cup of tea. As she drank, she continued to debate with herself whether she should or shouldn't call the police. She had to do so and risk being called an interfering old bag if everything turned out to be all right, or she had to ignore the situation and hope everything truly was all right.

Chapter 22

Jackson reached his home and found Sheila frantic with concern.

"Don't worry," he consoled. "Almost every child who goes missing turns up safe and well."

"I suppose they told that to the parents of the murdered boy," she protested.

"That's an isolated incident. We're not looking for a serial killer," Jackson responded, wishing he could be sure of that.

"Where can she be?" Sheila asked, close to tears.

"She's most likely gone off with a friend and lost track of time."

"I told you, I phoned all her friends."

"Perhaps she made a new friend, one you don't know about. It is the new school term. There'll be new girls there."

"I hadn't considered that," Sheila admitted. "I hope you're right. She wouldn't go off without telling me where she was going, though. Karen isn't like that."

"She might have forgotten," he said although he knew he hadn't convinced either Sheila or himself. "Where's Daniel?"

"I sent him to his room, out of the way."

"Is he all right?"

"He knows something's wrong. He went to his bedroom under protest, but he's okay, yes," she replied.

"Perhaps I should go and see him."

"I'd rather you did something about finding Karen. Daniel will be all right. He isn't going to disappear."

"There isn't much I can do."

"Surely you can use your influence with the police. Get a helicopter out or something."

He put his arm around her. "Sheila, they won't do that. Not at this stage, she hasn't been missing long enough."

"Not even for you?"

"Not even for me. It's just too expensive." He didn't want to tell her Karen wasn't the only child who had gone missing and resources were stretched to the limit. She already knew about Jake.

"What about that other young lad?" she asked as if reading his mind. "Have they found him yet?"

"No, but there can't be any connection. Jake went missing yesterday."

"So, he might be dead?"

"We haven't discovered a body."

"It doesn't mean he hasn't been slain, like the other lad."

"Sheila, you mustn't think that way. We don't know Jake's been killed, and even if he has, it doesn't mean anything has happened to Karen."

"You can't be sure there isn't a serial killer about, can you?"

It was no good. He would have to tell her.

"I'm sorry, Sheila. No, I can't be certain. And I might as well let you know you before you hear it on the news. Another child didn't get home from school today either. A boy. As it happens, he attends the same school as Karen."

"What!"

"Don't panic. It's almost certainly a coincidence."

"Don't you see? The other girls said Karen was chasing a boy! It might be the same one."

Jackson went to the phone to call Abercrombie.

* * *

Frank Churcher thought he was safe from Angela, leastways for the time being, as he walked back towards the church. He had a shock when she stepped from around a corner right in front of him. She must have doubled back along a different street.

"No, Angela. Please, let me explain," he pleaded as she came menacingly towards him. He still held the knife but realised she wouldn't consider it a threat as the large woman lumbered towards him.

"Explain, then!" she screamed. "And it had better be good, or I'll squash your balls."

It was no idle promise, and she grabbed his testicles to prove the point. Frank dropped the blade and moved his hands to his groin in a belated attempt to protect himself.

"Let go first, please. I can't talk like this."

"Start talking or I'll squeeze."

"I can't. You don't understand what it feels like."

She increased the pressure slightly.

"Aghh! All right. I'll tell you."

She relaxed her grip but kept hold. "Go on then."

"Okay, I was going to hurt Jake. Not kill him, though. It was just to punish him for what he did to Brian."

"Why? You didn't like Brian."

"I did, honest."

"Why punish Jake? He didn't kill Brian. If it wasn't you, it must have been that chap who escaped, Ewan."

"Jake might not have murdered Brian himself, but it wouldn't have happened if he hadn't left him by himself on the canal bank. You've got to admit he deserves to be punished for that. Besides, you said yourself it might be Jake that killed him."

"What were you going to do to him?"

"I'm not sure. Frighten him. Cut him, maybe. But not cut his throat as you thought."

"That fishing knife can cut deep, can't it?"

"Yeah, but I'd be careful. Now, please let go."

She did so, and he breathed out a sigh of relief. Did it mean she believed him, he wondered?

"Why stop there," she said. "If it were Jake's fault Brian got killed, then he should die too. If we find him, I think you really should cut his throat."

"What! You can't mean that. You want me to commit murder?"

"You owe me that much, and it would prove you were telling the truth."

"Well, we're not going to find him now, anyway, are we? In fact, there's a good chance he's already dead."

"But if he isn't, they will locate the lad eventually. Then there'll be other chances to get him. It doesn't need to be today."

"If you're sure that's what you want."

"It is. But if I ever find out it was you who killed Brian, I'll use that knife myself to hack you into a thousand bits."

* * *

Jake felt a little better once he'd finished his bath, even though he still couldn't stop shaking. He had a towel wrapped around his midriff and leaned against the wall looking down at the other two boys squatting on the floor, their backs against the bathtub.

Mark returned the look, wondering what was going through Jake's mind. But he was the oldest, not Jake. It was up to him to take the lead. They had to get out of here. There were three of them now; they should be able to overpower Ewan.

He looked at the youngest boy. Although a year younger, Anthony was physically bigger than Jake. On the other hand, he hadn't stopped crying since Ewan pushed him into the bathroom. No, he wouldn't be much help, Mark thought. It was going to be just himself and Jake.

"We need to get out of here, kid," he told Jake.

"How?" Jake replied, still trembling.

"He has to come back in here sometime. Why don't we jump him then?"

"We tried that before, remember. He's too strong."

"We've got to try. He might still kill us, you know."

Anthony cried harder.

"He needs us alive if we're going to be hostages," said Jake.

"Not all of us. You said yourself, one's enough for that."

"Even if we overpower him, what then? I've no clothes, remember."

"I'm sure you'd sooner be seen naked on the street than wind up dead."

"What about Karen? We can't leave her."

"She might have already found a way out."

"Then she'll fetch the police."

"He might even have killed her by now."

"He promised he wouldn't hurt her."

"Jake, people don't always keep their promises."

"Well, they should."

"I know, but they don't. It's a thing you grow out of. I've broken promises myself."

Jake looked horrified at this admission. A promise wasn't something you made lightly. But he agreed he'd met adults before who had let him down after promising something.

"He hasn't got a gun," Mark said, "or he'd have shown it to us by now to scare us."

"He has hard hands, though, and knives."

"Hard hands?"

"He hit me."

"So, he's sadistic. All the more reason to get away."

"Not without Karen."

"If she hasn't already escaped, we can get the police to rescue her once we get out. Don't you see, once we're out we can tell them where she is?"

"If we get out, he'll take her somewhere else."

"There won't be time."

"How would we escape? If we got out of this room, I mean?"

"Downstairs, we find a door or window we can go through."

"They'll all be locked."

"Then I'll throw a chair through the window. We'll find a way, don't worry about that."

"What about Anthony?"

"He must run with us."

"He's too scared."

"Listen, Tony, you can run, can't you?"

Anthony nodded, and then through his tears blurted, "I'll get killed if I'm home late for tea!"

Mark couldn't avoid laughing. "You might get killed for real if you stay here. You must help us fight the man, though, okay?" Despite his reservations, Mark decided Anthony needed to be involved somehow.

"I can't fight," Anthony answered.

"You can bite, though, can't you?"

"That's not fighting fair."

"Who the hell cares about being fair at a time like this? To get away from here, we must do whatever we can, whether it's fair or not."

"What do you want me to do?" Anthony was still sobbing, though not quite as audible now he knew they were going to try to escape. He wondered if they should, though. Wouldn't the guy hurt them badly if he caught them again?

* * *

Mrs Chegwin couldn't figure out where Mark had got to. He was always coming and going without telling his parents what he was doing or where he was going but always turned up for mealtimes. Using the vicarage as a hotel rather than his home was one of the many arguments between the vicar and his son. But today, he hadn't only missed lunch, but tea too.

Mark's mother wasn't unduly concerned about his safety. She was more annoyed her son had failed to say he would not be in for his meals. This was the last straw; if he were going to start this game, she would insist he told her his plans before any more food got wasted. Where could he go to in a small town like Staffington for the whole of the day?

* * *

Karen heard the kidnapper go upstairs. She threw down the potato she was peeling and dashed to the front door. It was locked and bolted as she expected. She tried the windows but found those locked too.

She desperately looked about for something to smash the glass. There was nothing in here. She rushed back into the kitchen and searched in there. There must be tools lying around, she thought, but succeeded only in finding the usual domestic items. A brush, a mop with a plastic bucket. None of those would be strong enough. There was a vacuum cleaner - that was more substantial, but she'd never be able to lift it to the height of the window. She needed Mark to help, but he was still locked in the bathroom. They were going to be given a meal, though, so maybe the kidnapper would allow them down here to eat. If so, she would wait for an opportunity then.

As she was wondering how to warn Mark about this, she heard the man returning downstairs and hastily returned to her chore.

If she annoyed him, perhaps he would put her back in the bathroom and then she could talk to the others. But supposing he punished her more severely? No, she'd better take the chance the boys would be brought down to eat, and they would be left alone long enough for her to enlist their help.

"Haven't you finished those spuds yet?" Ewan growled as he came into the kitchen with Jake's clothes and bundled them into the dryer.

"Nearly," she said.

"Well, hurry up," he said, switching on the dryer then turning to face her.

Karen flinched, half expecting him to slap her for being too slow, but he walked out, leaving her alone again.

* * *

Abercrombie addressed the team in the incident room. "We now have three missing children on our patch," he said. "The last two have no connection with Jake Swift's disappearance as far as are aware, but one of them is Jackson's daughter."

"They've not been missing long enough for us to be involved, though, have they, Sarge?" asked Hook.

"Technically, no they haven't, but because it's Jackson's kid the boss wants us to do what we can because Jackson won't be a lot of use to us while he's fretting about his own child. Once we find her, we can get back to looking for Jake. Besides, both these kids were together when last seen. That points to kidnapping rather than wandering off somewhere."

"No chance of them running off together of their own accord?" Gloria queried.

"No. Karen isn't like that and, as far as we know, neither is the lad. Besides, they're both rather young for that sort of thing."

Abercrombie waited for the contradictions. They didn't come. Everyone sat looking solemn.

"Uniform are interviewing the young ladies who saw these kids last. They've already talked to them earlier, but now we think it might be more serious they're going to put a bit of pressure on them to see if we can find out exactly what happened, like why Karen was chasing the boy?"

* * *

Ewan sat down on his sofa, trying to forget about the young girl in his kitchen. He tried again to tell himself they had cured him. He didn't want to abuse kids anymore.

Damn it! It was too easy. How could he resist all this temptation? The girl and those two young boys in the bathroom? He wasn't interested in the older youth; he'd put up too much resistance. But the others? There was no escaping jail now if they caught him, so what difference would it make?

No. He was determined not to go back to that. All the trouble it had caused before. Not just the prison sentence, but the attacks on him by his neighbours. Even after moving here, he had been sure to put strong double locks on all the doors and extra strength glass fitted in triple-glazed windows. Anyone wanting to break them would need to use something stronger than bricks.

He wouldn't do anything to the kids, he decided. He had to resist. Avoiding contact with them as much as possible until it was time to leave would be best.

* * *

Under Mark's direction, the boys in the bathroom had set up an ambush.

Jake had tied two corners of the towel around his waist hoping it would stay in place, and he was standing on a chair to one side of the door waiting to pounce on Ewan when he came into the room.

Mark crouched behind the door, ready to spring. Anthony, looking terrified, was poised behind Mark.

"Now, don't forget," Mark said, looking round at Anthony. "Once we get him on the floor, bite him on the thigh, sink your teeth in as hard as you can. Then run. Got it?"

Anthony nodded, even though he looked unsure.

Mark turned back to face Jake. "As soon as he comes through the door, leap on his neck, but make sure it's him and not Karen before you jump."

"Right," said Jake.

It seemed ages before anything happened and Jake was tiring of his position on the chair, but Mark insisted he stayed there. "If he hears us moving around when he comes up, he might suspect something," he pointed out. "Better to stay where you are."

Eventually, they heard someone coming up the stairs. "It won't be Karen," Mark said. "He wouldn't allow her to come up by herself. Get ready."

Jake became alert. Anthony trembled.

"Don't let us down now, Anthony," Mark warned.

The key turned in the lock, and Jake bent his knees to get a better spring.

The door opened, and Ewan walked in.

Jake was on him first; his arms around the man's neck in a tight stranglehold. Before Ewan got over the shock, Mark jumped onto his back as the man twisted around seeking to throw off the first attacker. Ewan's arms flayed about as he sought to brush both boys off, but the surprise ambush had taken him off guard, and he fell to his knees. Anthony, taking this as his cue to do his job, knelt beside Ewan, and bit into his leg as Mark had instructed.

"Aghh!" Ewan screamed, at the same time punching Mark in the face, sending him reeling.

This left only the two smaller boys attacking Ewan, and Mark knew they would not be able to hold onto him.

"Run!" he shrieked.

The towel around Jake came loose and dropped to the floor, leaving him naked. He didn't dare waste time trying to pick it up.

Mark recovered quickly from the blow and scrambled to his feet, jumping over Ewan, who was still disorientated and rubbing his injured thigh.

The three boys raced down the stairs, meeting Karen at the bottom who on hearing the commotion, had come to investigate.

"Go on. Get out!" Mark called out to her.

"All the doors are locked," she responded. "We'll need to smash a window. I'll get the vacuum cleaner. It's all there is."

"Quick, then."

She rushed back to the kitchen and in moments was back with the boys who'd now got to the front room. She gave the cleaner to Mark, who swung it at the window.

The window seemed to bend outwards, and the vacuum cleaner bounced back, leaving the window intact.

"Again!" Karen shrieked.

It was too late. Ewan had recovered and followed them down the stairs. He now stood behind them still rubbing his sore leg.

He hadn't intended the house to be used as a prison. The extra precautions were to keep people out, not in, but he was glad to see it worked both ways.

The youngsters, all in a straight line turned towards him, their backs to the window.

"So, you thought you'd get away, did you? Well, now you'll all have to be punished."

He looked into each of their frightened-looking faces.

Jake suddenly remembered Karen was present and tried to cover his nakedness with his hands. Ewan sniggered at this. As if it mattered, he thought.

Anthony started crying and Ewan went towards him. "We'll start with the youngest, our little cannibal," he said as he grabbed a handful of Anthony's hair and dragged the screaming child into the kitchen. He knew the others had no way of getting out.

Chapter 23

Ewan dragged the boy into the kitchen and closed the door, pleased with himself at having resisted the temptation to grab Jake, who was naked. Perhaps the treatment had worked.

The kid he'd chosen instead looked terrified. Tears streamed from his blue eyes, and he screamed loud enough for someone several doors away to have heard if the building wasn't almost soundproof with the installation of the strengthened triple-glazed windows.

"You're the little brat who bit my leg, aren't you? Well, you'll get extra punishment for that." Ewan kept a death grip on the boy's hair as he spoke.

"They made me do it," the child sobbed.

"I don't care why you did it. I'm still going to punish you. I've just not decided how yet."

Seeing there was no way out of the situation and knowing his kidnapper meant what he said, the boy wailed.

However, Ewan decided he would not hurt the child. Since the kid was already afraid, he didn't expect there'd be any further trouble from him. He'd scare him a bit more to make sure.

Still holding the boy, he went to one of the kitchen drawers and took out a breadknife. Anthony struggled when he saw it, but Ewan gripped him tighter and held the knife against the whimpering boy's cheek.

"Now, if you try to get away again, I'll slice this into your face, and you'll be scarred for the rest of your life. Do you understand?"

The boy nodded, but couldn't keep completely still and the blade scratched against his cheek, drawing a bead of blood. Ewan saw this and removed the knife. The boy had felt nothing, but as he put his hand to his face to rub where the blade had been, blood ran onto his fingers. He panicked on seeing it and screamed even louder.

* * *

In the next room, the others heard Anthony's shrieks and assumed the kidnapper was torturing him. They all knew their turn would come.

"We've got to get out," Mark said. "Let's all attack him together again."

"It didn't work last time," Jake reminded him.

"We've got Karen now. She's bigger than Anthony."

"Not that much, and she's a girl."

"I can fight as good as any boy," Karen protested.

Jake ignored this. "Even if we overpower him, we can't escape."

All went quiet for a few moments before Mark spoke again.

"He must have the keys with him. We'll take them from him."

"Why don't we use the phone while he's in the kitchen?" Karen suggested, looking towards the instrument fixed to the wall by the door.

"He'll hear us. There might be an extension in there," Mark responded, pointing to the kitchen door.

"I didn't see one," Karen told him.

"If we dial 999, they'll phone back here to make sure it isn't a hoax call, and he'll hear it ring."

Karen thought about this for a few seconds. "They still have to respond."

"By then he'll realise what we've done."

"I don't think we should annoy him more than he is already," Jake intervened. "He's going to punish us now anyhow, but if we attack him and it goes wrong again, he might kill us next time."

"Can you hear what he's doing to Anthony? Do you want to go through that?" Mark asked.

"Anthony's soft. For all we know, Ewan could simply be giving him a few slaps. Anthony would scream just for that," Jake answered

"It doesn't sound like he's slapping him," Karen said.

"What do you think he's doing to him?" Jake asked.

"Something worse than slapping. I think Jake's right, Mark," Karen said, "That guy's mad. There's no telling what might happen if we upset him again."

"So, you want to let him torture you, or rape you?"

"He won't rape me. If he wanted to do that, he would have done it when you were in the bathroom. Besides, I think he's queer."

"Shit! So, he might rape us then. You don't think he's at it now, do you, with Anthony?" Mark now regretted what he had forced Jake into doing when they were in the church basement.

"I don't know."

* * *

"I'm going back to the police station," Jackson told Sheila. "It will be easier to find out what's going on if I'm there."

"Do you think you should?"

"Probably not, but I'm going, anyway."

"Okay. You will phone me as soon as you find out anything?"

"Yes, of course." He turned away from his spouse's tear-smeared face and drove to his place of work. He went straight into the incident room, surprising his team with his return.

"You should be at home, sir," Hook said. "Your wife needs your support."

"She's all right. I can be more useful here. What's the situation?"

"Well, er—"

"Come on, Alan, tell me. What's happened?"

Abercrombie entered the room. "Tom, what are you doing here?" he asked.

"You didn't expect me to stay at home and not do anything while my daughter's missing, did you? Let's go to the office."

Once they reached the office, Jackson remained standing and leant against his desk.

"Now, what is it Alan didn't want to tell me? What's happened?"

"We can't be certain there's a connection."

"With what? Come on, Harry, out with it. What's bothering everybody?"

"There's another misper been reported."

"What! Another child?"

"Not exactly, it's a boy of seventeen. It's the vicar's son, Mark."

"So, we have three kids missing besides Jake."

"Yeah."

"And whoever killed Brian is still out there somewhere."

"Yes, but that's almost certainly Ewan. He'll be miles away by now. There's got to be another explanation for the kids' disappearing."

"And what if the murderer isn't Ewan? You know I have my doubts about that."

Abercrombie didn't respond.

"You believe we've got a serial killer on our hands?" Jackson continued.

"It's possible," Abercrombie said. "There is something else you should know, though."

"Come on, Harry, stop pussyfooting about. If you know something about Karen, tell me. I'm a cop, remember. I know how things are done. If she's been harmed, I want to know."

Abercrombie looked into Jackson's eyes. "It isn't anything like that. It's only that I know how you feel about bullying."

"She's been bullied?"

"No. You might consider this is worse. We've found out she was chasing the boy intending to hurt him."

Jackson stared at his sergeant.

"What! That's not possible. She'd never harm another kid."

"Sorry, Tom. Uniform have interviewed the other girls. They've admitted to taking part in some sort of initiation ceremony. Karen was with them."

"Initiation ceremony? But they're usually harmless things done in fun. They don't hurt anyone."

"I'm afraid in this case they did. In fact, if the victims' parents decide to press charges, the girls could be charged with assault."

"And Karen?"

"We don't know the extent of her involvement. Our priority, of course, is to find her."

"And when we do, I promise you she'll be grounded forever."

"Don't be too harsh. We don't know yet if she actually hurt the boy, and they could both be in danger."

"Yes, as usual, you're right. We need to find them both fast. And Jake."

"And Mark Chegwin," Abercrombie reminded him.

"Oh, yes. Wait a minute, you don't suppose that youth has kidnapped them, do you? I believe he's quite a rough lout."

"Why? There have been no ransom notes or anything. Besides none of the kids come from particularly wealthy families."

"Chegwin wouldn't realise that, would he? I admit ransom isn't a likely motive, but you never know. Anyway, it's a theory, isn't it?"

"Chegwin's parents are just as concerned about him as the other victim's parents."

"Well, he isn't going to hold prisoners at his home in full view of his parents, is he?"

"Where, then?"

"Some disused building or shed or something like that."

"We checked them all searching for Jake."

"But before the new disappearances."

"Yeah," Abercrombie admitted.

"Let's do it again."

"We're very short of manpower."

"I know that, but we have to do it, and the sooner the better."

* * *

"It's getting dark. We won't find him now, let's go home. I'm getting hungry." Angela decided she'd had enough for one day.

"Okay," Frank agreed. "The lad's probably dead by now, anyway."

"If he isn't, you'll get another chance to make certain he is when they find him."

"Yeah, right."

They turned towards home and as they rounded a corner, almost collided with P.C Peart.

"Where the hell have you been?" the constable asked angrily. "I've been looking for you everywhere. They need you at the police station. Not you, Mrs Churcher, just your husband."

"What do they want him for, he hasn't done anything?"

"I can't say, but you've got to go right away," Peart said to Frank.

"I'm not going there now. We're going home. And I ain't taking orders from no nigger."

"Then, I must arrest you."

"Just try it." Frank turned and ran, leaving Angela and Peart together.

"Try to persuade your husband to see sense, Mrs Churcher. We will catch him if he doesn't come forward voluntary, and it will look worse for him if we have to do that."

"What would be worse, what's going on?"

"I don't know, but Inspector Jackson wants to see him."

"Oh, God! You think he killed Brian, don't you?"

Angela's earlier suspicions about her husband surfaced again. Had his threat to hurt Jake been a bluff to throw her off track? Or had he meant to kill Jake because the boy might be a witness as she first thought?

"I don't know," Peart repeated, breaking into her thoughts.

"You could be right, you know. But if I find one shred of proof, I'll save you the expense of a trial, I promise you."

"Don't do anything hasty, Mrs Churcher. Get your husband to go to the police station."

Angela didn't reply. She walked away from Peart towards her home.

* * *

Gloria was still seated in her car, wondering if the Swift's would ever get fed up of waiting. It was getting dark, and there was no hint of the Churchers' coming home. Yet, the Swift's car remained stationary, its occupants staring ahead. One of them occasionally glanced into a wing mirror. Gloria wasn't sure if it was her they were looking at, or if they were watching for the Churchers' coming from that direction. It was well past the time she should have clocked off, but she wasn't going anywhere while the Swifts stayed here.

She'd been told via her mobile phone about Karen Jackson's disappearance and speculated how Jackson was reacting. Knowing Jackson, he would go home to see his wife and son, then almost certainly go back to the station to supervise things himself. The superintendent would try to stop him, but it was doubtful he would succeed.

Her thoughts came back to the more immediate issue. She couldn't prevent the Swifts from speaking to the Churchers'. She hoped it wouldn't be confrontational. If it was, there wasn't much she could do. Not unless someone broke the law. But she still felt she needed to be on hand.

In her driving mirror, she saw Angela turn into the street and come marching along towards her. In the dusk, she couldn't see Angela's expression, but her pace made Gloria suspect she wasn't in a good mood. It wasn't the stride of a mother mourning her son, but of one who had recently had an argument. The Swift's didn't appear to have spotted her yet.

Angela got to the tail end of Gloria's car before the passenger door of the other vehicle opened, and Mrs Swift climbed out.

Gloria wound down her window.

"Mrs Churcher, can we have a word?" she overheard Jake's mother ask.

"What the hell do you want, I'm busy," was the response.

"I understand. I'm sorry about Brian, but we need to talk to you."

"Go on then, talk. But make it quick."

"Jake's run away."

"I know that. We've been looking for him all day."

"We wondered if you might know where he could be. Somewhere he and Brian used to go together, perhaps?"

"If I knew that, we'd have found him, wouldn't we? Besides, you know he might have—"

Angela noticed Gloria sat in the car.

"What's she doing here? This is some kind of trick, isn't it?"

Mrs Swift's husband now joined in. "I promise it isn't," he said. "She insisted on staying here. It's nothing to do with us."

"Then we'll talk inside where the nosy bitch can't listen," Angela answered. She led her visitors into the house.

Gloria waited, hoping she wouldn't be needed after all. She was sure Angela had been about to tell the Swift's that Jake might have killed Brian. If she continued along the same lines, there was no saying how Jake's parents would react.

* * *

Jake, still naked and conscious of Karen's presence, had grabbed a cushion from a chair in the living area and was holding it in front of him. Karen did her best to avert her eyes to save him from embarrassment, but she couldn't avoid looking at him altogether. She realised he was uncomfortable about her being there even though he had said nothing. Well, she supposed, it might take his mind off the danger they were in and make him less frightened. He seemed to be coping better than she was. She was scared. When she had been comforting Anthony, things hadn't seemed so bad; she'd had something to do. Now, she was determined not to be the first to cry though it would not be long before she couldn't hold back her tears. Where was her father?

* * *

Mrs Milward was on her second cup of tea, still unsure about what she should do. She hadn't seen the two boys leave the house. It was now getting quite dark; surely, the truant officer couldn't keep them there after school time?

Perhaps they'd left while she'd been in the kitchen. Her eyes focused on the telephone. She still wasn't happy about involving the police, but she could phone her son. He'd tell her what to do.

She dialled his number and got his answering machine.

"Damn these new-fangled things," she said to herself. "I'm not talking to no machine."

She put the receiver down and went back to her drink. She'd try to remember to phone Barry later.

Chapter 24

"Do you think the three of us can move that piano?" Karen asked, indicating the instrument to one side of the kitchen doorway.

"I suppose so, why?" Mark responded.

"That door opens this way. If we block it, he won't be able to get at us."

"We still can't get out of here."

"It'll give us more time to try - and to use the phone."

"What about the kid?"

"Anthony? We'll have to leave him. It can't be helped. The sooner we bring the police, the sooner he'll be rescued."

"Right let's do it. Come on, Jake."

Jake joined the other two at the end of the piano. He was reluctant to let go of the cushion he was still using to cover himself.

"Drop the cushion, I promise not to look," said Karen, realising Jake's predicament.

With a sigh, Jake threw the cushion to one side and added his weight to pushing the piano. Karen tried to keep her promise but couldn't resist letting her eyes wander. No different than Daniel's, she thought, wondering why Jake was making such a fuss.

* * *

In the kitchen, Ewan was trying to pacify the screaming boy.

"You're not hurt. It's only a scratch," he said.

"You cut me!" Anthony screamed.

"I didn't do it on purpose. It was an accident, honest."

"I want to go home. Let me go."

"I can't do that. Not now."

"Why not?"

"You've seen where I'm hiding."

"I won't tell anyone. Please let me go. I promise I'll not tell anyone where you are or what you've done to me."

"I can't take the risk, sorry."

The boy continued screaming, and Ewan started to feel sorry for him, though not sorry enough to prevent him from punishing the other kids. Who would he deal with next? Not Jake, he'd keep him until last. He'd already decided what his punishment would be.

The girl then. Yes, she would be next. No knives this time. He'd give her a proper punishment. Spank her. Yes, that appealed to him. Smack her bare backside. He'd enjoy that. He made Anthony sit on the floor, his back against the wall. No harm in letting the kid watch.

There was a noise from the other room as if something heavy was being moved.

"What the hell are those kids up to now?" he said to himself as he sprang to the door. He tried to open it and found it would move only an inch or so before being stopped by what he now saw was his piano.

"Open this bloody door right now, or I'll kill you all," he stormed.

* * *

George Millward was marking the work of his year eight students in the spare room that served as a study in his house. He was frustrated, yet amused, at some of the errors he found in most essays written by the class of twelve-year-olds. Hadn't they taught them even the basic rules of grammar at primary school? Did he have to start all over again with them?

The telephone rang downstairs. He ignored it, deciding to let the answer machine deal with the call while he continued working. He wasn't expecting anyone to phone, probably either a salesperson or wrong number.

Regretting the number of students on whose creations he had written 'see me', George finished marking the work, then went towards the kitchen to prepare his tea, knowing it would be a few hours before his wife would be home.

As he passed through the living room, the flashing light on the answering machine caught his eye. He went over to it and pressed the play button.

He recognised his mother's voice, 'Damn these new-fangled things, I'm not talking to no machine.' George smiled as he dialled her number. The double negative reminding him of his pupils' work.

"Hello, Mum, did you want me?"

"How did you know?"

"The answering machine."

"I didn't leave a message. I don't speak to those stupid things."

"Yes, you did. You talked, and the machine recorded your voice."

"It had no right to. I didn't tell it to take a message."

This was getting as bad as the kids' essays.

"Never mind, Mum. What did you want?"

"Oh, I forgot. I want to know if I should call the police."

"Why, what's happened?" George started to panic.

"I saw a man take two boys into his house."

"What's wrong with that? They might be relatives."

"I don't think the lads wanted to go with him. He said they were truants."

"Truants?"

"That's what he told me. He said he was a truant catcher."

"Mum, there hasn't been any truant catchers for years."

"Are you sure?"

"I'm a teacher. Mum. I can assure you there's no such thing as truant catchers."

"You believe I should ring the police then?"

"Yes, I mean no. I will. I'll come round to your house now so I can see what's going on for myself, then if we need the police, I'll phone from there."

"Yes, I'd like that."

* * *

The three youngsters quaked at the anger in Ewan's voice.

"What if he hurts Anthony?" said Jake.

"We have to take the chance," Karen responded. "Get to the phone, fast."

It was Mark who sprang to the phone. Relieved to get a dialling tone, he keyed in 999.

The operator's response was almost immediate. "Emergency, which service do you require?"

"Police," said Mark.

"What number are you calling from?"

Mark looked at the phone for the number, but there was no indication of it on the instrument.

"I don't know," he said. "We've been kidnapped. We need help, quick."

"Where are you?"

Mark had no idea.

"What's the name of this street?" He called out to Jake and Karen.

None of them knew.

"We're somewhere near St Peter's Church," Mark screamed into the receiver. "This isn't a hoax, honest. Do something, please."

* * *

It didn't take Ewan long to realise all he needed to do was unlock the rear door and walk to the front. Too late to stop those brats getting to the phone, though. The one thing he hadn't thought about when he'd left them in the living room.

He heard the tinkle of the phone and realised one of them had already got to it. Damn the kids. He'd need to leave earlier than he'd planned now. There wouldn't be any point in tying his victims up; the police were probably already on their way. He'd have to let the kids go. He'd make them pay first, though, somehow. The boy in the kitchen with him still hadn't stopped wailing. Ewan ignored the child as he planned quick reprimands for the others. He felt some regret that he wouldn't now have time to slowly enjoy their tortures.

Taking the keys from his pocket, he unlocked the back door. Then he picked up the knife he'd used to frighten Anthony, grabbed the boy by the wrist, and pulled him to the door. He opened the door, dragged Anthony through with him then turned to lock the door again.

Fumbling with the knife and keys forced him to let his grip on the boy go while he locked the door. "Wait there," he ordered.

Anthony didn't wait. That moment was enough for the terrified child to bolt towards the gate and race up the cul-de-sac screaming. Ewan was sure a few people in the neighbouring houses heard the boy but hoped they would assume the screams to be boisterous kids at play.

"Come back, you little toe-rag!" he shouted. By the time he reached the gate, Anthony was out of sight.

It didn't matter that much, he thought. All the kids would be free soon, anyhow. Perhaps he'd keep one as a hostage as he'd first planned. It would have to be Jake, his original prisoner; the other boy was too big to handle.

Then he had second thoughts. The girl? She'd said her dad was a cop. That would give him better bargaining power, a cop's kid. Yes, he'd keep the girl. Karen, he remembered one of the boys calling her.

He ran round to the front door and unlocked it, stepping through it as Mark was putting down the phone.

"So, you decided to play a little trick, did you? Well, now you will be punished even more." He turned to Mark, brandishing the knife towards him. "Who did you call, the police, I suppose?"

"No, honest," Mark replied. "I tried, but I didn't know where we were, and I didn't know the phone number."

Ewan laughed. "You know, I think I believe you."

"It's true."

That gave him more time, but not much. They would trace the call, eventually. How fast depended on whether the operator believed the kid's story.

* * *

"Why did you come?" Angela asked the Swifts, "You know Jake is responsible for Brian's death."

Mrs Swift sobbed.

"How can you say that? Jake didn't harm Brian," she replied.

"He might not be the one who killed him, but if he'd stayed with him..."

Now Angela cried too.

"Look, this isn't doing anyone any good," said Mr Swift. "We shouldn't have come. Let's go, Freda."

The two weeping women ignored him and each other until Angela dried her tears and said, "I'm sorry, I shouldn't have said that. Please stay, have some tea."

The Swifts agreed, and Angela went into the kitchen to make the drink. It was true she shouldn't have blamed Jake, not in front of his parents. What did it matter now, anyway? Jake was probably dead too by now. And if he wasn't, he would be once Frank found him.

Frank? Why did he run from the police? They'd have found the knife on him of course, but why hadn't he ditched it once he was out of sight then given himself up. That would seem to be the logical thing to do unless he had something else to hide.

Why did the police want to see him again, anyway? Especially without her being there.

As she watched the kettle boil, like the bubbles of the boiling water, her earlier suspicions bubbled to the surface of her mind.

* * *

"Why did you come into work? Don't you consider you'd be better off at home supporting your wife?" Superintendent Everett asked Jackson.

"I can't stay at home, sir. My daughter's missing and I have to help in finding her."

"Well, I won't be able to stop you, so I won't waste my time trying. Any ideas about where she might be?"

Before Jackson could reply, the phone rang on the Superintendent's desk. He answered it, not too pleased about being interrupted.

Jackson started to leave, but Everett beckoned him back as he listened to the phone.

"This isn't a night to be messed about with kids playing pranks. Are they sure it's genuine?" he spoke into the phone.

He listened for a moment then said, "Right. I'll get Sergeant Abercrombie on to it." He replaced the receiver.

"There's been a report that some kids are being held in a house. Might be a hoax but you never know, do you?"

"We do have kids missing, and Karen could be one of them."

"I know. That's why I'm sending Abercrombie and not you. You realise I can't let you take any part in this while you're personally involved, don't you?"

"I'm not involved. You're only guessing Karen's there. I want to go, sir."

"Absolutely not, and that's an order. Understand me?"

Jackson knew Everett wouldn't be persuaded. In his position, he would say the same thing. Reluctantly, he left the office and made his way to the incident room to find Abercrombie. He needed more information.

"You've heard?" Abercrombie asked as Jackson walked into the room.

"Just the basic details. I was with Everett when he got the call. He won't let me take part."

"I recognise how you feel, but you can't blame him."

"I know."

"One good thing, anyway. One of the kids has returned home."

"What! Who?"

"Not Karen, I'm afraid. It's the boy, Anthony."

"Does he know anything about the others?"

"We can't get anything out of him. There's a WPC with him now, but all he does is shake and cry. Won't say anything. He's obviously been through a trauma of some kind. I'm going to send Gloria when she's free."

"Is this boy at his home?"

"Yes."

"What's the address?"

"Do you think you should?"

"Never mind that, give me the bloody address. Shouldn't you be getting those kids rescued instead of talking to me?"

"We're waiting for an A.R.U."

"Armed Response Unit. Why, for God's sake, they're just kids?"

"You've not been told, have you?"

"What?"

"The address—where the kids are allegedly being detained. It's Ewan's home."

"And Karen might be there! I'm coming with you, whatever Everett says."

"That's not a good idea, Tom."

"I'm coming. What makes you think Ewan's armed?"

"We're not sure he is. But we don't want to take any chances."

"What are we waiting for then? We can be at the scene and wait for the A.R.U there."

"We don't want to panic Ewan. He might see us before the A.R.U gets there to give us support."

"What's their E.T.A?"

"An hour."

"An hour! He could kill the kids in that time. Let's go!"

"Sorry, Tom, this is my operation. I say we wait."

"It might be your operation, but you can't give me orders. I'm off duty. I'll see you there."

"No, Tom. Don't be stupid. You can't go alone."

Jackson had left before Abercrombie finished speaking. Reluctantly, Abercrombie picked up the phone and reported to Everett. He couldn't wait any longer now. Jackson may have acted rashly, but he still had to be protected. He looked down into the car park to see the waiting vans already loaded with officers standing by to go. He gave the signal for them to leave and hoped the armed cops wouldn't be required.

At least he had been spared having to give Anthony's address to Jackson.

* * *

Gloria was getting concerned. The Swifts had been in the Churchers' home for some while. She was tempted to knock on the door to check everything was all right. She had decided to do this and put up with abuse from Angela when the front door opened, and she saw the Swifts shake hands with Angela before leaving.

Relieved, she started her engine and drove towards her house. She thought she'd better tell them at the station she had eventually clocked off and pulled over to use her mobile phone. It rang before she dialled, startling her.

It was Hook. "Gloria," he said, "are you free yet?"

"Just. But I was on my way home. I've not seen it for about twenty-two hours."

"Fourteen, actually," he corrected her exaggeration. "But I'm afraid there's another job for you before you sign off."

"What? Can't someone else do it?"

"Sergeant Abercrombie specially asked for you. He says you're good with kids."

"Kids? What kids?"

"One of the boys who went missing has returned home, but he's too frightened to talk. There's a uniformed WPC with him, but she can't get anything out of him. He only bawls his eyes out whenever she speaks to him. Abercrombie wants you to have a go. The child might know what's going on."

"Okay, it doesn't sound as if I have much choice."

"You don't. We think we know where the other kids are, but if this lad was with them, he might be able to tell us what the situation is."

"Situation? What do you mean?"

"We believe the others are being held by David Ewan, the escapee. We want to find out whether he's armed, the layout of the house. That kind of thing."

"Ewan! He's still in the district?"

"Yes. In his own house."

"Has he got Karen Jackson?"

"We think so."

"Where is the Inspector?"

"He's gone to the house."

"What's happening about Jake?"

"No news of him, I'm afraid."

So, at least, no dead body had been discovered yet.

"Have they called off the search for him, then?"

"Not exactly. It's become more low profile, though. Priority has to be to rescue the kids we're sure are still alive."

"Right. What's the address of this boy?"

She wrote it down as Hook dictated it to her over the phone. Then she sped her car towards the location.

* * *

Angela made herself more coffee after seeing her visitors out. They had separated on more friendly terms, on the surface at any rate. She still couldn't help holding a grudge against their son, though.

Why couldn't it have been their boy instead of hers?

If Jake didn't run off when they were attacked, the two of them might have been able to fend off the murderer. Why had he deserted his best friend?

She no longer believed Jake killed Brian but held him to blame for not preventing it. If she could get hold of him now, she'd strangle him herself. Still, if the boy wasn't already dead, Frank would soon change that. Where was that husband of hers?

* * *

Frank thought he had given the cop the slip and paused to regain his breath. He considered ditching the knife. He didn't want to have to explain carrying an offensive weapon if they caught him. And if he found Jake Swift, he could kill him with his bare hands; he was only a kid.

But the blade would be easier and quicker, he decided. Less time for anyone to hear the boy scream. He left the knife in his pocket and walked towards the woods near the church.

Chapter 25

George Millward got to his mother's house and let himself in.

"What's going on, Mum?" he asked. "What exactly did you see?"

She told him.

"And you haven't phoned the police?"

"No. I didn't want to make myself look stupid."

"They won't think you're stupid, I promise you. I'll call them myself now."

He went to the window and glanced towards the building she had pointed out. The curtains had been closed, and all looked quiet. Nothing seemed amiss, but his mother didn't imagine things. He walked to the phone.

Wondering if the situation warranted a 999 call or the regular police station number, he hesitated a moment. He decided he couldn't justify the emergency number. Even if the kids his mother had seen were still in the house, nothing showed they were there against their will. He dialled the local police number.

When the operator answered, he was a little surprised to be told they already knew of the situation, and officers were on their way.

He told his mother.

"How did they know?" she asked.

"I have no idea. Are you sure you haven't contacted them?"

"I might be old, but I'm not senile." She peered at her son through her spectacles.

"I know. I'm sorry. Someone else must have been suspicious too. I'll see if I can find out what's happening."

"Be careful," she cautioned, wishing he would leave things to the police.

"It's all right. I won't go barging into the house. Besides, this is Staffington, not New York."

He went outside and made his way to the rear of the suspect house. He found the dustbin upturned. Could have been dogs, he thought.

He looked toward the windows at the back of the house, once again finding himself staring at closed curtains. Everything was peaceful. There didn't seem to be any children around now. Maybe they'd left without his mother seeing them. She couldn't have been watching through her window all the time. Then, there was the possibility they had left the back way where she wouldn't have seen them, anyway.

Perhaps he should knock on the door and ask the bloke who lived there about the kids. If there were an innocent explanation, no damage would be done.

Then, if there was an innocent explanation, why were the police coming and where had they got their information? His mother had told him that no other neighbours seemed to be around at the time she saw the boys.

The sensible thing would be to wait for the police. Why were they taking so long? If the householder had the boys inside the house, he could hurt them - or worse.

That thought caused him to decide to go to the front door after all. He didn't have to say what he wanted. He simply needed some excuse to look inside.

Trying to think of this excuse, he retraced his footsteps towards the back gate. As he walked through the gateway, he collided with a tall, smartly dressed man.

"Sorry," he said to the stranger.

"Who are you?" the other man replied.

"What's it got to do with you? Do you live here?"

"No. Police." Jackson produced his warrant card.

"Thank goodness," said Millward. "You took long enough."

"You haven't answered my question."

"Sorry. I'm George Millward. My mother lives in one of the neighbouring houses. She saw something suspicious earlier on. I was trying to find out what was going on."

"How were you going to do that?"

"I was about to try to get into the building. Pretend to be a salesman or something. It doesn't matter now you're here, though."

"So far, I'm on my own. The others should be here soon, but it might not be soon enough. I suggest you carry on with your plan. Not pretend to be a salesman, though, he'll give you the brush-off. It needs to be something he has to let you into the house for."

"Now, hold on a minute. If you're a police officer -"

"I can't do it. Ewan, the fellow who lives here, knows me."

"Is this bloke violent?"

"You'll be safe. He's a child molester. He won't attack an adult." Jackson was aware that he was asking a member of the public to place himself at risk. He couldn't be sure Ewan wouldn't attack, or that he wasn't armed, unlikely as he believed this was. But his daughter was in that house, and he wanted her out - he didn't care how.

"What do you want me to do?" Millward asked.

"Go to the front door as you planned. Tell him you're a cop. He'll have to let you in then."

"If I tell him I'm a cop, what's the point of me going instead of you? He already knows you're a cop."

Jackson stood silent for a moment as he gathered his thoughts about this. He had his reasons but hadn't intended to share them with Millward. Then he decided if he was asking a civilian to put himself in danger on his behalf, the man had the right to know the facts.

"I think one of the kids he has might be my daughter. I can't guarantee I'd act rationally if I got in there, and that could put lives at risk," he said.

Millward gasped. "What if he asks for I.D?"

"Use mine," Jackson reached into his pocket and offered his warrant card to Millward.

"He'll see the photograph isn't me," Millward protested.

"Nobody ever gives the warrant card more than a glance. He won't notice, don't worry."

"Is this legal?"

"Probably not, but we're desperate. We have to get those kids out."

"What happens when I get in?"

"Find the children. Make sure they're safe and, if possible, bring them out with you. If you can't get them out, stay with the kids and tell them the police are on their way."

"Okay. I don't like this, but I'll do it if there are children at risk. I have an interest in kids. I'm a teacher."

At that moment, Jackson didn't care about Millward's profession. He was just relieved he had agreed, though a little apprehensive about whether he was doing the right thing. He hoped they were being over-cautious at the police station in assuming Ewan was armed.

Jackson watched Millward until he'd turned the corner then glanced up at the windows of the house. There was nothing of interest there; the upper and lower floor curtains were closed.

It looked as if he'd been mistaken all along, and Ewan was the killer. If so, it meant the kids inside were even more at risk than he'd first thought. Why hadn't Ewan left the district after his escape as everyone presumed? Staying here, knowing the police were searching for him made little sense, especially returning to his home. He must have known they were bound to carry out periodic checks on the house and would find him eventually.

Unless the whole idea of remaining in the locality was to do precisely what it had done, put the police off track and make them believe he was now in someone else's area.

As his thoughts continued, Jackson realised this made it even more likely Ewan was guilty. If not, surely he wouldn't have added child abduction to his already serious crime of escaping from custody.

If he had killed once, he had nothing to lose by doing it again. Indeed, the children in the house might even now be dead. He swallowed as he remembered one of those children was Karen.

* * *

In case he was caught and searched, Frank Churcher threw the knife into the trees, having changed his mind about keeping it.

He emerged cautiously from the wooded area near the church into the street. There was nobody around.

He couldn't stay in those woods, he decided. At this time of day, it was too dark in there. He couldn't go home. The cops were bound to be waiting for him. Besides, how was he going to explain to Angela why he had run away from Peart? That he refused to be arrested by a black cop? He could try that. She knew how he felt about blacks. Not that he was racist, of course.

He didn't want blacks living in his country. That wasn't being racist. There was plenty of room for them elsewhere in the world.

But resisting arrest? Even from a black cop? Would Angela believe he was stupid enough to do that, or would she think there was more to it?

He leant against the church wall as he mulled over what to do, all the time keeping his eyes on the street for any sign of Peart or any other cops.

Why did the cops want him, anyhow?

* * *

Jackson knew perfectly well that Millward had no chance of being let in through the front door. Telling Ewan he was a cop would give him even less chance of being admitted than if he'd stuck to saying he was a salesman. Ewan was running from the cops - he wasn't going to open the door to one.

What Jackson hoped would happen was Ewan would be distracted by the visitor long enough to give him time to force entry at the back and get in the house himself. He had told a little white lie to Millward; it was better he didn't know the full story. It would help him to play his part well. Jackson was sure the front door would not be opened to the caller, or he would certainly not have put the civilian in such a position.

He had already examined the rear door and discovered it had only a single lock. If this were a cheap lock, as he knew most people around here used, and provided there were no bolts on the door, it would be a simple matter to lever it open with the large screwdriver he had retrieved from his car.

Pressing the edge of the tool between the door and its frame, he tried to prize open the door. He took seconds to realise the lock would not be as easy to force as he'd hoped. It was far more secure than usual and probably had one or more bolts in addition to the lock. He turned his attention to the windows.

* * *

Inside the building, Ewan strolled towards the three trembling youngsters; the knife still held menacingly in his hand.

Karen screamed.

"Shut up! You stupid kid. No one can hear you," Ewan snapped.

But the scream was heard. Millward heard it as he stood at the front door, trying to pluck up the courage to carry out his mission. He could leave now and tell Jackson he wasn't getting involved. Then a high-pitched scream seemed to come from the letterbox. It wasn't loud, seeming to be muffled somehow, but it was unquestionably a scream.

That made up his mind for him.

He knocked. "Open up! Police!" he shouted.

Inside, Ewan froze on hearing the knock. "Damn! He'd left it too late to run."

"Get back upstairs!" he ordered the kids.

While he was in such a mood, and with that knife in his hand, all the youngsters were prepared to do whatever he said and made their way up the stairs and into the bathroom. Ewan followed them.

Once in the bathroom, Ewan grabbed Jake's arm. "You come with me."

He pulled Jake out of the room before locking the bathroom door, then roughly pulled the boy down the stairs and ushered him towards the front door.

"I've got no clothes on!" Jake protested as he realised Ewan was dragging him to the outside door.

"Do you think I care?"

* * *

Abercrombie held his officers out of sight of the cul-de-sac while he assessed the situation. There was still no sign of the A.R.U. What was taking them so long? He made his way, with Kevin Gibson, towards the target house.

"Ewan knows me," he told Gibson. "So I don't want to get within view of him yet. You carry on and see if you can find out what's happened to Jackson."

"He didn't say he was coming here, though, did he, Sarge? Wasn't he going to see the boy that got away?"

"That was before he found out his daughter is probably here. If he thinks his kid's in that house, he'll be somewhere around, perhaps even inside the house."

"Yeah, right."

Abercrombie backed into the shadows, and Gibson continued walking along the cul-de-sac towards the house.

Anyone seeing him would assume him to be a late-night visitor to one of the houses.

* * *

Gloria sat holding Anthony's hand as she tried to talk to him.

"You're not in any trouble, Anthony. We only want you to tell us what happened. Can you do that?"

The boy simply sat and quivered.

"We need a child psychologist," said the WPC sitting on the other side of Anthony.

"No, we don't," Gloria responded. "Not yet, anyhow. Anthony has had enough excitement for one day. Isn't that right, Tony?"

There was no response. Anthony just continued to shake.

"We'll have to have him medically examined, in case anything nasty happened," the WPC said.

"You don't think..." Anthony's mother now started to ask.

"We need not worry about that yet," Gloria answered, glaring at the police officer.

"I only thought..." the policewoman said.

"Leave it to me, will you," Gloria demanded. "In fact, I think it would be better if you left the room."

"What! Why?"

"Come outside for a minute." She led the way to the door with the constable following. Outside the room, Gloria turned to her, "Don't you realise, it might be your uniform that's frightening the boy?"

"I never thought of that."

"Stay in the house, but give me a bit of time with him on my own, just me and his mother."

The policewoman nodded, and Gloria went back into the room, glad to be rid of the constable and her unhelpful comments. She found Anthony weeping; his mother had placed her arms around his shoulders. He was still shaking but looked a little more relaxed. Gloria resumed her seat beside him.

She let him cry for a few minutes without disturbing him. When she judged the time right, she asked, "Are you feeling better now, Tony?"

This time, she was rewarded with a slight nod.

She paused, giving the boy time.

"Are you ready to talk now?" she asked, eventually.

Another nod, this time, a more definite one.

"Tell us what happened. In your own time," Gloria said.

Once Anthony did start speaking, he was difficult to stop, and Gloria had to work hard to keep up as she took notes. Anthony told her everything that had taken place, starting with the big kids chasing him.

"Do you know the names of the other children in the house?" Gloria asked him after he finished his story.

"One was called Jake."

"Jake!"

"Yeah."

Gloria rushed to her car to make a phone call.

Chapter 26

"Get away, copper. I've got a kid here, and I'm gonna kill him if you don't go away right now!"

The voice came from the letterbox, and its tone convinced Millward the threat was real. He wasn't trained to cope with this. "All right, all right, I'm going," he called back. He withdrew from the doorway and went to find Jackson.

Detective Constable Gibson watched the stranger leave the front door of the target house and hesitated. He had no idea who this person was, but the fact he'd been there at all changed things. The visitor might be an accomplice or an innocent caller. Either way, if he remained in the vicinity, it would lead to complications when the ARU arrived, not the least of which was getting in the line of fire.

He pulled out his mobile to call Abercrombie, then replaced it, deciding it would be better to walk back to the sergeant. If Ewan wasn't aware of police presence yet, he'd rather it stayed that way as long as possible. It might give the game away if the suspect heard him on the phone. He could text, but he wasn't that skilled at texting, and it would use up valuable time. Gibson went to report the new information to Abercrombie in person.

* * *

Behind the house, it amazed Jackson at how tight the building was. It would take more than his puny screwdriver to force a way in here. As he tried to think of another plan, Millward re-appeared. Though surprised he had come back, it relieved Jackson to see him safe.

"He has got a kid in there," Millward told him. "He'd have killed him if I didn't come away."

"Him? You said him?"

"That's right. He definitely said he would kill him. Why?"

"Never mind," Jackson answered, trying not to show his relief.

* * *

Inside the house, Ewan still held the knife at Jake's throat. The boy trembled with fear as he tried to twist free.

"Stop struggling!" Ewan ordered. "I'm not really going to kill you. Remember our deal?"

Jake remembered but was no longer sure he could trust his captor. He didn't know if he'd ever done so.

"Let me go, please!" he made another desperate plea.

"Let you go? I can't do that now. You're my insurance. The only way I can get out of here."

It had been a few minutes since he'd ordered the cop away. He needed to make certain he'd left, and there weren't any others snooping around.

There wasn't a good enough view from the window. He would have to open the door, confident using the boy as a shield would keep him safe.

* * *

Angela fumed as she pondered where Frank had got to. She was still confused. Jake, she was sure now, couldn't have killed Brian by himself. It must have been Ewan. But Jake was there. He had escaped without helping Brian and hadn't even helped the police to catch the murderer. Yes, he deserved to die. Could she trust Frank to carry out the mission? No, she decided. Frank was basically a bungler, whatever he did. And now, the police wanted him. She still wondered what they wanted him for and why he'd run off. The knife was the only reason she could think of. She'd get an explanation from him when he eventually came back home, but that would wait. If she couldn't rely on Frank to kill the boy for her, she'd have to persuade someone else. That was going to be a problem; she hadn't got the cash needed to pay a hitman.

Could she do the deed herself then? She didn't see why not. Jake was only a small kid; it shouldn't be too difficult to dispose of him.

A ring of the doorbell interrupted her plans.

It was Peart.

Angela's face flushed with guilt as she opened the door and saw the police officer. How had he found out about her intentions so quickly? Then, she realised Peart hadn't come to arrest her. He'd come to look for Frank.

But Peart had already noticed the guilty look and misinterpreted the reason for it.

"Where is he? I know he's in here."

"He isn't. I haven't seen him since I left you."

"I can get a search warrant and come back."

"There's no need for that. You can come in and look for yourself."

Peart accepted the invitation and entered the house.

He quickly ascertained no one else was in the building. Then he spotted the still unwashed teacups on the coffee table.

"You've had visitors?"

"Yeah, the Swifts. Jake Swift's parents."

"What?"

"Yes. Ask that woman detective you have. She saw them."

"So, it wasn't Frank?"

"No. I told you. I haven't seen him."

"Why did he run off if he'd nothing to hide?"

"I've no idea. He must have panicked or something."

"Why would he panic?"

Angela wanted to know that herself. She couldn't tell Peart about the knife. "He's not too comfortable about going to police stations," she said.

Peart wasn't convinced but realised he was getting nowhere so left the house, much to Angela's relief. She sat down in the fireside chair and went back to thinking out the best way to kill a twelve-year-old and dispose of the body in such a manner it would never be found. Frank intended to cut the boy's throat, but that, she decided, wasn't sufficient punishment for what Jake had done. Why should he have the luxury of a quick death? No, the boy had to suffer first. She hoped she'd have the opportunity to make him do so, and that he hadn't already been drowned in the storm.

* * *

Gibson got back to Abercrombie and told him what he'd seen.

"Might have been a salesman or something," Abercrombie answered.

"He didn't go to any of the other homes as far as I know."

"But Ewan didn't open the door?"

"No. He didn't seem to answer at all. It was as if there was no one at home."

"He's there all right. I've just had a phone call from Gloria. It sounds like he has Jake Swift in there too."

Gibson stared at him. "The other missing kid?"

"Yeah. It seems the lad's alive, or, at least, he was when the other boy got away. Did you see anything of Jackson?"

"No. Isn't he answering his mobile?"

"He probably has it switched off. Besides, I don't want to phone him if I can avoid it. If he's hiding anywhere within earshot of Ewan and hasn't put the phone on silent, its ringing might give him away."

* * *

Ewan restrained Jake with an arm around the boy's neck, holding the knife in the hand of the same arm as he fumbled for the door keys with the other hand.

He withdrew the keys from his trouser pocket and unlocked the door. Then, tightening his grip on the prisoner, he warily opened the door. There was nobody in sight.

Suddenly, he screamed as Jake saw his chance and bit hard into the arm around his throat. Ewan cursed as he let go of the boy who bolted out into the street.

"Come back, you stupid kid. You're naked!"

Ewan rubbed his sore arm. This was twice in one day a kid had bitten him. Jake had sunk his teeth in far deeper than the other boy. Inspecting his arm, he found not only teeth marks but also that the boy had drawn blood.

Looking back outside, he watched Jake streak between two of the neighbouring houses and climb a fence behind them. At least, he had the pleasure of knowing the kid must be feeling some pain in his feet as he scrambled the rough fence in his nude state.

He locked the door and went to select a new hostage.

* * *

Jake ignored the shouting behind him and bolted along the alley between two of the houses. This, he thought, was the quickest way to get out of Ewan's sight and reach. Where was that copper who knocked?

He found his passage barred by a wooden fence. Without stopping, he glanced along the fence looking for a gate. Unable to see one, he decided not to spend time trying to find one. He scrambled up the barrier, the rough timber scraping against his bare skin. He was too scared to notice the pain. It was getting dark, but there was still enough light for him to watch for nails ready to spear him. Dust from industrial wastage covered the fence, but, in spite of his recent bath, Jake didn't care about keeping his skin clean.

He did care about his nakedness. Though the light was to his advantage for the climb, he wished it were darker so there was less chance of anyone seeing him in his birthday suit until he got home. He jumped down the other side of the fence, paused for a moment to recover his breath and tried to find his bearings. He had no idea where he was, but in the declining light, he could see the outline of the church tower and headed towards it.

* * *

Frank Churcher sat in the archway of the church gates. He stood and withdrew further into his refuge when he thought he heard someone coming in his direction. He watched anxiously, ready to flee if it turned out to be the police.

Then he saw a young male streaked approaching and smiled. Somebody had played a joke on the kid, he supposed. Nicked his clothes while he'd been swimming or something. Or maybe some older kids had attacked him and taken them as a prank.

As the boy drew closer, the figure seemed familiar. With a start, he realised it was Jake. Almost unrecognisable in his scratched and dirty condition, but it was Jake.

Damn! He'd got rid of the knife now.

* * *

Jake was doing his best to keep out of sight of anyone and wanted to reach his home in the shortest time possible. Going through the churchyard would be the quickest way, and he was less likely to be seen. He considered for a moment if he should call at the vicarage and tell Mark's parents where he was. They would be able to contact his own parents for him too. But that would mean having to expose himself to the vicar, and even worse, the vicar's wife might answer the door. He couldn't bring himself to do that.

He almost got to the church's main gate when he noticed a figure in the shadows. Jake stopped, ready to retreat in the other direction. How did Ewan get there before him?

Then as his eyes focused on the man, he realised it wasn't Ewan but Brian's father.

With relief, he ran towards the familiar, safe, figure.

Chapter 27

"Help me! Please! I've been kidnapped." Jake ran to the first person he had seen since fleeing the house, glad it was someone he recognised. He'd forgotten about his earlier fear of Brian's father.

Frank Churcher didn't believe it. They'd been looking for this kid all day, and now here he was, trotting straight towards him. There was a God after all.

"Take me home, please," Jake begged. He would feel safer if he had a grown-up with him.

"I'll take you home. But not your home, not yet. We'll go to mine so you can get cleaned up and we'll find you some clothes."

That sounded reasonable to Jake. The Churchers' house was closer, and they could contact his parents from there - and the police. He mustn't forget Dave was still holding Karen and Mark captive.

"Okay," he agreed and walked with a slight limp by the side of his rescuer, still conscious of being naked and hoping they wouldn't meet anyone else before arriving at the sanctuary of Mr Churcher's house.

Frank was happier than he'd been all day. Angela had told him to kill the boy, and he would, but not yet. Now he had the luxury of doing it in his own time.

Perhaps he might even get the chance first to… no, better not do that, not after what happened with Brian.

* * *

Gloria was at the Swift's house. She was tired and realised she should have gone home after reporting her discovery about Jake's whereabouts, but she had to tell his parents about this fresh hope.

"We believe we know where Jake is," she told them.

"So, he's safe," Mrs Swift responded. "Thank God for that."

"I didn't say he was safe. Just that he's probably alive."

"So, you consider he's still in danger."

Gloria had yet another dilemma here. She'd wanted to give the Swifts hope, but if she told them Jake was with the man suspected of killing Brian they would panic.

"There is still some danger," she admitted. "We can't get at him yet."

"What's wrong? Is he trapped somewhere, or hurt, tell me?"

Gloria wished she hadn't come.

"We think Jake has been abducted," she said.

"What! Who'd want to do that? We're not rich enough to pay a ransom."

"This is like something out of a book," Mr Swift chimed in. "It doesn't happen in actual life. What do they want?"

"There's no question of any ransom," Gloria answered. "The person holding Jake is using him as a hostage."

"What!" Mrs Swift screamed. "Who is it? What have they done to him?"

"According to my informant, the man who captured Jake might have given him a clout or two during escape attempts, but he hasn't hurt him, not seriously, anyway."

"Who is this informant?" Mr Swift asked.

"I can't tell you that at present."

"What are you doing to get my boy, then? This is all your fault, you know. If that Inspector of yours hadn't scared him, he wouldn't have run away in the first place."

"We're doing all we can. I promise you."

"Whatever you're doing won't be enough until he walks through that door, unharmed."

"I do know how you feel."

"You still haven't told us who it is that has captured him?" Mr Swift reminded her.

"I can't say."

"Why? What have you got to hide?"

Gloria's mind struggled to think of a way out. She couldn't find one.

She didn't need to as realisation dawned on Mrs Swift. "It's him, isn't it? That bloody murderer you let escape, and now he's got my child."

* * *

The van containing the armed response unit arrived at the location Abercrombie had specified. An officer clad in full protective gear alighted and approached the sergeant.

"Sergeant Hoyle," he introduced himself. "What's the situation?"

Abercrombie pointed towards the cul-de-sac. "A man is holding a group of kids in his house. We haven't discovered for sure if he's armed or not."

"Until you establish that, we can't do anything."

"I'm aware of that. You can give us back up while we find out, though, can't you?"

"Yes. We will cover your men. But once you find he has got a gun of any kind, you must pull your people back and leave everything to us."

"I know. There may be an officer somewhere near or even in the house, though. He isn't officially part of the team. One of the kids might be his daughter. We've also seen a civilian around. We're not sure if he is involved."

"What's the officer doing there? That could damn well complicate matters if we need to fire."

"He was told to stay away. He disobeyed. It is his child in there."

"Well, I hope he doesn't get in the way."

"He has enough sense to keep clear when he hears your warning. He knows we've called you in."

"All right. How many kids in the building?"

"We think three, might be more."

"Right. I'll get my men in position. Wait until I tell you, then give your target a shout. Tell him it's his last chance to surrender."

* * *

Gloria left the Swifts' home, relieved to be away from the resentment they felt for the police. She was tired but couldn't finish work now; she had to see what was going on at Ewan's house. If anything untoward had happened to

Jake, it would have to be herself who came back to tell his parents. She couldn't expect them to hear it from uniform, or anyone else. Not now.

Because of her fatigue, she didn't feel safe to drive, so she left her car where it was and walked. She was in no hurry to get to the scene - her presence there would make little difference.

It was becoming dark by this time though she was glad there seemed no threat of more rain for the moment. Not having expected to take this walk she hadn't dressed for wet weather.

She was surprised to come across some of her uniformed colleagues who seemed to be searching the streets. Surely, they knew by now that Jake Swift had been found at Ewan's house.

She recognised Vincent Peart and approached him.

"Hello, Vince. You're not still looking for the boy?"

Peart turned towards her, his black face looking stern. His expression softened when he saw who had spoken to him.

"Oh, hello Gloria. I thought you'd gone off-duty hours ago. No, we're not looking for the kid. They reckon they know where he is. They're mounting a rescue attempt. Sending in the guns, I hear."

"They've called in the A.R.U. Oh, God!"

"So I've been told, anyway. The kid'll be all right. Those men are crack marksmen."

"I know. It just seems over the top to get a child out of a house."

"Not only one kid. Jackson's daughter's in there too."

"Oh, I'd forgotten. Is that why?"

"No, Jackson's at the scene, but he had nothing to do with calling in the A.R.U. In fact, I don't think he's supposed to be there at all, but it's his child, so..."

"Yes. Well, if you're not looking for Jake, why are you still here?"

"We're after Frank Churcher. They want him at the station and when I told him, he did a runner."

"Why?"

"That's what I want to find out, especially now they know Ewan's the killer."

"Are they sure?"

"Well, he's abducted the kids, hasn't he? What other reason would he have for doing that?"

"Something doesn't seem right. You've checked Churcher's house?" Gloria rubbed her chin as she tried to think of an explanation for Frank's odd behaviour. Peart was correct that Ewan seemed the obvious suspect for the murder, but what did Frank Churcher have to hide? She knew they were going to question him about the sexual attacks on Brian, but he wasn't aware of that himself yet. So why had he run?

"Yeah," Peart answered. "He's not there. She is, though. He seems more scared of going home and facing her than he is of us."

"But he can't be far away."

"I know. The trouble is we only have a few officers left for the search. Most of those that would have been available are giving backup at Ewan's house."

"Yes, they would be. I'm on my way there now myself. Let me know if there's anything I can do."

"You could stay and help us look," Peart shouted as she walked away. She turned, hoping he was joking. Seeing the look of desperation, she realised he wasn't. She ignored him and hurried on.

* * *

Frank unlocked the door of his house and ushered Jake inside. Angela, hearing the door open, came from the living room ready to pounce on Frank and demand an explanation for his strange behaviour. She stopped in her tracks on seeing Jake.

"What's he doin' here? And why's he naked?"

"He came to me for help."

"What?"

"He was kidnapped."

"So, why've you brought 'im here?"

"I thought it'd be easier to kill him here, in private."

Hearing this, Jake made a bolt for the door. Frank threw his arm around the boy's neck and restrained him. Jake struggled, but weak from his lack of food and sleep, the resistance was feeble, and Frank soon had him under his control.

"Get me a kitchen knife," he said to Angela.

"Don't be stupid. There'll be blood all over the place. Besides, he's not getting off so easy."

"You don't want him killed now?"

"Oh, we'll kill him all right, but not 'till he's suffered a bit."

"Why?" pleaded Jake, his face once again awash with tears.

"Shut up!" she told him. Then to Frank, "Wait there, and don't let go of him."

She went into the back of the house.

"Why are you doing this?" Jake screeched at Frank when Angela had gone. "I thought you were going to help me."

"Well, now you know you thought wrong, don't you?"

Angela returned with some short lengths of rope she had made by cutting up a clothesline and gave them to Frank.

"Take him upstairs and tie him onto Brian's bed, face down."

"Why?" Jake pleaded again. "What have I done?"

"What did you do? You killed my son."

This accusation stunned Jake into silence as Frank pushed him up the stairs.

"I didn't," he screamed as they reached the last step.

No one answered him, and Frank shoved him into the bedroom.

* * *

Jackson had given up on finding a way into the house. He would have to leave it to his colleagues. Reluctantly, he left by the back gate, taking Millward with him.

"Get yourself away from here," he told him once they were in the alley. "There could be gunfire. Thanks for trying to help."

"Gunfire! What about my mother?"

"She'll be okay as long as she stays inside the house."

"I'll go to her."

"It would be better if you didn't show yourself at the front right now. We don't want any mistakes made, do we?"

Millward nodded he understood and walked round to the rear of his mother's house.

Jackson hesitated as he tried to decide his next move. He heard what sounded like someone climbing the wooden fence a few houses away. He didn't think Millward was as agile as that. Running towards the sound, he was just in time to see a boy's head disappear over the fence. Could have been a child at play but the boy looked familiar in that one brief glimpse he'd had. Jake? Surely not, and if it was Jake, where had he come from?

Jake or not, any kids around here needed to be got out of the way before any shooting started. He ran to the other side of the fence, but by the time he got to it there was no sign of the kid or any pals he might be with. Had it really been Jake, and had he come out of the house? If so, he must have escaped, and that meant there was a chance for Karen to do the same.

"Would you leave the area, sir? Armed police."

The voice came from behind and Jackson spun round.

"I'm a police officer," he said. He produced his warrant card; glad he had remembered to retrieve it from Millward.

"I must still ask you to leave, sir. If you're on this case, please join your colleagues. We are about to surround one of these homes. You're in danger if you remain here."

"I'll go," Jackson answered. "But watch where you fire if you need to do so. My child is in that house."

"Don't worry. Every officer here is well-trained."

"I know. It isn't that I don't trust you. It's just that when it's your kid..."

"I understand, but you're better out of the way."

Jackson nodded and walked away to find his team– or what was now Abercrombie's team.

* * *

Jake was spread-eagled face down on the bed. His wrists and ankles tied firmly to the bed's frame. Tears ran down his face mingling with the dirt and transferring some of it onto the white pillowcase.

He wished now he hadn't escaped. He had more to fear from his present captors than he ever had with Dave. Dave had hit him, but never really hurt him. Here, it was clear he would be tortured, then murdered.

Brian's father checked the bonds were tight.

"Why are you doing this, please tell me?" Jake pleaded again through his sobbing. "I didn't kill Brian, I promise."

"I know you didn't. But Angela thinks you did, so that's all that matters."

"Tell her, please."

"I can't do that."

"Why?"

"Because if I do, she'll know it was me, won't she?"

For an instant, Jake stopped crying. His face contorted in shock as he realised the truth.

"You?"

"I might as well tell you since you're not going to be able to tell anyone, are you? Yeah, it was me."

"Why?"

"He ran away, didn't he? I told him he'd not to go out that day. He was grounded."

"That's no reason to murder him."

"I didn't plan to kill him. I only followed him to bring him home."

"H-he t-told me what you did to him."

"Well, then, I suppose you might as well know the whole story." He checked the doorway to make sure

Angela was still downstairs out of earshot before continuing. "He threatened to tell about me. Well, I couldn't allow that, could I? They'd have sent me to prison. I followed you both, keeping out of sight. I saw that bloke playing with you and pretending to strangle Brian. That gave me the idea. You see, I knew that chap's fingerprints would be on Brian's neck. You were lucky, if you'd stayed with Brian, I might have had to kill you both, but when Brian hit you and you ran off, it made it easier for me. I caught Brian and throttled him, but then I realised my own fingerprints would need to be explained too, so I used water out of the canal to wash his neck. Great plan, don't you think?"

"If you kill me, you'll get caught."

"Oh, we'll get rid of your body where no one will ever find it. You don't need to worry about us. I'm sorry, but we do have to kill you, you must see that. Especially now you know everything."

"I won't tell."

"I can't trust you. Besides, Angela wants her revenge, doesn't she?"

Seeing there was no escape, Jake buried his face into the pillow letting the tears flow freely. He screamed, making himself hoarse, hoping someone, somewhere, would hear and come to his rescue. In his heart, he knew this was unlikely, or Frank would have gagged him. He awaited his fate, wondering if while in this position there was any way he could kill himself. That would deprive his captors of being able to torture him.

Frank proudly checked his knots again to be sure they hadn't come loose with the struggling of the boy. He wasn't good at many things, but knot-tying was one of them. Satisfied they were still holding tight, he stood back and looked down at the naked, screaming prisoner. The screaming didn't bother him; there was no one next door to hear.

What was he supposed to do now? Angela hadn't given him any instructions other than to tie Jake to the bed.

Surely, she didn't want him to …

No, she didn't even know he was that way inclined. Pity to waste the opportunity, though.

* * *

Jackson found Abercrombie with his men, waiting for the A.R.U to get into position.

"What's the situation?" he asked.

"Tom! You shouldn't be here."

"I know, but I am. It's my kid in there, and there's no way I'm not going to be here. Don't worry. I understand this is your shout. I won't interfere. Tell me what's going on, though."

"As soon as the armed response people to get into place, I'll give Ewan the chance to come out with the kids. We understand Jake Swift, the missing boy's in there too."

So, he'd been right. It was Jake.

"Not anymore he isn't."

"What?"

"I saw him clambering over a fence, or thought I did."

"Damn! He'd have been safer where he was."

"We don't know that. Ewan might have killed him anytime. We already know he has it in him to murder a child."

"Yes, I know, but now we must tell the ARU there's a kid loose in the area."

"I think he got well away. I saw no more of him."

"How was he dressed?"

"Couldn't see. I only saw his head briefly, but his description will be on the misper report. He hasn't had any chance to get changed."

"No one has contacted me to say he's reached home. I'll call the station to be sure."

"Good idea," Jackson agreed.

"He's not got home," Abercrombie told him after making the call.

"Pity."

Hoyle appeared. "We're ready," he said. "Shout from the front of the house. We still don't know whether the suspect is armed, so keep well back. My men are ready to cover you just in case. Do everything they say, instantly. Even if it doesn't seem to make sense, do it. You understand?"

"I understand," Abercrombie said, taking the megaphone handed to him.

"Do you want me to go?" Jackson offered. "It is my child we're trying to get out."

"No," Abercrombie insisted. "You said no interference, remember. Stay here."

Jackson found it difficult to bear being left out, but his sergeant was right. He watched Abercrombie walk into the cul-de-sac, Hoyle in full protective gear beside him, gun at the ready.

* * *

Frank Churcher decided to leave the boy alone unless he got specific instructions from Angela. He couldn't risk annoying her now. However, he could not resist giving Jake's bare buttocks a pat before leaving him.

Jake flinched, expecting something more and braced himself for a spanking or worse. He felt a moment of relief when it didn't happen and Frank left the room.

Once alone, Jake struggled to free his bonds, but it wasn't long before he had to accept the knots were expertly tied and all he was doing was causing the ropes to cut into his wrists or make friction burns that his sweat caused to sting. He gave up.

* * *

Downstairs, Frank found Angela sitting in the living room.

"Have you done it?" she asked.

"Yeah, he can't get away."

"Good."

"What are we going to do with him?"

"Hurt him, of course. I just haven't decided how, yet."

"I can use my belt across his backside. Give him a good thrashing."

"No. It has to be worse than that. Let me think."

Worse, Frank thought. What was Angela thinking about? What could be worse than a good hiding to a kid that age?

"I wish it were the old days," Angela said. "If we still had a coal fire, we could put a red-hot poker across his ass. That'd make him yelp."

"There's the electric iron."

Angela stared at him. "For once you've come up with a brilliant idea," she said. "Go and plug it in."

Chapter 28

The police searched the area around the cul-de-sac and satisfied themselves that neither Jake nor anyone else was in the vicinity. They also warned all Ewan's neighbours to stay inside their houses.

At Hoyle's signal, Abercrombie switched on the megaphone and lifted it to his lips.

"David Ewan," he shouted. "We know you're in there. The house is surrounded by armed police. There's no way out. Send the kids out first, then come out with your hands up."

There was silence. Curtains from the neighbouring houses moved back as their occupants came to the windows to watch the excitement.

Abercrombie heard footsteps behind him and turned to see a constable holding a battering ram walking towards him. Jackson was at his side.

Damn! He should have known Jackson wouldn't stay out of it. Still, the enforcer was a good idea. Preferable to using the guns, though he hoped they wouldn't need either.

Jackson joined him. "I thought you might need this," he said, indicating the object in the constable's hands.

"Thanks," Abercrombie responded, knowing full well Jackson could have sent the constable alone. He also knew that if it had been his child in the house, he would have found an excuse to get on the scene too.

"What's happening?" Jackson asked.

"Nothing. I've called out the first warning, but he hasn't responded."

"Let me try."

"What will you say?"

"Don't worry. I won't spook him into hurting any of the youngsters. Don't forget, one of them's mine."

Hesitantly, Abercrombie handed him the megaphone, unsure whether he was doing the right thing, but years of working under Jackson had accustomed him to taking orders from him.

Jackson raised the loudhailer to his mouth.

"Ewan! Let the kids go. You can't get away now."

This time, the door of the house opened slowly, and those police officers who were not part of the A.R.U breathed a sigh of relief, expecting Ewan to come out and surrender.

The gunmen, however, did not relax. As soon as the door opened, all their weapons were trained on it, ready for action at the first hint of trouble.

Ewan appeared in the doorway, but he was not alone. He held Karen around the waist and had a knife against the terrified child's throat.

"This kid belongs to one of you, doesn't she? Well, if you don't want her throat cut, pull your men back. We're going to walk away from here. You won't shoot. Not while I'm holding the kid."

"That's my daughter," Jackson yelled. "You touch her and I'll–"

Abercrombie retrieved the megaphone before Jackson said more.

"Where are the others?" he asked through the loudspeaker. "We need to be sure they're not hurt."

As he spoke, a youth came from the house prodded by Ewan's foot.

"This one, you mean? I don't need him anymore. You can see he isn't hurt. That doesn't mean I won't harm the one I've still got, though. You've got ten minutes to call your men off." As Ewan shouted the threat, he yanked Karen back inside and kicked the door shut.

"Armed police! Lie down on the floor and don't move, someone barked an order to the youth."

Mark froze with fear.

"Lie down!" The command was yelled again.

This time, Mark obeyed. Two police officers rushed to him, one keeping his gun aimed at the door. The other grabbed Mark and pulled him to his feet. "Don't be scared," he said. "We're just getting you out of here."

He hustled Mark to where Jackson and Abercrombie were standing. Abercrombie told a uniformed police officer to take the boy away to get medical attention. As they walked away, Jackson looked at the boy's frightened pale face.

"Just one thing," he said. "Has he hurt the girl at all?"

Mark trembled. "Slaps, that's all. I'm certain he'll kill her if you don't let him go, though."

"Has he got a gun?"

"No. Well, I didn't see one, anyhow."

As the officer led the youth away, Jackson turned to Hoyle.

"That means he's unarmed apart from the knife, then."

"Yes, but now he's threatening to kill his hostage. You still need us."

"If you fire there's a chance the kid - my kid - will be hit."

"Don't worry, the guys here are well trained. They won't shoot unless they're confident they won't hit the girl."

Jackson wasn't reassured but had little say in the matter. He'd seen scenes like this in films where they invariably ended satisfactorily. But no one here was following a script. In real life, mistakes happened.

"Well, it's your shout. What are you going to do?" he asked Abercrombie.

"I have no idea."

* * *

Gloria continued walking towards Ewan's cul-de-sac. She hadn't been there before but had a good idea of its location.

She thought about what Peart had told her. Why did Frank Churcher run off? Had he somehow found out about being suspected of child abuse, or was there something else he had to worry about? She would have to pass close to where he lived. Perhaps she should call in to see Angela and find out what she had to say about her husband's behaviour.

* * *

Ewan appeared at an upstairs window, still holding the blade against Karen's neck. Feeling safer there, he threw open the window so he could shout to the police.

"Time's running out!" he yelled. "I can't see you moving."

Abercrombie didn't bother to use the megaphone but shouted back. "Let the child go. Then we can talk."

"You must think I'm stupid."

"You know there's no way out."

"Either I get out, or the girl dies."

Jackson could contain himself no longer as he heard the threat to his daughter. "You need a trained negotiator," he told Abercrombie.

"I know. The Guv's seeing to it already."

"Then what's taking him so bloody long to get here?"

"It's a she, and she's tied up on another case."

"Some use that is to us."

"There's nothing we can do about it."

Jackson turned to Hoyle. "You must have seen this sort of situation before. Haven't you any suggestions?"

"I'm not in a position to tell you what to do, but if your sergeant wants my advice..."

"I'll listen to anything you suggest," said Abercrombie.

"Okay. The negotiator might be delayed for some time, and you can't afford to wait. This bloke knows we have him cornered and while I don't consider he will hurt the girl -" he paused and looked back into Jackson's face, "He might panic, and anything could happen if he does. I recommend you keep him talking here while some of your men force entry at the back. I assume you have another battering ram you can get around there without him seeing what you're doing?"

"Yes," Jackson said. "But that back door is built like a fortress. I've already tried."

"You've what?" said Abercrombie, accusingly.

"Save your arguments for later," Hoyle said. "When you tried you didn't have a proper enforcer to do the job, did you?"

"No. But it will take several blows. He's going to hear it."

"By then he won't be able to do anything about it."

"He'd have time to kill my kid, though. I don't like it."

"I doubt he'll do that, but my men will shoot him if they have to before he can hurt the girl. He can't protect himself on all sides."

"It's hell of a risk."

"No more so than standing here doing nothing."

Jackson agreed with that even though he was still anxious. Hoyle might not believe Ewan would carry out his threat, but the boy who had come out of the house seemed more convinced, and he'd been inside with the man.

* * *

Still crying and trembling with fear, Jake lay on the bed, waiting for his fate. He was sure Frank would give him a good thrashing or something before killing him, despite not having already done so. He'd most likely gone to fetch a belt or stick to hit him with. Or maybe Angela would do the hitting. It was she who wanted the revenge. Revenge for something he hadn't done. If only he could convince her of that, but there seemed little chance. He wondered how they would murder him after the battering was over. How bad would the beating be? Perhaps they planned to do it all in one go - beat him to death. If he pressed his face into the pillow, perhaps he could smother himself before they came back. That would spoil their fun.

* * *

Abercrombie had issued orders for his team to follow the plan Hoyle suggested and they were now moving into place, unseen by Ewan. He had, however, seen Abercrombie leave his position and return a few minutes later. Still holding Karen in front of him to protect himself, he shouted from the window.

"What's going on, where have you been?"

"I've been contacting my boss. I can't agree to your request without his permission."

"And what does he say?"

"He hasn't decided yet."

"He'd better hurry up. The clock's ticking."

At that moment, Superintendent Everett arrived on the scene.

"What the hell are you doing here, Jackson? I told you to go home, didn't I?"

"I'm off duty, sir. I can go where I please."

Everett saw there was no point in arguing. He turned to Abercrombie. "What's the situation?"

Abercrombie briefed him and warned him to stand by for them to charge the house and be ready for possible gunfire.

"Gunfire?"

"If the girl is thought to be in danger when the officers at the back of the building enter, they're going to have to shoot Ewan."

"It's a bit drastic, isn't it? If he isn't armed except for a knife, don't you think?"

"With that knife, he could kill Karen in a second."

"I know. I suppose there isn't any choice, is there?"

"Having already killed one kid, he has nothing to lose. We can't take any chances."

"He didn't kill Brian," Jackson interjected.

Abercrombie spun round to face him, "What! You still believe that after all this?"

"I had my doubts for a while. But he's had Jake with him in that building. If he was guilty, do you honestly think he would have let the chief witness get away? No, he'd have killed him when he had the chance."

"Then, why the kidnappings?"

"I don't know. Panic, probably. He's convinced himself he won't get a fair trial, so he tried to make sure he wasn't caught. Once he started the game, he got himself in too deep. Now, there's no way he can avoid going back to prison, even if it isn't for murder."

"Then Karen's safe."

"I hope so. But as Hoyle said, we can't be sure. Because he hasn't killed before doesn't mean he won't."

"Who killed Brian, then?"

* * *

Inside the house, Karen struggled frantically as Ewan held her by the hair, the knife against her throat.

"Keep still, you stupid kid or I'll cut you," her captor threatened.

"No!" Karen screamed. "Let me go!"

For a moment, she considered biting the man's arm, but she didn't think he would fall for that a third time. Besides, the blade of that knife was already touching her neck. She couldn't take the risk.

"Shut up," Ewan growled. "I can't think with you screaming in my ears."

Karen did shut up, sensing that Ewan was scared himself and not wanting to panic him into using the knife. She closed her eyes, and her body stiffened. Reluctantly, she accepted she would have to let Ewan use her as a human shield, and she could do nothing about it.

Suddenly there was a crash at the back door and Ewan spun round, wheeling Karen with him. She opened her eyes, now wide with fear, as police with guns came rushing through the house into the bedroom.

One of them quickly grabbed hold of her as others pounced on Ewan before he had time to react.

* * *

The police outside heard the crash before Jackson had time to answer Abercrombie's question and realised the people around the back had gained access.

Immediately police officers ran to the front door, taking with them the other battering ram.

It was all over in a matter of seconds, and Ewan was brought out between two constables.

Karen, screaming, ran from the building and into her father's arms.

"I'm sorry, Dad," she cried. "I'll never do it again, honest. Not as long as I live."

"Calm down, love. It wasn't your fault."

"I mean the bullying." She let her tears freely flow down her face. "I know what you think about it. I was chasing a lad when that man captured us." She hesitated briefly before continuing her confession. "I was going to hurt him. I'm sorry."

Jackson felt a surge of relief that she could even remember this after the trauma she'd been through. It meant she probably would not suffer long-term effects.

"It's all right, Karen. Just part of growing up, as your mother would tell me."

* * *

Frank came through to the living room, the hot iron in his hand.

"About time," said Angela.

"You wanted it hot, didn't you?"

"Give it to me."

Frank was reluctant to do this. He wanted to inflict the pain himself, but it was no use arguing, and he gave the iron to his wife then followed her upstairs to where their prisoner waited.

Jake had failed in his attempt to smother himself. He braced himself for the beating he expected as he heard Brian's parents coming up the stairs.

Angela entered the bedroom just in front of Frank. She looked at the pillowcase now stained with the dirt from Jake's face and glared at Frank. "Why didn't you take the bedding off first, you fool?"

Frank looked sheepish. It hadn't occurred to him that his wife would consider putting Brian's bedding into the washing machine to be a problem.

Angela didn't dwell on the subject. The iron was getting cold.

"Now, you horrible child," she said. "I'm going to scorch your arse."

"No!" Jake screamed, seeing the iron and realising what she was about to do with it. "P-please, don't. It wasn't me. It was Frank. He told me. He wanted to stop Brian telling you he bummed him."

"What?"

"He's lying," said Frank. "Go on. Burn him."

Angela turned towards Frank. Suddenly, everything fell into place. She'd been right when she suspected him earlier.

"You bastard," she said. "It was you. All those bruises Brian got. He didn't get them in fights at school, did he? That was you too."

"No, Angela. The kid's just trying to wangle his way out of it."

"No, you are. Just like you did last time." She stepped towards him and thrust the hot iron flat against his cheek.

Frank screamed and turned towards the door. Angela chased him with the iron. He reached the front door and tried to escape through it, but Angela pursued him into the street.

* * *

Gloria had decided to pay a visit to Angela and got to the Churchers' pathway when she was amazed to see Frank come through the door screaming with Angela chasing him, a cordless electric iron in her hand. Angela didn't stop to close the door behind her.

Curious as to what was going on but also concerned the home had been left insecure, Gloria went to the door to close it. As she reached it, she was sure she could hear whimpering from inside.

She listened harder. This time, she was certain she heard a child crying. She knew Brian had been an only child. She went into the house and followed the sound of the crying until she discovered the boy.

"No!" pleaded Jake through his tears, assuming one of his captors had come back to torture him.

"Oh, God!" Gloria murmured. She quickly untied Jake's bonds and wrapped a sheet from the bed around his naked body. By then, Jake was past caring about his nudity and fell into her arms where he soon fell into oblivion.

Gloria ran downstairs and called for an ambulance. Before replacing the handset, she saw Jackson,

Abercrombie and two uniformed officers escorting Frank and Angela back into the house.

"Gloria, what are you doing here? Where's Jake?" Jackson asked.

"I came to talk to Angela. When I got here, I found Jake tied up upstairs. He's fainted, but he's okay otherwise. I've sent for an ambulance."

"Good. The time he's been missing he needs to be checked out, anyway."

"Why are you here?"

"I realised Frank had to be the killer. I first suspected it when we knew for sure he'd been molesting Brian. Ewan's behaviour made me feel I might be mistaken, then when Frank did a runner from Peart, I knew I was right. Ewan has problems, but murder isn't one of them. After we arrested him, we were on our way here when we came across these two attacking each other."

The angry red mark across Frank's cheek left no doubt who had done the attacking.

"Once we apprehended them, Angela's conscience got the better of her and she promptly confessed to kidnapping Jake and we came here to rescue him, but you beat us to it."

Epilogue

Jake woke up between clean sheets. Had the whole thing been a dream? It felt comfortable - but he knew this wasn't his bed. Had he died and gone to heaven? His wrists and ankles hurt a bit where the ropes had dug into his skin. Not a dream then. But it couldn't be heaven; there would be no pain there. Someone had rubbed some ointment into the wounds. He looked more closely at his wrists. Apart from the rope burns, the other thing he noticed was they were clean. In fact, he was clean all over. Someone, he realised, washed him while he'd been asleep. He knew of only one place where that would happen. Hospital! He must be in some hospital. Thinking he was alone, panic started to set in and he raised himself to a sitting position to get a better look around. He felt a flood of relief when he saw his mother dozing in a chair beside the bed.

"Mum!"

She woke with a start. "Oh, Jake, thank goodness you're all right," she cried.

Jake threw his arms around her neck, and they both sobbed in relief.

"Where's Dad?"

"He's helping the police?"

"Why?"

She couldn't tell him. He'd had enough distress. Yet, he needed to be told before the detectives asked him questions.

"I'm sure everything will be okay," she said.

"What's wrong, tell me?"

He had to know, and she needed to know the truth too.

"Jake, when they examined you, they said you'd been interfered with. You understand what I mean?"

"I know what you mean - but it wasn't Dad, honest."

"Thank God for that. I believe you, but you must tell me who it was. The police have already done tests on both the men who kidnapped you, and they know it wasn't them. Who was it, Jake?"

"No, I can't tell you. I promised."

"That kind of promise doesn't count."

This was the second time someone had told Jake promises didn't matter, both times by an adult. Didn't grown-ups have any standards?

"I can't. But it wasn't Dad. Anyway, I don't know his name, just that he had rotten teeth."

* * *

After leaving the Churcher's' house, Abercrombie went back to the police station to charge them both formally with the attempted murder of Jake Swift and Frank with the murder of Brian. He would also have to charge Ewan with child abduction and assault. Before doing so, he went to the locker room to change into his spare suit, identical to the one he was wearing. He smiled as he realised how Jackson still hadn't discovered how he always appeared so immaculate, no matter what kind of day he'd had.

* * *

Jake did not have to break his promise. Mark made a full confession once he recovered, and the youth with the bad teeth was found and arrested. Having a string of other offences behind him, he was convicted, and the court sentenced him to a period of Youth Custody. For his part, Mark himself was ordered to do one hundred hours' community service, which served not only as a punishment but made him realise, to the relief of his parents, the need to become more responsible now he was approaching adulthood.

* * *

The Jackson household went back to being almost normal, though Jackson was a little less preoccupied about his children being bullied. He now knew they could give as much as they got.

The End